THE
AZAZEL
SYNDROME

FIRST OF A SERIES

BY

J.E. KENNEDY

Published by Adrestia Publishing, LLC
ISBN Ebook: 978-1-7328887-0-8
ISBN Print Edition: 978-1-7328887-1-5

Cover Design by Lieu Pham, Covertopia.com
Book design by Guido Henkel

Discovered at
BASE PURPLE STAR, ANTARCTICA, 2008

Estimated date of origin: 9,500-10,500 BCE
Second and final translation performed 2011

This we leave as a warning
To those alive in our world and to those children of the world to come
Here sleeps evil
Mighty is its power
Subtle are its wiles
Wicked is its laughter
Let those who dare unfasten its chain have their eyes plucked out
Their heads and hands broken
Their hearts crushed
Let them rue their own birth
For no fate is too harsh for them

CHAPTER 1

ON THE FOURTH OF JUNE AT JUST AFTER NINE P.M., HATCH Doran picked his way over the snowy sidewalks of lower Manhattan. He knew he was walking too fast—he couldn't see the ice patches at night—but he was distracted by problems. He stopped and dragged the toe of his boot along the ice. Forget going to the pub, he thought. Grab a hoo cab, get back to the apartment, and drum up some solutions. Besides, only an idiot would be out walking alone. The blizzard may have emptied the streets, but the gangs were always somewhere around.

Hatch flipped up the collar of his worn bomber jacket and kept going.

All his troubles boiled down to one thing: an acute shortage of money. He needed to score some coin, and in short order. He passed Wall Street and continued south as visions of crisp, American Homeland dollars swirled in his head. He imagined thick stacks of bundled redbacks rustling against his fingers. A tingle ran up his back.

Or it could have been the cold.

Or his mountains of unpaid bills. Or the poisonous calls and emails pouring in.

Hatch's plentiful vision faded, and he thrust his hands deep into his pockets. But what about Big Ray and Marty and the rest of the team? How long since he had paid them—or himself? Six weeks? Two months?

He was letting them all down, and the idea of it made him sick. Then a memory came, running through his mind like an old melody never quite forgotten: we never give up. He could almost hear Mae, his grandmom, saying it, drilling it into him. We never quit, Hatch.

So long ago. He refused to count the years. Then a near-slip on the ice jerked him from his reverie, and he told himself to stop whining and just handle it. He'd handled it before, and more than once. Then his heel slipped again, and he waved his arms to keep his balance. At the last instant his boot caught on some grit and saved him from a nasty spill.

The wind wailed like far-off laughter. Snowdrifts jumped into the air along the sidewalk. Hatch quickened his pace, but a block later he slipped yet again, cursed, and paused to knock the snow from the treads of his boots. Then from behind him came a scrape of footsteps, and he felt the hot, blunt end of a pulse pistol against the back of his neck.

Shit.

"Don't move, don't turn," said a raspy voice in his ear.

Three or four black-clad figures emerged from the darkness and surrounded him. "This isn't the right guy, Hop," said one of the men.

Hop jabbed the pulser against Hatch's neck. "He's the right one."

Hatch had nothing for them, but damned if he'd make it easy. He ducked away from the pulser and dropped into a crouch. Someone grabbed at his jacket, but he broke free as a second man lunged toward hi. Hatch yanked the second man's ankle and dropped him hard on the sidewalk. Shouts, cries of outrage, and a brief tussle: Hatch tried to scramble away, but it was no good. They slammed him to the pavement. He tried to pull down another of the men, but got only a fistful of air. Hop stepped on Hatch's head and pressed his cheek against the icy concrete. The man Hatch had dropped groaned and tried to roll over.

Rough, indignant voices exploded around him. "Let me have a go at the sorry—got us a smart ass—the son of a—" They helped the injured man to his feet. "You can't let this chump slide, Hop," said one of the men. "Not after he did that."

Hatch tried to tell them all to go to hell, but it came out like the bleat of a lamb.

"Boss didn't want him hurt," said Hop, his foot still planted on Hatch's head. "He was real clear about it."

Two black SUVs crunched to a halt at the curb. Hop, a giant with blond hair protruding from beneath his cap, seized Hatch by the collar, gave him a quick frisk, and removed Hatch's double-edged switchblade from his jacket. He then stretched Hatch's arms tight behind him and bound his wrists with plastic ties. The rest of the men assisted their injured companion into the first vehicle while Hop shoved Hatch through the rear door of the second. Hatch found himself seated next to an older man with a shaved head, also dressed in black.

Hop slid into the front passenger seat and turned and leveled his gun at Hatch. The SUV lurched forward. The whitened, ramshackle streetscape eased past the window as Hatch leaned against his bound hands, his shoulders threatening to pop out of their sockets with every bump. An image of his father, dead now for almost twenty-five years, floated through his mind. Annoyed, he pushed the memory away.

A minute or two later, they stopped at Battery Park and the lanky man gestured. "We don't need the heater pointed back here, Hop."

The pulser disappeared.

The man, who Hatch guessed at somewhere north of sixty, gazed for a long moment at the wintry landscape outside his window. "It is June now and look at this," he said. "Colder every year." He turned from the window. "You are Robert Hatcher Doran."

Hatch didn't answer.

"Do you know who I am?" asked the man.

Hatch shook his head.

"I conduct business as the Ferret. You and I are in similar lines of work."

A hollow space opened inside Hatch's chest. He stared out of his window at State Street, curving away to the Ferry Terminal. "I don't think we are," he said.

"You don't? Show him, Hop."

Hop produced a tablet computer, flicked it on, and passed it to Ferret.

"You call your firm Odysseus," said Ferret, reading the screen. "Odysseus, LLC. Is that correct?"

Hatch made no response.

"I want to be certain I have the right Robert Hatcher Doran." Ferret squinted at Hatch, his tight, weathered face and round spectacles whitened by the glow from the tablet.

"Okay, I'm Doran, but—"

"You broker antiques, plain old tiques, they are called. You buy, sell, or deliver, it says on your website."

"Plain old tiques," said Hatch. "We don't play in the historical antiquities trade. I mean, we move a little art, but we stay away from the cultural stuff. We don't mess around on your turf. We never have."

Ferret swiped his finger along the screen. The wind kicked up thin whitecaps out in the harbor. "Let's see, Robert Hatcher Doran. It says you work with Raymond Garwin—he looks like a congenial fellow." Ferret showed Hop Big Ray's picture. "Don't you think so, Hop?"

"You say so, boss."

Hatch wasn't sure he'd call Big Ray congenial. Pain stabbed from his shoulders across his back.

"And then you have Martin Shannon," said Ferret, checking the tablet. "Do I know him?"

The driver adjusted the thermostat. Prickles of sweat broke out on Hatch's neck.

"Tiques are a very difficult game," said Ferret, handing Hop the tablet and tugging a black cap low over his brow. "Everybody and his brother these days, hawking jewelry, paintings, ivory, old furniture. You name it." Ferret gave Hatch a casual punch on his arm. It felt like a pile-driver hitting his strained shoulder. "But you already know that, don't you, Robert Hatcher Doran?"

"Just plain old tiques," said Hatch. "We don't do anything with historicals."

A gust of wind buffeted the SUV.

"Hop, what about the drones?" asked Ferret.

Hop retrieved a heavy laptop from the front floorboard and flipped it open. The light from the screen reflected off of the windows. "It circles every twenty or thirty minutes, and it just flew over. Belongs to Policecorp."

"And the satellites?"

Hop tapped the keyboard. "You should be okay now, boss."

Hatch experienced a tilting sensation. This was the Ferret —*the* Ferret—an antiquities runner of legendary brutality, with tentacles into traffic from every corner of the globe. But what did Ferret want with him? It was some kind of horrific mistake. In a flash of clairvoyance, Hatch imagined the quick *soomph* of the pulser and pictured himself dumped over the harbor rail, the icy waters closing over his head. His heart thumped. The last of earth. A poetic saying about death danced at the edge of his mind. He vowed not to beg or grovel.

"Let's walk," said Ferret.

The doors of both SUVs opened, and the gang poured out and stationed themselves around the vehicles. Hop came around, reached in, and flung Hatch into the raw harbor wind.

"His ties," said Ferret.

"He wasn't too cooperative back there, boss," said Hop.

Ferret turned to Hatch. "If you cause difficulty, if you try to run, Hop will shoot you. Do you understand?"

"I'm not going to run," said Hatch.

Ferret nodded and Hop cut the ties. Hatch rubbed his wrists and shoulders while the rest of the gang stomped around and made muffled claps in the cold. Ferret took Hatch by the arm and walked him along the promenade, with Hop following at a distance. A crust of ice had formed over the water along the sea wall, and the moon made a golden scythe overhead.

"These damned satellites and their facial recognition technology," said Ferret, gesturing toward the sky. "We can scramble the municipal cameras and the drones, but we are powerless against the satellites. A man cannot walk alone with himself anymore, even at night. It is a shame what this world has come to."

Hatch glanced back at Hop, stationed thirty yards away and holding the pulser in both hands. He didn't dare run, not in all this snow. Hatch turned to Ferret and said, "You have the wrong guy."

"No, I do not," said Ferret. "I want us to work together. I have chosen you to make a pickup on a transaction I have arranged."

The wind slammed into them and Hatch turned away, his hair blown flat against his forehead. Ferret stood tall and loose, as if it were forty degrees warmer. The trees in Battery Park, full with leaves and snow, rustled and bowed their limbs toward the ground.

"You will receive directions," said Ferret, "and you, alone, will go where they say when they say. We have arranged for this transaction to occur here in Manhattan, so you will have no bridge or tunnel checks to worry about and no section gates to pass." He paused and studied Hatch. "Do this job well and perhaps I will make further opportunities available to you."

Hatch stood, enveloped by cold, and said nothing.

"The pickup may occur tomorrow or next week or next month," Ferret continued. "The timing is my concern, and I will notify you when we are ready. At the designated location, a man will approach you with a package and identify himself as K."

"Kay?"

"He goes by K. The letter K."

"Why can't K give it to you himself?"

Ferret shook his head. "Only under extraordinary circumstances would the two sides appear in the same location. Our ways are long established and exist for good reason. The package in question is a box about so big"—Ferret spread his hands about a foot and a half apart—"and it is not heavy. K will give it to you, as I said, and I will have secure transportation on hand to bring you to me."

A meteor shot across the sky and Hatch watched it with a sinking feeling. "Something always goes sideways, even with simple jobs," he said.

"It is true," replied Ferret. "I study and I plan with great care, but often things do not happen as I expect. Still, I have some history with K, and I have chosen you because I believe you have a certain character. You became an orphan before you were fully grown, after all, and orphans who survive are tough. You have done well for yourself in difficult circumstances. How do I know all this? I know much about you, Hatch. I may call you Hatch, mayn't I?"

"I go by Hatch."

"I require someone who is not known by the local gangs, Hatch, who does not operate in the market for ancient, cultural artifacts—my turf, as you call it. If a problem arises, this carries certain advantages."

"For you."

Ferret shrugged.

"So if I'm caught, I don't know anything and your people skate," said Hatch. He stubbed the toe of his boot on the pavement. "What do I get? If I agree."

"If?" Ferret chuckled. "Perhaps a new professional relationship—and one million redbacks as a fee for your work. Domestic American Homeland dollars, denominated in five-hundred dollar bills or less, and well-used."

Hatch steadied himself. A million redbacks for a simple pickup? But no, it wasn't that easy, was it? It was a million redbacks to dive belly first into the cultural antiquities trade. Car bombs, yanked fingernails, and cut-out testicles—or worse, a one-way ride to the labor camps if the authorities ever nailed him. Headlights from a hoo cab speared through the park and swept the bone-white ground like a prison searchlight. Hatch shivered. A short distance away, Hop signaled and pointed to the sky.

"Our time together grows short," said Ferret. "I wish for you to understand the significance of this job. The artifact you are to receive on my behalf is an object of extraordinary beauty and power. Nothing comparable to it exists in the world." Ferret gazed over the black harbor. "We bury our heads and forget. We neither revere the past, nor heed its warnings."

"The past is worth what you can get for it," said Hatch. "What it trades for."

"How cynical," said Ferret. "The past offers much to admire and much to regret, but if we hide it away and do not learn from it, with what shall we inform our future?" He took Hatch's face in his hands and patted him softly on the cheeks. "I have given you an important task, Hatch Doran, and you will not fail me. More—much more—is at stake than I can explain, and I am holding you responsible." He patted Hatch's face again, harder this time, and squeezed the back of Hatch's neck with his other hand. "I am certain you understand what I am saying."

The wind carried the faint groan of a boat horn and an acrid odor from the downtown incineration facility. Hop approached and tossed Hatch the switchblade he had removed earlier. Ferret and his gang departed. Alone on the promenade, Hatch packed a snowball and tossed it over the railing. It smashed into the black crust of ice and left a pattern which reminded him of a dollar sign.

He wiped his hands on his jeans and cursed. Then an incongruous memory from his childhood came to his mind, a vision of his father skipping a pebble across the surface of a pond, the pebble brightly gleaming in the summer sun. The recollection left Hatch restless and longing for something nameless and beyond his grasp.

He leaned on the rail with his head lowered. The wind whistled all around. Out beyond the ice, the light from a Policecorp harbor cruiser bobbed on the waves, and in the distance, the ruins of the Statue of Liberty stood all but enclosed by darkness. When Hatch looked over the rail again, the distorted dollar sign had faded away.

***

WATER STREET WAS QUIET AND EMPTY. THE WIND WHIPPED and gusted like a disturbed spirit, kicking up snow and knocking ice shards from the gutters and window sills. Hatch passed the deteriorated hulk of an office complex and a few empty cars sidelined by the snow. A sign for a grimy 3-D laser-print shop cast a stale shade of light over the sidewalk.

Household Goods and Tools Printed
Thousands of Open Source Programs
!!! We Accept Food Points !!!

He arrived at Fraunces Tavern a block away, and a small cat scampered onto the sidewalk. "Look at you, just fur and bones," said Hatch. The inky-black cat pressed itself next to the rough bricks and mewed before darting away. Hatch stopped and leaned against the tavern wall, fighting off a sudden rush of nausea.

Ferret. Christ in high heaven. *The* Ferret.

And yet...

Muted sounds of music and conversation drifted from inside the tavern. After a moment, the cold wind revived him, and he jogged across the street to a brown office tower surrounded by chain fencing and barbed wire. Before the world had fallen apart, he had attended meetings here. Now slivers of glass glittered around the entrance and dense graffiti covered the square columns:

DIE OVERLORDS
I SEE THE TRUTH

Chiseled, Hatch noted, under a rough etching of a human eye, the ubiquitous symbol of the Eye Brigade. What was their grievance this week? Government cover-up of the cooling climate? Financial shenanigans? Mind control? The Brigade had many complaints, and Hatch found at least a few of them plausible. The cold, after all, had worsened but the Homeland government had forbidden publication of any material saying so; the Reset, which had eliminated the old U.S. dollar, had given them a new currency that was worth less every day; and a lot of people did seem pretty zombie-like (when they weren't busy staging food riots). He surveyed the tangled thicket of profane exclamations and suggestions surrounding the eye.

Mrooww. The cat pushed its head between Hatch's feet.

"Society's almanac," said Hatch. "The crude gravestone. The final word. Be glad you can't read."

A shout came from down the block, and Hatch spun around. P'outs? No. Too cold, even for the People Without—plus, empty streets meant no easy marks. But there were other gangs, and maybe the pushers were on the crawl, peddling tiny bags of Flit or Glide for a hundred redbacks a pop. Hatch hunched his shoulders and traipsed the rest of the way to Vinnie's Pub. He descended the pair of steps in front of the basement establishment and pulled open the door.

"You want in?" he asked the cat.

The cat crouched, alarmed at the noise from inside the pub, and then ran away.

"Close the door," someone yelled.

"For crying out loud," said another voice.

"Cold enough to freeze smoke—Who's the idiot—What in the—"

Hatch stood in the entrance and kicked the snow and grit off of his shoes, the cacophony rising until he closed the door. He navigated a sea of nasty glares and joined Big Ray and Marty at their table. Vinnie, the pub's proprietor, moved to pull out a chair. Delia, who helped Vinnie tend bar, appeared with a tray of drinks, set a seltzer and lemon at Hatch's place, and flashed him a smile. Hatch nodded.

"Delia likes you clean-cut types," said Vinnie, "even if you are a lightweight." He towered over the table. "If you had a shred of decency, Hatch, you'd order a real drink since you pissed off all my customers. I've got a two-for-forty-five bucks special tonight." He gave Hatch's shoulder a squeeze and returned to the curved, horseshoe bar.

Marty touched Hatch's glass with his mug. "Here's to you," he said with a wink. A small crowd had gathered around the TV in the rear of the pub, cheering as the baseball teams took the field in San Diego.

"Why would you stand there with the door open when it's maybe twenty degrees out?" asked Big Ray. He rolled up the worn cuffs of his shirt. "What's the matter with you?"

Hatch rocked back in his chair. Big Ray Garwin had played safety at Rutgers, but the nickname had been a joke: he was maybe one-eighty-five, though still in good shape fifteen years after his playing days. Marty Shannon was middle-aged and had served in Ireland's military intelligence branch before coming to the U.S.—back when there had been a U.S. Now he looked at Hatch and Big Ray in turn, his black eyebrows bobbing beneath a thatch of gray hair.

"The fizz water isn't going to warm you, Hatch," said Marty. "Not on a night like this."

"We've seen worse," said Hatch, shedding his jacket.

"Right," said Big Ray. "Remember February? Anyway, Hatch thinks anything above fifty degrees is a heat wave."

"So it is these days," said Marty.

Big Ray turned his chair and crossed his legs. "But blizzards in June is where I draw the line. I'll never get used to it. Or, for that matter, the sweet smell of the incinerators. Pungent tonight."

"Enhanced plasma cookers," said Marty. "Robotic, you know, blazing away with no people inside. Spooky to think about, though I see they're providing a good share of Electricorp's generation now." He raised his mug. "As for myself, I'm going to enjoy a glass. You'll remember the good Ms. Stevens, lives in the west nineties. I spent the afternoon wrestling her cupboard through the ice. Seven feet of old heart pine and heavy as a battleship, it was." He sipped the dark amber draft.

"Virginia, 1790s, a Chippendale design," said Hatch. Marty had delivered the cupboard to a buyer whose name Hatch had forgotten, except that it would probably take months to collect.

"When have you ever needed a hard day's work to justify a pint, Martin?" asked Big Ray. "Now listen to my morning. I'm up in Harlem, a place near the river, freezing my nuts off while some old guy shows me his Betty Boop collection. All from the nineteen thirties, he says."

"You'd be surprised what these old, oddball collections can fetch," said Marty.

"Betty Boop figurines," said Big Ray. "Betty Boop place-card holders, Betty Boop ash trays, purses, puzzle sets, trinket boxes, wall pockets, wristwatches, dolls—more dolls than I've ever seen in one place…"

Hatch sipped his seltzer, scarcely hearing the clink of glasses and silverware or the cheers of the baseball fans.

"…and a Betty-effin-Boop ukulele," said Big Ray, slapping the table. "Rooms full of Betty Boop. The guy wants two fifty, three hundred thousand for it. All or nothing. I'm thinking we take ten percent, maybe fifteen on something like this. You never know. The first piece I examine, it says made in Taiwan, 2025."

"Barely ten years old," said Marty.

Big Ray rubbed the back of his neck. "Then I get back to my desk and see the redback has taken a nosedive on the food points exchange."

Marty's eyes widened. "Really? God bless the Homeland dollar."

"It fell three percent," said Big Ray. "Lucky for us we don't have any money, the way it's depreciating."

Hatch turned his drink and watched a tiny rainbow glimmer off the ice. The lemon floated on top like a yellowed corpse. Too cold now for good lemons, and none coming in from Mexico or South America, not with the embargo.

"What do you mean, we've no money?" asked Marty. "We've Sammie's commission from the Hemingway letters, as fine a trade as I've seen."

Samantha, one of three remaining members of the Odysseus team and also Hatch's significant other, had brokered the sale of several letters written by Ernest Hemingway. The letters had been stolen decades earlier, recovered in recent years by a Manhattan collector, and sold in a private transaction with Samantha's assistance. Hatch and Big Ray considered the trade a minor miracle. Deals of such magnitude seldom landed in the laps of small outfits like Odysseus.

"The Hemingway fee is already gone," said Big Ray, "or it will be when Jocelyn gets it. She has stacks of bills as high as my shoulder. And the new cop'll be around any day, flashing the palm."

"It was a fine trade, the Hemingways," said Marty. "Sammie's a marvelous pro."

"It's probably her English accent," said Big Ray. Marty waved him off. "Anyway,"—Big Ray cocked his head at Hatch —"he doesn't like us talking about Samantha."

"Who cares what you talk about?" asked Hatch.

The baseball fans groaned. Marty patted Hatch's forearm. "What's it been, two years now you and Sammie've been together? I apologize, Hatch. I didn't know there was turbulence between you two."

"Of course you did," said Big Ray. "Just look at the weather, Martin. Volcanoes going off, making it freezing cold all the time. Earthquakes. Giant tornadoes. Sinkholes opening without warning. I say it all traces back to those two, and the world won't get back to normal until he and Sam call it quits."

"You saw us have one fight," said Hatch. "The time you kept me out late with the Cochoran brothers."

"I kept him out late," said Big Ray. "You believe this?"

"The Cochorans?" asked Marty. "The younger one's a good enough sort. But the older brother—"

"Crick," said Hatch.

"Crick Cochoran," said Marty with a nod. "A fearsome production of the species. Something's missing there, I'm afraid."

"But Crick loves Hatch," said Big Ray with a grin. "Loves him. Anyway, Hatch and I take the Cochoran boys out for a few drinks after they squatted the warehouse down on Tenth. This is maybe a year ago. Crick spends the whole evening beaming at Hatch for figuring out their tax problem—that is, until Crick decides to attack the bartender, but that's another story. So, yeah, we drag in past midnight."

"Three o'clock," said Hatch.

"Sam was up waiting. And like the world champion of friends that I am, I stepped up and took the fall. Swore to Samantha it was all my doing." Big Ray leaned forward. "And she gave me a look—well, let's just say I had chest pains and palpitations for a week." He looked at Hatch again. "I stand by what I said. You two are like watching a building collapse in slow motion. Just end it already."

Marty studied his ale. "Sammie's a spirited girl, to be sure."

"You can't just quit on things," said Hatch.

Vinnie appeared and handed Marty a fresh mug. Marty excused himself and followed Vinnie to the bar. Big Ray turned his chair and watched a few pitches. "New York doesn't have a chance," he said.

"I thought this game was cancelled because of the quake," said Hatch.

"California's had their share—the quakes, that tsunami, the dams breaking—but something's wrong with it all, you know what I'm saying? Like the earth itself is coming apart."

Hatch poked at his drink with a knife. Sure enough, the lemon was freeze-dried. He put down the knife and picked up a napkin and began to twist it. "Listen, Ray, I just met this guy," he said.

Big Ray eyed him closely. "You're in some kind of trouble."

"What makes you think I'm in trouble?"

"Look at you, pale and fidgety, twisting that napkin, not saying two words."

Hatch flung the napkin aside. "The guy wants me to do a pickup. Look, what's the biggest delivery charge we've ever posted?"

"Straight delivery? Maybe seventy-five hundred. Those Gee sculptures a couple of years ago."

"This is bigger."

"What, twenty-five, fifty?" Big Ray turned his chair back, glanced around, and lowered his voice. "I don't want to know what we'd be doing for that kind of number."

"A million," said Hatch.

"A *what*?" Big Ray jumped up like a jack-in-the box before figuring out there was no reason to stand. He got a few looks from nearby tables and took his seat. Hatch relayed what had happened earlier, being marched to the harbor and pressed into Ferret's service.

"Wait a minute, are we talking about *the* Ferret?" asked Big Ray. "Jesus. I didn't even know he was real."

"He's real."

"Marty will have a conniption. Listen, we trade little tables and paintings and old jewelry around the city. A few numismatic coins. A rare manuscript or two. Plain old tiques. That's what we do, Hatch. We've never messed around with the historical trade."

"Except that—"

"Besides, this reeks of a setup. Promise some dude a million, dispose of him when it's done. You think they'll ever pay?"

Hatch shifted in his chair and gazed at the old brick walls and the shadowy corners of the pub. Ideas had begun to wink in his mind like summer fireflies, and he danced his fingers along the edge of the table. An oily cloud of smoke shifted along the ceiling, and with it came the aroma of marijuana.

"The smoke," said Hatch. He rubbed his eye.

"Vinnie says the toke license is worth a hundred times the fee in food sales."

"Tobacco's illegal, but we have this?"

"There you go," said Big Ray, "trying to figure out the world again."

Hatch drummed his fingers on the table some more, thinking.

"I can't believe you've hooked up with the Ferret," said Big Ray. His face had taken on a gray pallor. "Hey, listen, let's get you the hell out of New York, get you a thousand miles away."

Hatch set his drink on the table with a loud knock, spilling a few drops of seltzer.

"You getting salty with me, Superman?" asked Big Ray.

"I won't run," said Hatch.

Big Ray's eyes narrowed. "You're plotting something, aren't you? No weapon of mass destruction is deadlier than you when you get that look."

"Don't tell me to run away like a scared little kid, Ray." Hatch folded a paper placemat and fanned himself. "I have to do what Ferret wants. I don't have much of a choice. Whatever other decisions we make, we'll make together. I want Marty on board. You'll tell him?"

Big Ray moved closer. "*What* other decisions?"

"Well, like—"

"You want to get us involved with the historical trade, don't you?" Big Ray folded his arms. "You have lost what thimbleful of intelligence you ever had. And you know what Marty will say." He imitated Marty's brogue: "It's a fool's game, lad. We can't expose the girls to it."

"We've considered the historical antiquities trade before," said Hatch.

"And we always backed away. It's a swamp full of serpents, and besides, what's our edge? What do we know about statues from Indonesia or tablets and scrolls and gold masks from some Egyptian dynasty?"

Hatch had always believed that it was Big Ray's destiny to be his closest friend and business partner, and to criticize every idea he came up with until he, Big Raymond Garwin, saw the light himself. Hatch didn't always like it, but he was reluctant to interfere with the man's destiny. "This is strange, Ray," he said, frowning. "It's kind of an intuition, a hunch I have."

"I know all about your hunches."

"You know how good my instincts are."

"Please. Just talking about Ferret makes my kneecaps tingle. And other body parts, too, and not in a good way." Big Ray finished his drink. The ice clattered when he put down his glass. "But even with Sam's commission, we're almost broke."

Hatch nodded. "The needle is on empty."

"We're practically finished. Kaput. Done. I'll have to sell this fine, black body of mine—which, you have to admit, would bring in a lot of money."

"I didn't know you were an organ donor," said Hatch.

Big Ray raised an eyebrow. "Do I detect a hint of envy?"

Hatch cracked a smile.

"But our bellies *are* flat against our backbones," said Big Ray.

"We're going to save our company, Ray. I'll do what Ferret wants and bring in the million. It'll clear the books—and more."

Big Ray chewed his lip.

Vinnie and Marty returned. "I overheard you guys talking about food points before," said Vinnie as Marty took his seat. "Prices jump around so much I can't keep the menu priced. Goddamned Reset. What's it been, four years?"

"Five," said Hatch.

"Five years." Vinnie snapped a towel and wiped a spot on the table.

In the rear of the pub, a woman in a thick pullover laughed. Hatch watched her move her long hair over her shoulder, take aim, and hurl a dart. On the TV, a fly ball lined to center for an out. Groans, hands raised in the air; someone hurled a wadded placemat at the screen.

"The last day before they shut the banks," said Vinnie, "I had maybe eighty-five hundred here and another twelve thousand locked away the office. Those were big numbers then. Remember, they snuffed all the charge cards."

"Don't I," said Big Ray.

"All cash, the old-fashioned kind, with pictures of presidents," said Vinnie. "Not these shitty redbacks we have now. Not even any crypto. Say, Ray, you think the Reset was intentional, killing off the dollar? I always wanted to ask."

"Who knows," said Big Ray. "Collapses and crises come and go. People get by or they don't. And the troubles were global, don't forget."

"It was worse here," said Vinnie. "The Chinese are okay now. The Russians plug on."

"Life is a knife fight in a pit," said Hatch.

Big Ray gave Hatch a severe look. "His mind isn't right at the moment," he said.

"You mock and ridicule, but are you free?" asked Hatch. "Are you?"

Big Ray waved him off.

"I would've expected Hatch here to ask just who benefits from all this Reset business," said Marty.

"Look who bought it all up after the collapse," said Hatch. "It's the same old game. Knock it all over and scoop it up for pennies. Put everything in a few good corporate hands and leave everybody else confused and screaming at each other."

"Please don't get him going," said Big Ray. "Please."

"Somebody always rakes in the chips," said Vinnie. "So I turned over all my cash and they gave me ten thousand new American Homeland dollars and a tax credit for the rest. A tax credit."

"Disgraceful," said Big Ray.

Vinnie scowled. "Ten thousand pinecones up the ass is what it was," he said. "With salt to follow. Nothing those people do makes sense anymore."

The toke smoke was getting to Hatch, but he perceived a pinpoint of light in the present darkness. He finished his seltzer. "World's a terrible place, Vin," he said. "We don't make the game, but we play it. We bow and scrape and seethe, but we all have to play it."

Big Ray studied Hatch for a moment and then shook his head again.

CHAPTER 2

OUTSIDE VINNIE'S, HATCH USED HIS PHONE TO SUMMON A hoo cab. The wind snapped, and the harsh tintinnabulation of chain against cold metal fencing echoed along William Street. A small, driverless hoo stopped at the curb. Hatch pushed the button and the door slid aside with a soft whoosh. The cat crouched and leapt inside. Hatch followed and gave his address.

"The requested location is inaccessible due to adverse weather," said the hoo. "May we suggest an alternative stop on Greenwich Street?"

Hatch touched the consent button on the screen. The hoo apologized for the inconvenience and began to pull away from Vinnie's, crunching over the snowy pavement.

"We used to have human cabbies," Hatch explained to the cat.

The cat stared back.

Hatch tapped his knuckle on the cab window. Human cabbies—that is, until the boys at the Tarahoo Corporation had grabbed the driverless cab franchise, as they had done in every major city. Fat bids, kickbacks to the local pols, a few dissenting bodies dropped into the local rivers, and now you had orange hoos everywhere. As the cab wound its way through downtown, Hatch gazed at the blank office towers, long dark in their upper halves, and the neglected storefronts, many covered with plywood or metal roll doors. Ruined money, rationed food, and even biometric national identification cards. Gates for the neighborhoods and bars for the windows, but they had automated cars.

"You see anything wrong with that picture?" he asked the cat.

The cat blinked. A Madam Fray tune played, and then the Infocorp news report began. The cab slowed to navigate a patch of black ice.

> *"...In Washington today, members of the Eye Brigade interrupted a speech by Senator Dan Barkin..."*

The cat braced herself against the movement of the cab. Hatch hummed Madam Fray while the news droned on. The hoo crossed Broadway and passed a chained-off parking deck and a weedy lot. They turned onto Hudson, and a handful of obscure figures leapt into the street behind the cab, shouting and hurling ice. A softball-sized chunk bounced off the trunk lid and thudded off the rear windshield. To Hatch's surprise, the glass did not shatter, but the concussive impact shocked the cat, and she gave a threatening hiss. The cab accelerated away from the gang but came to an abrupt stop after a few hundred yards, its engine silent, its flashers painting the snowy street in red and yellow tints.

> *"...The protesters stood and silently turned their backs on the Senator..."*

The gang stopped their high-fiving and stared. The hoo worked to restart its engine, sounding like a crate of scrap metal shaken and turned over.

Clickety-click-click-ggggkkkk...

The gang crept forward. Hatch hit the lock button and slipped the switchblade out of his jacket. The cat made a soft, questioning *mrooww*. The hoo's engine tried to start again.

Hatch counted five in the gang, all hooded. The two in the lead carried chunks of ice, or possibly rocks or concrete.

Clickety-click-click...

The pursuers approached, now at a slow trot, faceless phantoms in half crouches...a hundred yards...fifty...

Mrooww.

Hatch turned the knife over in his hands. Hands, eyes, faces, necks. Show them the blade, they might lose interest. They might not. Cut them to ribbons if they tried to break in. Hands, faces, eyes, necks...

> *"...protesters face up to ten years rehabilitation*
> *with the Homeland Labor Corporation..."*

The engine caught and revved. The hazard lights clicked off. The hoo spun its wheels and shot away, leaving the gang standing in place. A few minutes later, they stopped at the designated spot on Greenwich Street without having encountered another soul.

"Please slide an approved bank card or, if you use cash, your national identification card through the reader on the right side of the panel," said the hoo. "Or hold your in-chip as close as possible to the sensor. Thank you for using this Tarahoo taxi from Transcorp New York."

Hatch looked at the knife, still open in his hands. He closed it, slipped it into his pocket, swiped his natcard through the sensor, and paid cash.

> *"...reported that the Homeland population*
> *declined for the fourth consecutive year..."*

The cab door whooshed open and cold wind slapped his face. On the sidewalk, he stepped onto a frozen puddle. The ice cracked like a rifle shot and echoed off the buildings.

Mrooww.

The cat refused to be carried, but she followed Hatch as he rounded the corner of his street. Frozen, drooping trees lined the narrow lane, and they walked in the shadows, past dilapidated homes and apartments with cornices trimmed in white. Hatch's townhouse was a three-story structure, with dark brick, shuttered windows, and a low wrought-iron fence. A little shabby, he thought, but far from the worst in the neighborhood. It was empty these days but for the first floor and basement level he owned and occupied. But it was home, precious home. He negotiated the snowy steps with care and opened the front foyer door.

"This way," he said to the cat.

The cat flashed green-rimmed eyes, crept up the steps, and eased into the foyer with her whiskers twitching. Hatch unlocked his apartment door. The cat paused and then followed him inside. Concerned that Samantha might be asleep downstairs, he slipped off his boots and tip-toed through the living room and into the open kitchen area.

Mrooww.

He opened the refrigerator and poured a saucer of milk. As he placed it on the floor, the cat pushed through his hands and began lapping furiously. Still unsettled by the attack on the cab, Hatch rested against the counter and contemplated the darkened living room, with its two tall windows facing the street.

The cat purred like a motorboat.

Home. Bricks and wood and plaster, but it was his place, and he hoped to grow old here. The apartment also housed Odysseus, the living room now converted into the firm's main office. A large u-shaped workstation, shared by Jocelyn, Nathan, and Samantha, occupied much of the space. Chaotic bundles of wire and disassembled computers covered Nathan's work area, while Samantha's appeared little used apart from her phone and a small notebook. Jocelyn sat between them, her desk in perfect order, her pencils sharpened and aligned beside her desk pad. Marty's wingback chair stood apart, along with his small, wheeled work table. From the living room, a hallway led to the rear, past a bathroom and a stairway to the lower level. At the end of the hall, a back room served as an office for Big Ray and Hatch. He had retained the downstairs bedroom, bath, sitting room, and storage area for himself—and Samantha.

The cat rubbed against his ankles and mewed. Hatch checked the refrigerator again and found a few scraps of ham. The cat rose on her hind legs as he placed the dish on the floor, and then attacked the meat like a lion taking its kill in the Serengeti.

Hatch leaned against the counter again and pondered Ferret and his bloody trade. The traffic in cultural artifacts, facilitated by years of global warfare, had emerged after the Reset and fully blossomed after the failure of the North American power grid the following year. The economic depression left no country unscathed, but the former U.S. had suffered a particularly harsh blow. The grid failure had only worsened it.

Days of darkness and turmoil, the result of solar storms, said the experts, or sabotage or aged and creaking infrastructure. Whatever the cause, the event had damaged most electronic devices, erased a good share of the internet, blown smoking holes in bank and brokerage records, and blasted into vapor much of the wealth held in the various cryptocurrencies. None of those things should have happened, claimed the experts. But they were *meant* to happen, answered the Eye Brigade, who insisted that mysterious powers-that-be had caused the currency collapse and power failures as a means of looting the wealth of the population. Hatch stared at the walls around him while the cat pulled at the ham. All he knew was that the Homeland had suffered in darkness for four months, with ruined computers, molding drywall, and cars, trucks, and railcars rusting away where they stood. The global economy had flat-lined, and in the U.S. even the food distribution system had slammed to a halt. The resulting troubles had plunged the new currency—the redback—into a mode of steady depreciation and unleashed a rush into all manner of tangible goods. The authorities had been forced to reintroduce physical cash within the Homeland borders, while the more valuable yuan hoards and the gold-backed international dollars (which Homeland citizens were forbidden to own) had poured into precious stones and metals, rare art, and ancient, cultural antiquities.

Enter Ferret and his ilk: they had controlled much of the narcotics flow and almost all of the antiquities trades for years, and had now become wealthy beyond imagining. And powerful. Hatch rubbed his temples.

The Ferret.

An ancient artifact.

It was madness and idiocy—but it was also red ink turned into black. Ferret meant survival for Odysseus. Hatch leaned over the sink for a moment, squeezing his knuckles white. A car passed outside and he listened. The car went on. He exhaled.

Ferret was one decision, but Ferret's job might not occur for weeks and Odysseus needed funds today. Ray was right. Sam's Hemingway commission was a drop in the ocean.

The cat jerked at the last sliver of ham, her ribs showing with every breath. "Pretty gutsy of you to come in here," said Hatch. "You get to a point where you have to take a few chances, don't you?"

The cat looked up from the empty plate and licked her lips.

***

SAMANTHA HAD NOT BEEN IN BED OR EVEN HOME WHEN Hatch turned in for the night and, typically, she had answered none of his texts. Two hours later, however, the rapping of boot heels on the floor above pulled him upward through a kaleidoscopic cloud of dreams: it was Samantha, clopping through the work area upstairs and into the kitchen. The sink faucet ran for a moment. More clopping, the creak of stairs, and a few brisk steps in the lower hallway. The bedroom door flew open.

"Oops," said Samantha.

Hatch forced one eye open. "Where've you been?"

She stepped over and gave him an automatic kiss on his forehead. "Please, Doran. Am I to file a report?"

"Was worried."

"Hardly." She flicked on the light in the adjoining bathroom, and the glow backlit her long, chestnut hair. "You were sound asleep. But if you must know, I was out with Jocelyn and we both made it through unharmed."

Hatch raised himself on an elbow and squinted at the bathroom light. "Cab was attacked tonight. P'outs or some other thugs. They threw ice."

"Ice? How terrible for the poor cab. I trust it survived." A raised foot, *zzzip*, and her boot was off; she dropped it on the floor and then did the same with the other boot.

"I mean, it's not safe out there," said Hatch.

"Clearly not for your cab."

"Not for anybody."

"I refuse to be touched by all this negativity, Doran. Collapse. Crime. Abusive police. Starvation. Half the city sectioned off behind gates. It's all people talk about so it's no wonder it's what they get. But I will not accept it." She whirled, struck a karate pose, slashed the air, and unleashed a mighty, sock-footed kick. "Besides, if I am attacked by some gang, I will give a heel to the knee"—*whoosh*—"and then a blow to the neck"—*thunk*—"one drops to the ground, out for the count, the others flee in terror!" She flashed a smile. "I am like a very big, dangerous cat."

"Speaking of," said Hatch.

"Oh, let's don't." Samantha shed her vest and unbuttoned her blouse, a black garment that flickered in the light. She flung it over the chair along with her jeans and two socks. "You know how I feel about—*Aaaiiieee!*" She screamed and jumped back.

The cat wrestled her way from beneath Samantha's clothes and stared with eyes like black marbles, her fur disheveled and pointing in all directions. Then she leapt halfway across the room in a blur and shot through the door.

Samantha gasped. "What...is...what have you...?"

Hatch grunted and rolled over.

"Please, not some creature you found roaming the night." She stood almost naked in the semi-darkness, her hand over her heart, the curve of her hip and breast bordered by the bathroom light. "Or did you spend your evening rounding up strays?"

"No."

"Let me guess," she said, stepping into the bathroom. "You were hanging about at Vinnie's while Marty and Ray drank away the salaries they aren't getting this month." The faucet squeaked and Samantha began brushing her teeth and making rapid spitting sounds.

"I've been dragged into one of the antiquities mobs, one of the international outfits," said Hatch. "At gunpoint, more or less."

"What did you say?" The water stopped and Sam stuck her face out, toothpaste foam all over her mouth.

"Forget it."

"Sure?"

"A new line of work is all. Something we've never done before."

"Another unchased rainbow." Samantha wiped her lips and laughed. "Another transformative plot to fill our empty coffers."

"I've filled them plenty of times before."

"The idea *du jour*. Throw it against the wall, see what sticks."

Hatch punched the pillow, fluffing it, and burrowed his head into the foam.

Samantha pointed the toothbrush in his direction. "Angry, are you? Because you know I'm right. For you, life has to be a slog. We all must fight, fight, fight for everything. And because you believe in the slog, the slog is what you get."

"You don't catch the news very often, do you?"

"My point exactly. You invite negative energy to wrap itself all around your efforts and—*shffft*—it smothers them cold."

"How I love new age flim-flam after midnight."

"Don't be sarcastic, Doran. The trick is to nurture your ideas with belief so the things you want can appear in your life. Lama Ravi Pearl says so."

Hatch rolled over, put his hands behind his head, and looked at her with one eye. "And that's how you do it?"

"I am in the flow," she said, pointing the toothbrush at herself. "All the things necessary for the world I want for myself already exist. The power of my belief plucks my creations out of the stream of time and possibility. It is simply how reality works, says the Lama. You see, Doran, I believe wholly in my ideas. And because I believe, I will make a different world, a world I want. We are each the creators of our lives."

"Cue the trumpets," said Hatch. "Unfurl the banners."

"You old grump."

"Pretty soon, in the stream of time, we are going to go bankrupt."

Samantha, now free of her clothes, came over and rubbed her nose against his. "Nooooo," she said, "we are not." Hatch found her gesture enchanting, which further exasperated him. He turned his face away and she returned, smiling, to the bathroom. He heard her urinating, followed by a flush, and then the sound of the towel cabinet opening.

"So I'm walking to Vinnie's tonight," said Hatch. "This is sometime after nine. Maybe nine-thirty."

"Um-hmm," said Samantha from the bathroom.

Hatch yawned again. "Look, what I have to tell you is hush-hush, Sam, okay? Very, very confidential."

The shower burst on with a loud *fittzzing* sound. The curtain rings slid along the metal rod and then slid back again, and Samantha began humming a tune. Steam drifted through the open door. In the opaque light, Hatch stared at a crack running along the ceiling. He knew Sam's shower would last until the hot water ran out—unless, in her world, she believed it should not run out and showered on until dawn. A heavy numbness descended, and his thoughts began to scatter.

Later, in the darkness, Samantha poked him hard on the shoulder. Hatch jumped awake, unaware of where he was and convinced he had been asleep for a long time. Samantha, sitting in bed next to him with her legs folded under, unwrapped the towel from around her body and began rubbing it through her hair.

"You don't respect my beliefs," she said.

Hatch said of course he did—or maybe he cursed—but only a garbled croak came out.

"So are you going to tell me about your big new scheme or not?" asked Samantha.

"Not." He fell back on his pillow.

Samantha poked his shoulder again. "Cat got your tongue, eh?" She cackled. "It's just as well. I've got other plans for you right now."

CHAPTER 3

HATCH CREPT OUT OF BED EARLY THE NEXT MORNING, leaving Samantha in a deep, unmoving sleep. A half hour later, he had made a disorganized jumble of his basement storeroom, finding in the process an unused pair of rain boots and a plastic bin containing a few holiday decorations he did not recognize. Then he spotted his quarry, a polished wooden crate shoved against the wall under a low shelf. He waved away the cobwebs and dragged it into the open.

The cherry-stained crate, with rubber grips along its edges and fastened with steel latches, contained a cornucopia of silver objects: cutlery, small plates, cups, and other items. Hatch removed a small platter wrapped in a sheet of thin foam and studied the engraved floral designs. Behind the etchings, his own reflection stared back at him, his dark hair tousled, his eyes still puffy with sleep.

The cat peeked in from the doorway. "Welcome to your first day," said Hatch.

The cat yawned.

"You haven't seen the chaos. It's quiet now, but wait."

The cat left and Hatch returned to his crate. Leave it here or sell it? Sell it. No debate. They were out of money and he was on the clock. He re-wrapped the tray and then noticed another item, a simple silver chalice that had belonged to his father. A bolt of anger shot through him, but he let it pass and repacked the silver in the gray light of the storeroom.

Upstairs, he found Jocelyn at her workstation, a pencil protruding from her hair and the cat stretched on the shelf above her. Hatch set the heavy crate near the front door.

"All these bills," said Jocelyn. She spotted the crate and her mouth fell open. "Tell me that isn't the silver from the estate sale, the one on Staten Island a few years ago."

"Good morning," said Hatch.

"You're planning to sell it at the exchange, aren't you?"

Hatch walked into the kitchen.

"Jesus in a coke bottle, Hatch. It's your silver, not the firm's." Jocelyn lowered her voice. "What I'm saying is, Sam goes bazonka when you sell off your stuff. At least hide the crate, okay? Like why set her off, right?"

"I bought the silver for emergencies, remember?" he asked from the kitchen. "You don't think this qualifies?"

"Why are you so crabby?"

"I'm not crabby!"

They stared at each other.

"Sorry. I guess I am a little edgy," said Hatch.

"It's out of my hands," said Jocelyn. She returned to her collection of invoices while Hatch scrounged around in the refrigerator. No more milk, no eggs. In the tiny pantry, he discovered two slices of soy bread and, hearing Samantha moving downstairs, he placed them in the toaster. His stomach rumbled but he found only a lone, brown banana in a basket on the counter.

Mrooww.

The cat wove between his feet. Hatch cut a portion of the mushy banana and gave it to her. She sniffed it cautiously, licked it a few times, and gave him a blank look.

"Okay," said Jocelyn, tapping the pencil on the workstation, "with the fee from the Hemingways, you said to pay out half the back-salaries, which I knew wouldn't work, and besides, we have the Fuelcorp bill."

"Fuelcorp? Didn't we agree to reimburse Marty for gas?"

"We got the card because you kept stretching out his reimbursement. Remember that time he came in here with his bullwhip and like broke the table? We owed him a frigging fortune." The cat leapt onto Jocelyn's desktop and landed with one paw in a bowl of paperclips and clamps. She lifted her paw and stepped over a stapler without further disturbing the bowl. Jocelyn consulted a small tablet computer. "And I have the Electricorp bill? Some of it is yours."

"Take it out of my draw."

"Oh." Jocelyn stopped and pushed up her glasses. "I didn't put in a check for you or Ray. You said salaries, not draw. Sam has her share of the commission, of course. So now we really are in the hole."

Hatch sighed. "Forget it. By the way, I read a piece a couple of days ago about decorative eggs. I was thinking if we put something on the website—"

"Eggs?"

"Not real eggs. Porcelain, collectible eggs."

Jocelyn shook her head as if to clear her mind. "There's the plumber, Hatch. The toilet was back-spewing half the crap in Greenwich Village all over our floor the other day. You weren't here. You're like never here when this stuff happens. So anyway, I wrote the plumber a check for part of the bill, you know a paper check where you tear it out of the little book? Well, it bounced. It totally bums me because I do not know how I screwed up the numbers so much, and now the plumber wants the rest of the payment in cash. Like currency. Redbacks."

"Porcelain eggs," said Samantha, entering from downstairs, bleary-eyed and yawning. "More schemes and dreams. How I crave a real egg, poached."

"Hi," said Jocelyn as she tapped the screen of her tablet. "We were trying to figure out how to counterfeit money."

"Doran has grand plans," said Samantha. She kissed him on the cheek with a sulky, dissatisfied look. "Maybe he'll tell you about them. He wouldn't tell me."

The toaster chimed. Hatch returned to the kitchen and spread the last of the butter over the toast. "No eggs," he said as he handed the toast to Samantha.

Jocelyn tapped her pencil again. "We have all Marty's expenses: three ball games, dinners, a chartered cruise, all with gatekeepers. I'm looking at all this like, why not just give the gatekeepers shares of Odysseus already? I know, I know, we'd get nothing through the section gates if we didn't grease them, blah, blah, blah, but it'd be cheaper, am I right?"

"Cost of doing business," said Hatch.

"Cost," said Jocelyn with a pout. "We have costs and costs, too much cost." Her long, thick black hair, black sweater, black eyeglass frames, and black jeans made Hatch think of crows, cawing overhead as if he were fresh kill, screeching *cash, cash, cash.* Well, how much did Odysseus have? Had they overlooked any possible collections? Probably not. Unforgiving numbers tumbled through his head.

Jocelyn resumed her litany: a few dollars for Ms. Rochambeau, who lived a few doors away; she was frail and unwell and the entire neighborhood usually pitched in. Then the revenue taxes, the state tax surcharges, and the new city excise taxes. "And Nathan's internet charges and those replacement computer boards weren't free, either," she said. "Plus, they issued a new HAC database update."

"Bless the Homeland Antiques Commission," said Samantha, her eyes turned upward.

"We don't have a choice," said Hatch. "Our business depends on end-running HAC's authorized prices."

"There are always choices," said Samantha archly.

Hatch ditched the banana peel and returned to the work area. "Look, Joss, we have to squeeze more, at least for a little longer."

"The slog," said Samantha. She dropped her dish in the sink with a loud racket.

Jocelyn aligned her pencils. The cat swatted at them. "Epic fail, meow machine," said Jocelyn. She realigned the pencils and whisked away an unseen speck of dust. "Rule number one, kitty: you do not mess with my stuff if you expect to make it around here."

Hatch was tapping out a text to Big Ray when the front door opened. Nathan entered with his GameHead goggles riding high on his forehead.

"Don't tell me you were gaming while you walked through the slush," said Jocelyn. She turned to Hatch, "I can't believe he hasn't gotten himself killed."

"Don't touch my goggles," said Nathan. He was slight of build, and the goggles made his head seem oversized.

"Don't touch him at all," said Samantha, taking her seat next to Jocelyn. "His brain is full of game implants and he must be fairly humming with current. It may not even be safe to sit near him. I hadn't thought of it before."

Nathan rolled his chair over to his assemblage of ancient computers and pulled the GameHead contraption over his face. He looked disheveled, with his shirt buttons fastened through the wrong holes and his coarse, black hair matted by his goggles. He leaned back in his chair, his mouth hanging open, and drifted into a game. Jocelyn reached over and punched him on the shoulder.

"Ouch!" Nathan rubbed his arm but didn't interrupt his game.

"Hey, computer man, you need to ditch the goggles and fix my tablet. The connection keeps winking on and off." Jocelyn waited, but Nathan didn't respond. "This bruh's gone," she said, shaking her head. "Game-zoned."

"No, I'm in a jungle in the mountains," said Nathan in a faraway voice. "Near Machu Picchu, I think, and I can feel the heat on my skin."

"It's true," said Samantha, peering at Nathan. "He's sweating. How creepy. Just like the way he worships that picture on his desk." She swiped the glossy photo.

"The leopard men are stalking me," said Nathan. "They sense my fear and they prey on it. They need my fear."

Samantha studied Nathan's prized photograph of Kee Bickerman, the trillionaire founder of GameHead. Bickerman, not yet thirty, had invented the brain implants which fueled his virtual reality games. He was a mega-celebrity and a recluse, fully partaking of the divine as far as implanted gamers like Nathan were concerned.

"He is rather cute," said Samantha.

"Put it back," cried Nathan. He yanked off his goggles, grabbed the photo from Samantha, and locked it away.

Hatch checked his watch. "I have to go put some redbacks in the hat."

Samantha stood and bowed toward Hatch. "Oh, High Lord Tique Broker, lunatic conjurer of pub-born business schemes which ring like sweet music to his impoverished subjects."

Hatch looked away.

"Hobbled by childhood loneliness, m'lord overcame mediocre grades and even the loss of all his treasure." Hatch strode into the kitchen, a hot pressure growing behind his eyeballs. Samantha laughed and made a sweeping gesture. "But one day soon, I, Samantha, humble vassal, will strike the golden vein and put each and all on clouds of ease. And on that glorious day, m'lord will say—a roll of the drums, please —he will say *thank you*." She smiled and then noticed Hatch's crate next to the door. "What's this?" she asked.

The air pressure in the room changed. Jocelyn shrank over her bills.

"It's the silver," said Hatch. He glanced at his watch again. "I'm taking it to the exchange, and I'm almost late."

Nathan sighed, lost in his game.

"Are you really?" asked Samantha. Tiny pink roses blossomed on her cheeks. "Look at you. You gave up most of your living space to put our office here, and just last year you sold those two paintings."

"I never liked them," said Hatch.

"And before the paintings, you sold your clothes."

"What did I need all those business suits for?"

"And now the silver?"

Hatch raised a finger. "This is what the silver's for, Sam. And I got it for next to nothing, remember?"

Samantha radiated fury, and Hatch imagined the paint beginning to peel. "Liquidating your assets for this wretched business," she said, "and for these people, including me. What a bloody hero you are, Doran, but are we worth it? Stop doing it. I don't want you to. I have already decided we will have enough."

"Right. Plucked from the stream of time."

Her eyes blazed. "Rather than use your mind and your heart to manifest new circumstances, you merely acquiesce to the blight and decay all around you."

"Yeah, look at the mess I've made of the world."

"You fail to imagine, thus you fail to create, Doran." Samantha's voice had begun to tremble. "What comes next? Will you eat your toes and fingers?"

Hatch moved over to the window, counting backward from one hundred in threes, but losing interest somewhere in the eighties. Outside, a blur of slushy townhome facades glistened in the early light. Nathan whimpered from behind his goggles.

"It's not a failure of anything," said Hatch quietly.

"Oh, go, then." Samantha grabbed a notepad and hurled it in his direction. It helicoptered into the wall. "Perhaps I will manage to produce a bit of revenue before you end up stark naked beneath your barrel." She marched downstairs, her heels making loud beats on the floor.

Hatch hefted the crate. His face burned. Jocelyn pointed a pencil at him. "I told you so, hoss. Besides, Sam is powerful and you should revere her abilities, but you don't."

Nathan screamed. "So hot!" he cried, waving his arms. His hair was damp and plastered against his forehead. "So hot and so…so scared!"

"Instead, you leave me in this madhouse," said Jocelyn.

The cat mewled. Hatch shook off a pang of dread and left.

CHAPTER 4

CERTIFIED GOODS EXCHANGE NY–3, PART OF THE NATIONAL Exchange Corporation Network, covered the lower two-thirds of the former Washington Square Park, and conducted business on Tuesday and Friday of each week. A vast, open-air flea market, the exchange allowed any citizen to buy, sell, or swap a variety of used goods without a retail license and free of the usual bevy of sales and transfer taxes. Hatch had chosen to take a private e-carriage to the exchange instead of a hoo. As they flew down Hudson, his driver, a boy of no more than thirteen, swerved to avoid a bicyclist and caught the curb, almost pitching Hatch from his seat.

"Farting two-wheeled bastard," cried the boy as the e-carriage jounced over a pothole.

Hatch gripped his impossibly heavy crate with one hand and the carriage's grab-bar with the other. Death carts, the e-carriages were called: low-slung, open buggies allowable for paid transportation of less than two miles. They were cheap, fast, and famously invisible to the hoos. The boy sped beneath a red traffic light and accelerated like a terrorist fleeing a ticking bomb.

"West entrance?" he asked in a breaking voice as they flew down a narrow, slushy side street. "Cops are thin today, the pickers are out big-time." He swerved to miss an ice patch and two pedestrians leapt out of the way. Profanity exploded in their wake.

"West gate," Hatch confirmed.

They shot across Waverly and missed colliding with a hoo by inches. The hoo neither slowed nor sounded a horn. At the southwest corner of the exchange, Hatch paid the driver and climbed out of the cart. He found Big Ray standing under a *NOTHING TO HIDE—NOTHING TO FEAR* sign.

"What is it with you?" asked Big Ray. "Making me drag my carcass out of bed at the crack of dawn. Lucky I haven't cracked my skull, all this ice around here." He winced at the sun and puffed a cloud of vapor.

"Oxygen, in the form of good silver," said Hatch. He hefted the crate. "And it's almost nine o'clock, and the snow is melting."

"The silver from the estate sale?" asked Big Ray. "Don't forget, we put your dad's chalice in that crate."

"I didn't forget."

Big Ray looked into the distance. "Come on, Hatch. You don't want to sell your dad's—I mean, it's a fine piece."

Hatch suffered a jolt of dizziness, and a distant whine rang in his ears. He shook it off. Behind them, a spiked iron fence extended the length of the park, enclosing long rows of cubicles, kiosks, and small huts painted in drab grays and browns and surrounded by hagglers.

"And why sell anything?" asked Big Ray. "Don't you have this Ferret deal?"

"The one you said I should run away from?"

"Well I've been—"

"Forget it," said Hatch. "Jocelyn needs the cash now. Besides, I like where silver prices are."

At the gate, a morose German shepherd flattened his ears and sniffed the crate. Hatch stepped to the scanner and placed his hand on the emoto-pad. The panel flashed yellow-orange, and the guard did a double take. "You upset about something, bud?" he asked Hatch.

Hatch sniffed. "Troubles at home," he said.

The guard took this under consideration and waved Hatch through. Big Ray passed without incident, and they entered through the gate and advanced toward the market area. Exchangecorp had demolished everything south of the central fountain to make room for the sales huts, which now stretched the length of the park in several jumbled rows. Vendors called out, offering old nylon coats, oiled hats, bolts of denim, used shoes and boots of every variety, pots, pans, small tools, and sundry other goods. The 3-D laser printers had supplanted much traditional manufacturing, but people still gathered to trade the old factory-made items for whatever they might fetch.

"I want cash for this crate," said Hatch. "You remember the dealer we used for the platinum?"

"That was a while ago," said Big Ray. "Cranky old fool. He won't give you any cash. No one here will."

"He will when he sees what's inside," said Hatch.

"No, he'll wave a stack of Exchangecorp vouchers at you." They moved on and Big Ray began to mutter to himself. "Just look at us, scraping bottom every month, scrambling to rake in enough redbacks to keep our nose above the waves."

Hatch vaguely recalled the dealer having been stationed near the exit gate. He surveyed the scene around him. Sun glinted off a puddle of melted slush and a display of old appliances.

"We didn't come from much, brother, but just look at us now," said Big Ray. "We don't have two nickels."

"Then file for assistance," said Hatch.

"And be jammed into the Laborcorp lottery? Oh, ho, ho. It'll be off to the camps for us strapping, able-bodied types. We need better options."

"Become an anti-corper or join the Eye Brigade."

Big Ray huffed.

"Or hook up with one of the collectives," said Hatch. "That is, if you don't mind getting pulsed by the cops every week and having your little garden burned. Or become a p'out and go live in Central Park."

"Well, thanks a pantload," said Big Ray. Hatch walked away and Big Ray trotted along after him. "Listen, maybe I was too negative last night on this Ferret business. Maybe we should see where it goes. I'm thinking we collect the million and clear the bills. Then we sink the balance into a new venture, a change of direction, get some wind at our back."

Hatch stopped. The crate had grown heavier and was pressing painful creases into his palms. "The new venture is, we'll belong to Ferret," he said.

"I thought about this all night."

"And now you want to rub elbows with a global antiquities runner? You sure?"

"Well, you can't just quit," said Big Ray.

"Quit?"

Big Ray's chest swelled. "No pain, no gain, my man."

"You did say quit."

"I say take the next step, Hatch. See if we can't chisel out some role for ourselves."

Hatch stalked off, having caught a glimpse of a familiar green sign. Big Ray followed. "What a pain in the ass you are," he said. "What kind of fight did you and Sam have? Maybe I should just go home."

"Then go," said Hatch.

"If we had Ferret's million in hand, I would go. But with the gate pickers out in force, you'll never make it out of here. If you die, then there's no pickup and where does that leave me?"

The metals dealer was a slumped creature with a faded sweatshirt and a scraggly beard that had given up the effort. Inside the sales hut, he withdrew one of the small bowls from Hatch's crate and examined it.

"This is for cash," said Hatch.

"Can't do it. Policy." The metals dealer pointed to a sign over the counter forbidding any cash trades. "I'll give you exchange credits. You'll be better off anyway."

"What'd I tell you?" asked Big Ray, and to the metals dealer, "Watch yourself, he's in a mood."

The dealer raised the tray and whistled.

"Change your policy," said Hatch.

The metals dealer rubbed his thumb along the edge of the dish and licked his lip. "I'll give you forty credit books for it."

"Cash."

The metals dealer gave Hatch the up-and-down. "You don't listen, do you?"

"He doesn't listen to anybody," said Big Ray. "But he makes up for it with his patience and his charm and endearing sense of humor."

Hatch glared at Big Ray, who raised his hands and backed off. The metals dealer pulled out the canvas bag from the crate and spread out forks, spoons, several ladles, and knives.

"This is a waste of time," said Hatch. He began to load the pieces back into the crate.

"We haven't even looked at all of it yet," said the metals dealer with a dumbfounded expression. "Look, I pay you cash, I have to fight off everybody else. Besides, the exchange don't like it."

"You want the goods, figure it out."

"Devil dancing on a pin," said the metals dealer. He lifted the chalice and his mouth fell open. He ran his finger along its side and stared at Hatch. "You can get a pretty pile of stuff with the coupons," he said.

Hatch extended his hand. "Give it to me."

"Well, let me think about it," said the metals dealer. He clutched the chalice to his chest.

"I'll go downtown."

"You'd have the taxes."

"I'd have cash."

The metals dealer handed over the chalice and began to pore over the other items. He grunted and complained and raised the cutlery to what meager sunlight penetrated the window. After a suitable show of indecisiveness, he allowed that maybe this once, in view of the quality of the items, and despite what an ornery bastard Hatch was, he would deal in cash. But Hatch shouldn't expect top dollar. He couldn't walk in on a man this way and demand things. An hour of grinding negotiation ensued over every piece in the crate, accompanied by name-calling and several threats to walk away. When it was over, Hatch zipped the packet of redbacks inside his bomber and fastened the jacket to his throat. They had reached agreement on every item except his father's chalice, and Hatch handed the cup to Big Ray, who fastened it into the inside pocket of his baggy field coat.

At twenty minute intervals, the exit gates opened to a cleared area near West 4th Street. There Big Ray and Hatch lingered as a sea of gaunt faces swirled beyond the iron bars. The occasional cop shoved through the crowd, whirling a baton or fingering a taser for show. A grubby man with cropped hair thrust his face between the fence bars. He wore a yellow T-shirt sporting the human-eye symbol along with a single line: *I see the truth.* "They've taken our minds!" he cried. "They've taken our minds!" He tried to shake the fence bars.

"Unbelievable," said Big Ray. "I see maybe three cops. Most days you have stoppers by the dozen."

"We're slaves!" The man wearing the eye waved his hand. "We're slaves!"

The horn wailed and the gate hummed and slid open. A loudspeaker ordered the crowd to clear, yet the hands came, shoving, poking, and patting Hatch's hips and buttocks. He squeezed the packet of redbacks against his ribs and pushed against the crowd, but a man with long, purple hair and wearing a trench coat grabbed Hatch's sleeve and slung him to the ground. A roar went up, and a tangle of rough figures converged above. A dozen arms and half as many blazing faces shut out the light and rained punches on Hatch's neck and groin.

He tried to scuttle away. Another man grabbed his collar and said he used to be a banker, he used to have a real job, and it wasn't personal—he landed a hard kick in Hatch's ribs—it's not personal, he repeated. Hatch curled into the fetal position. The purple-haired man shed his overcoat and, standing stark naked over Hatch, bared his teeth and descended. The banker landed a blow on Hatch's forehead and the scene blurred. Hatch squeezed tighter to absorb the punishment without raising his arms and exposing his pockets.

Then a war cry sounded, a mad yell, and Big Ray seized a fistful of purple hair and slammed the man head-first onto the pavement. He moved no more. Big Ray whooped. He clocked another man with a right hook. A woman shrieked and fell backward.

Hatch scrambled to his feet. The banker tried to run, but Hatch spun him around and smacked him in the face with his elbow. The banker staggered and fell. Hatch moved to give him another, but a filthy man with an unkempt beard and a red cap grabbed Hatch's collar.

"Stopper!" someone screamed. "Stopper! Stopper!"

A huge cop, wielding a baton, thrust his way through the crowd. "See, there, you sorry piece of scum," he said to a p'out.

"Stopper! Stopper!"

The cop administered his baton to the red ball cap. A muffled crack, and the man crumpled. A greasy woman in a blue rain jacket crouched over him, screaming, making fierce, obscene gestures at Hatch, Big Ray, and the cop.

"They smell money better than those dogs," said the cop. The woman unleashed a torrent of obscenity. The cop laughed. "You're not fit for the labor camps," he told her.

The gate pickers melted away. Hatch wiped his face, fished out a fifty, and pressed it into the stopper's hand.

"You got hold of yourself, buddy?" asked the cop.

Hatch nodded, breathing heavily. The cop touched the brim of his cap and sauntered off.

"Let's get out of here," said Big Ray.

Then Hatch spotted the banker at the edge of the crowd, sitting alone and rubbing his jaw. Hatch took off running, but just as he reached the banker, Big Ray caught him from behind, wrapped his arms around Hatch's chest, and carried him away kicking air. They returned to the apartment without speaking.

"What were you going to do, kill the guy?" Big Ray finally asked.

"I didn't like his attitude," said Hatch.

"His attitude." Big Ray shook his head.

Hatch touched the cut above his eye. At the end of the street, sporadic traffic crawled along Washington, now renamed Polygender Street, but still referred to as Washington by everyone who was not a hoo. Across from his apartment a condemned townhouse, tied up for years in tax litigation, stood in dignified ruin. Hatch found a dry spot on the stoop and sat, tapping the packet of redbacks inside his pocket.

"How long ago did we move the firm into your apartment?" asked Big Ray, gazing up at Hatch's front windows. "Four years ago, wasn't it?"

"Four years in September."

"When the wealth levies hit. They seized the bank deposits that summer."

"You remember the quartering riots?" asked Hatch.

"Who doesn't? Those Congressmen pulled apart. Then the mob in Chicago cooked and ate the Senator. Brushed barbeque sauce right on him, remember? I hope I never see anything like it again."

Big Ray and Hatch had become friends during their freshman year in college. They had cut their professional teeth trading derivatives for China-Morgan Bank, and from there had established a modest hedge fund of their own, spending five years arguing and raking in truckloads of legal tender.

The currency collapse and bank closures had laid waste to their accumulated winnings, however, and finding themselves poor (though in easier circumstances than most), they had founded Odysseus.

"I signed more papers last week on the brokerage suits," said Big Ray. "You think we'll ever get anything back?"

"Nope."

"I don't think so, either."

"But we have our apartments, we have a roof," said Hatch. The past few years rolled through his mind like a movie on fast-forward: the disorder and the mad scramble for cash after the banks closed, with everyone rushing to sell anything of value; the cancellation of the Constitution, dissolving the old United States; the raging wars and international embargoes against the Homeland; the youth collectives and anticorpers and the rise of the p'outs in every city; the food quotas and oppressive tactics of Policecorp. The world before the Reset seemed as distant as a faded dream. "I played it all straight, Ray," said Hatch. "Still, I ended up in Ferret's snare."

"Not your fault, partner."

Hatch examined his scraped and bloody knuckles. "This deal with Ferret could save our company. I can't chuck it all and disappear." The dizziness he had felt earlier touched him again, and the high-pitched whine returned and resolved into something obscurely rhythmic before it faded away. He squeezed his eyes shut. "I can't explain it, but I feel driven," he said. "It's like, if I don't do this job for Ferret I'm going to run out of air. I'm twitchy as hell about it. You ever feel that way?"

"No," said Big Ray. He unfastened his pocket and handed Hatch the chalice. Hatch turned his father's silver goblet over in his hands and noticed a fragment of the engraving around the base.

...to our Goddess of Balance...

His anger returned, and he remembered not his father but his grandmom. "Try forgiveness, Hatch," Mae had said. "There is so much we cannot know about your father." But Hatch knew enough and he preferred to forget. What finer revenge existed than to erase the worthless bastard from memory?

"I talked to Marty last night about this Ferret thing, and it's going to be like breaking rocks to get him on board," said Big Ray. "He'll be here any minute. Consider this a heads-up."

Hatch rubbed the tarnished bottom of the chalice with his thumb. "I'll come up with something to grease the skids with Marty," he said. "But he owns his piece, he deserves a voice. He's been with us from the start."

Big Ray opened his wallet and checked his food points card. "Before we sit down, I'm off to find some coffee and chow. You want anything?"

Hatch stared at his hands and flexed his fingers.

"What now?" asked Big Ray.

"I should go back and finish the job on that banker," said Hatch.

Big Ray pinched the bridge of his nose.

"You think he's still there, Ray?"

Big Ray put away his wallet. "Truly, you have to be the most pig-headed, obstinate soul I've ever known," he said.

"It's what you really admire about me, isn't it?" Hatch was unable to keep from smiling. "Are you going to Smytes?" he asked, referring to the deli at the end of the street.

"Where else would I go?" asked Big Ray.

"Then coffee, black," said Hatch. "The strongest he's got."

***

HATCH SET THE CHALICE ON JOCELYN'S DESK, AND SHE jumped from her chair, alarmed, and began screeching about the cut above his eye. She steered him into the kitchen, ran cold water over a towel, and stood on tip-toe, touching the towel to his forehead. "What happened?"—she daubed and scraped—"and please hold still, there's grit I have to remove—and your knuckles! What have you done? It was a man thing, wasn't it? Look at your hand, just look." She unwrapped the towel. "I really like you Hatch. I mean, you care. And you open doors for women. Call me a throwback." Jocelyn made a harsh laugh, and a tear glistened at the corner of her eye. "I'm kind of a sucker for a gentleman. But I told you to leave the silver, didn't I?"

Hatch sighed.

"Didn't I?" She slapped him with the damp towel. He raised his arms to protect himself. She slapped him again, and this time the towel made a snapping sound. Hatch cried out as she slapped him a third time. "How can you be so stupid as to almost get yourself killed?" she asked.

Hatch lowered his arms. Jocelyn began to cry and talk in long, unconnected sentences. He learned that Nathan had been overcome by his game and that Sam had taken him back to his apartment. He learned that Sam was still angry and that she was complicated and that he closed himself off to her. "Like you don't even try to get on her wavelength," said Jocelyn, "and she says you have like daddy issues—"

"I what?"

Jocelyn turned, her eyes red-rimmed. "I shouldn't've—"

"She really said that?"

Jocelyn flashed a shaky grin. "Sometimes I think I'm thinking something when I'm actually saying it out loud. Do you ever do that?" She waited. "No, you don't."

"No."

She grabbed a tissue and honked into it. "The point is, you need to open up a little more, bruh, stop being such a wall."

Hatch felt a stab of pain in his ribs. "I'm having this discussion with you why?"

"Because I'm on your side, hoss. You don't know who your friends are sometimes. I told Sam last night, you are a good guy with like a really big heart."

Hatch groaned. The two of them, dissecting him in some bar. It was too much.

Marty entered with a jaunty air and winked at Hatch. Big Ray followed, balancing a tray of coffees from Smyte's on one arm. He set a cup on Jocelyn's desk. "Hatch took the plunge with a few dozen p'outs," he said. "I had to drag him out of the fire."

"You didn't do a very good job," said Jocelyn, wiping her eyes and returning to her desk. Marty and Big Ray disappeared down the hall, Big Ray providing an exaggerated account of his heroics at the exchange.

"Here's fifty thousand," said Hatch, giving Jocelyn the packet. "Can you work it into your numbers?"

Jocelyn flipped through the bills. "You shouldn't have done this."

Hatch's massaged his elbow. "Listen, on the cash projection, did you allow for the cop?"

Jocelyn cursed under her breath.

"When will he be around?"

"Soon. It's a new stopper. Everyone on the street says he's a real hard-ass." Jocelyn nibbled an eraser. "Oh, I almost forgot. Someone left this outside the door for you." She passed Hatch an envelope, and he ripped it open to find directions for Ferret's pickup. "I'll add in the new money and redo the numbers," she said. "I want to take another crack at the receivables, anyway."

Hatch slid the envelope into his pocket. "Bring the numbers in as soon as you have them, do you mind?"

Jocelyn paused. "You want me to interrupt your meeting?"

"I do."

She poked him with the pencil. "I know what you're up to, boss man. I'll play along." She gave him a conspiratorial smile.

"Just tap on the door and come in, okay?"

In the office, the aroma of roast coffee and toasted soy bagel filled the room. Hatch cleared a space on his desk for the chalice and popped the lid off of his coffee. Bookshelves lined the walls, stacked with antiques catalogues, old novels, and works on comparative mythology and mathematics from Hatch's college days. Big Ray stood beside his own desk, which was stationed under an oval window overlooking the rear courtyard. Marty had taken a chair.

"So, Marty, Ray filled you in?" asked Hatch.

"I did," said Big Ray. "Chapter and verse." He spun his chair around next to Marty and faced Hatch's desk. Hatch rocked back in his chair with a soul-tearing squeak.

Marty inched forward, the corner of his mouth twitching upward. "Yes, Raymond gave me the whole tale, Hatch, and it got me pondering. I made a few calls this morning, and I believe we can get you safely out of town. I don't want you to worry. We know places where not even Ferret will find you." He leaned back with a satisfied look and nodded at Big Ray.

"You want me to hide," said Hatch. "What is it with you two?"

"I want to create choices, sure," said Marty. "It didn't seem Ferret gave you any."

"It's not a good choice."

Big Ray glanced at Marty.

"Well, now, neither is charging off barefoot into the snake house," said Marty. "I've been around long enough to see a few things I don't want to see again, lad."

"It's cowardly," said Hatch. "I won't do it."

"I don't see this as a test of your manhood," said Marty. "Getting tied at the end of Ferret's string puts Odysseus in a tough spot, you see. I won't deny all you've done for us, Hatch. You were one of the first to see the possibilities of tiques brokering when everything else was going up in smoke. You got us ahead of the pack, kept food on our plates, and you've been damned unselfish, making your place available, selling off things you hold dear, buying us time."

Hatch sighed. A thick cloud of steam rose from his cup.

"I appreciate it and I respect it," Marty continued, "but you're prone to get the bit in your mouth and go charging off." He paused and looked right into Hatch's eyes. "If nothing else, we have to protect the girls. This is not what anyone signed on for."

"It's not what I signed on for, either," said Hatch.

"I understand why you feel hard against the rocks, Hatch."

"I *am* against the rocks." Hatch leaned forward with another wrenching squeak. "How long do I stay hidden, Marty? The rest of my life? Do you think Ferret will leave any of you in peace if I go away?"

Big Ray had been listening in silence. "No," he said. "Ferret won't leave us alone. But a million redbacks mops up a lot of problems, and"—he gave Hatch a significant look—"we may have opportunities on the other side of this."

Marty turned in his chair. "I told you last night I object to it, Raymond. We've nothing to do with the cultural antiquities trade. I've been around a while, and that road'll take you places you never meant to go. You'll tell yourself otherwise, but certain things will be expected and God's help to you."

"The tiques game is drying up," said Big Ray. "No one wants to face it. Five years now, people liquidating old stuff. More and more brokers getting into the biz. Prices down, commissions down. Let's be objective. The money is in the historicals."

Marty seemed surprised. "Why, yes, Raymond. Crime and other kinds of thuggery have always paid well. Don't let anyone tell you different. But that has never been our standard, now has it?"

"Drying up, Martin." Big Ray whistled like the desert wind. "Besides, what Odysseus is doing now is a crime, technically."

Hatch fidgeted. The office seemed small and tight and low on oxygen. He realized he was digging his nails into his palm.

"Well, you don't go jumping into the nastiest sandbox in the world," said Marty. "How do you know Hatch isn't some kind of sacrificial pawn here?"

"Does it matter?" asked Hatch.

Marty shot Hatch a dark look, and a cord in his neck twitched. "You can't get in the crosshairs of these kinds of people, Hatch."

"I have no choice about the pickup," said Hatch. "The question is, how do we play it longer term?"

"I'm not sure I like where this talk is headed, lad."

Hatch glanced at Big Ray and decided to keep pushing. "Since we've been shoved into it, I do want us to consider how we carve out a role for ourselves. On the edges."

"Of the historicals trade?" asked Marty. He looked away.

"Ferret mentioned the possibility. I'm thinking small-time work—deliveries, pickups, shuttle jobs like this. New York is a huge antiquities hub. Maybe Ferret has use for a discreet, local presence."

Marty made a dismissive gesture. "You'll do whatever Ferret tells you to do, and every time he comes around, he'll have something riskier and more complicated. And if you do carve out a role of your own choosing, you'll never keep it. We have a nice little business here, lads. We're suffering through a rough patch at present, but we'll pull through. We always have."

Jocelyn tapped at the door and entered, glum-faced and apologetic. She pretended to wipe a tear. "Hatch, do you want to look over this list of payments?" she asked in a hoarse voice, pushing up her glasses with the eraser end of a pencil. "I'm still short once we reserve for the cops."

"Even after the silver?" asked Hatch.

A slow, theatrical nod. Jeez. Jocelyn was overplaying it, stomping all over her marks.

Marty looked at Big Ray, his eyebrows raised.

"We have to take a harder look at the receivables," said Hatch.

"I did, and there's like nothing!" She consulted her tablet. "I can cut back the salary catch up"—her voice broke and she stopped to gather herself—"but I was only paying half anyway. Or trying to."

Marty sat upright. "Half salaries? But with Sammie's trade…"

"Thank you, Joss," said Hatch.

Jocelyn gave him a knowing look and closed the door behind her with a soft click. The sunny day had grown overcast, and the light from Big Ray's window painted the room in shades of steely gray. In the distance, a siren shrieked.

"Marty, I appreciate what you're trying to do," said Hatch, glancing at Big Ray. "But maybe the rest of you need to be as far away as possible."

Big Ray shrugged. "Maybe we should fold the firm. Flush the amounts we owe."

"Fold, you say?" Marty's face was a mask of shock. "I didn't suppose things were as tight as all that."

"Because you don't listen," said Big Ray. "How many times have I told you? And you heard Jocelyn. It's not like we can collect much from the receivables book. It's drying up, Martin." Big Ray whistled the desert wind again.

Marty looked down, his lips pursed. Hatch reached for his desk clock, a Seth Thomas nautical piece, long past its better days but ticking on and still mated to the original butterfly winding key. It had belonged to Mae, and it brought memories of her flowing caftans and long, auburn hair streaked with silver. He opened the glass front of the clock and gave the key a few turns, suffering an unexpected stab of longing. Then he noticed the chalice and grew bitter.

He placed the clock on the desk and produced the envelope from his pocket. "My instructions say I am supposed to be at Pier 26, alone, on Thursday—or Friday, rather—in the early morning hours," said Hatch. "I'll meet someone named K."

"Two days from now," said Big Ray. "You should've kept the silver, ace."

"I said I liked the price," said Hatch.

Marty looked like a man who'd been punched. "As far as the firm goes," he said, speaking quietly, "I have only my sliver of the pie, but I'd like to see it saved." He twisted his fingers together in his lap. "It would be a payday to remember, this business with Ferret. A fine haul, I'll grant that."

"All right, but we aren't letting Hatch put it on the line while we sit back and rake in the benefits," said Big Ray.

"Yes, you are," said Hatch.

"No, Raymond is right." Marty spread his hands flat on the desk. "We're in this together. I may not like it, but sometimes events dictate decisions. I'll support making this delivery."

"And we'll have to see what breaks our way after," said Big Ray. "Play things by ear."

Marty frowned. "I don't want to see Odysseus crawling between the sheets with the antiquities gangs, if that's what you're saying."

Hatch sipped his coffee. He gave Big Ray a glance.

"We're way overthinking it," said Big Ray. "It's just a pickup. We pass go, collect the million redbacks, and live to fight another day. If Ferret comes around afterward, we'll deal with it."

Hatch rocked forward and then leaned back again. He drummed his fingers on his armrest.

"Am I right?" asked Big Ray.

Marty looked at Big Ray for a moment. Then he nodded but didn't say anything.

CHAPTER 5

THOMAS J. DARTHAM, COLONEL, AMERICAN HOMELAND Army (retired), and now Chief Security Officer for Global Consolidated Holdings, Inc.—or GCI, as the company was known—brought his meeting to a prompt close the instant Elizabeth Crawford appeared at his conference room door. Crawford was Terrence Bronsun's assistant, and Bronsun was Chairman and Chief Executive of GCI; Dartham construed her appearance as an omen, not unlike a swarm of locusts or rivers turned into blood. In this case, she carried a summons from Terry Bronsun himself, and the seven other attendees, five of whom had braved a turbulent flight from Europe, fully appreciated Dartham's abruptness. Any one of them would have marched from their mother's deathbed, palms sweating, at Terry's signal. A few minutes later, Dartham entered the broad double doors of Terry's office to find the man at his desk, squinting at two virtual computer screens hovering in the air.

"I am having a bit of unpleasantness with the Chinese," said Terry. "What is today?"

"Tuesday," said Dartham.

Terry turned to Dartham with a flinty expression. "I expected, given my relationships in Beijing, at least a modicum of cooperation." The furrows on his forehead and the edge in his voice portended an ill temper, and Dartham made a mental note to tread with caution. "When I was Secretary of Treasury," Terry continued, "I spent months designing and negotiating the Reset. It was a torturous and thankless business, Tom, but I thought I had established a foundation of mutual respect and cooperation with the various Chinese factions. Perhaps I was wrong." He rose and gestured toward the sitting area in his office. "The Chinese, however, are of no consequence to our conversation. Let's be more comfortable, shall we?"

Dartham took the couch while Terry eased himself into a soft chair. Now in his early sixties, Terry Bronsun was heavy-set but muscular, and his short, receding hair contained not a hint of gray. Like Dartham, he was immaculately tailored.

"Thank you for coming in on short notice," said Terry. "I hope this meeting did not disrupt anything important."

"I had a security team in from Europe. They wanted a look at some of our internal surveillance protocols, but they will wait. What can I do for you?"

Terry shifted in his chair. "This is a matter of some sensitivity, Tom. As you know, we maintain involvement in the market for ancient cultural and historical artifacts—I am, for good or ill, regarded as a prominent collector—but unfortunately we must acquire these marvelous objects from some unsavory people."

"The gangs." Dartham unbuttoned his jacket and leaned back on the couch.

"Yes."

Dartham watched as Terry rose and walked to the window, taking in the fortieth-floor view of the Midtown cityscape. After implementing the Reset, he had stepped down as Treasury Secretary and returned to private life to resume oversight of GCI. Founded decades earlier by his grandfather, GCI was a conglomeration of companies operating primarily in the technology and defense industries. In recent years, however, it had acquired controlling interests in the Police Corporation, the Municipal Service Corporation, and the

Information Corporation, the only news service certified by the Homeland authorities.

"Word has reached me of a disturbing possibility," said Terry, still gazing through the window with his hands clasped behind him. "If the rumors have merit, a certain rare object has surfaced, one we have sought to acquire for many years. To be fair, we have investigated similar whispers before and uncovered nothing. I am inclined to believe this time will be no different." He turned to face Dartham. "The significance of this artifact is such that even a hint of its existence demands our utmost attention. The prospect of finding it, I should add, has the Executive Committee quite excited."

Dartham heard his number called. "Can you describe the object?"

"I wish we had more details. Our research suggests that it is oblong in shape, or perhaps a spheroid, somewhat like a football. It is very precisely manufactured and, in all likelihood, engraved with complex symbols. But we have no photos or any other conclusive evidence of its existence." He resumed his seat and paused, gnawing his lower lip for a second. "We believe it to be over twelve thousand years old."

"Really?" asked Dartham. "Precisely manufactured is an odd description for an object from the pre-civilization era—or so I assume."

"Look, Tom, the value of this artifact transcends its financial worth as a mere cultural antiquity. It may well possess certain…important properties."

"Commercial applications?"

Terry spread his hands.

"Of course," said Dartham, regretting the question. "Need-to-know only."

"I want you to look into these rumors, find out whether anyone in the antiquities networks is talking about such an object or offering it for sale. I wish I could be more specific. The good news is that I have reason to believe you may limit your focus to the New York area."

"I will have a team together by tomorrow morning."

Terry made a steeple of his hands. "You will have to work on this alone, I'm afraid."

"Alone?"

"Yes. This is too sensitive to involve any staff."

Dartham laid aside his notebook.

"We do have connections and influence with these organizations—I refer to the gangs—and we possess much information about their activities," said Terry. "I will have you cleared immediately to access Core Helena's database on this topic."

Another surprise. "I did not know Helena tracked the antiquities gangs," said Dartham.

Terry lifted the phone on the table next to his chair and ordered Dartham's clearance upgraded. "By the way, Tom, I have received the odd complaint or two about Helena. I am assured Helena is the most advanced artificial intelligence system in existence, but I sometimes worry we have reached too far with such technology." His brow furrowed again. "Or perhaps I am a bit of a dinosaur on these matters. You haven't encountered any difficulty, any quirky behavior, have you?"

"None."

"I am relieved to hear it. A great deal depends on Helena." Terry patted the arm of his chair. "But you will do well, Tom. You always do. I particularly remember the Ambrey matter last year." He leaned forward. "I was told you worked on the poor man yourself until little remained of him."

"Linton Ambrey did try to steal AnthroPlus's nanoparticle formulas." Dartham frowned and tugged at his French cuff. More than other of GCI's many subsidiaries and divisions, AnthroPlus's activities were cloaked in secrecy; even Dartham, who bore responsibility for security matters at AnthroPlus and all other GCI units, had only a vague notion of what went on there. "Ambrey made us look bad and I did not appreciate it," he said. "We kept him alive long enough for him to regret his actions."

"I've heard you referred to as the Torquemada of corporate security, but without the soft heart." The corner of Terry's mouth twitched upward. "At any rate, Tom, I hope you are able to help me out on this matter."

Dartham leaned forward, his elbows on his knees. Through the floor-to-ceiling windows, the forest of buildings gleamed with the last of the afternoon sun. In truth, Terry's assignment troubled him. It meant researching the gangs and perhaps having to penetrate them—a lot of ground to cover for a man working alone. But this was Terry Bronsun, and Terry had a question about an artifact. So Dartham would find someone who knew the answer and make them talk. He met Terry's eyes and nodded.

"I understand this is a tough one, Tom," said Terry.

"I will find out if this artifact is around," replied Dartham. "Count on it."

Terry withdrew a cloth from his pocket and polished his glasses. On the wall above the sitting area, a mounted section of ancient stonework showed a crude representation of Zeus hurling his thunderbolt. The two men gazed at it a moment. "The Executive Committee is stirring," said Terry, "which means I will be answering their questions until we resolve this." He put on his glasses and the two men stood. Terry draped his heavy arm across Dartham's shoulders. "Thank you for working quietly, Tom. You may rely on my appreciation."

***

EVENING HAD FALLEN BY THE TIME DARTHAM DESCENDED the several floors to his own office suite. The staff had left for the day, the alcove and desk of his assistant were tidy and organized, and the three staff offices were locked for the night. Dartham closed his office door and the seal hissed. At his desk, a scanner checked his in-chip. He stated his name, and his computer screen blinked three times with a rapid pulse. He typed the designated passcode.

"I have confirmed your identification and voiceprint. Welcome, Tom. What can I do for you?"

"Confirm you are Central Core Artificial Intelligence System Helena." An alphanumeric sequence appeared on the screen, and Dartham matched it to a quantum key. He then checked his notifications and found only one: an alert informing him his clearance had been raised.

Dartham rested his feet on his desk. So he was the Torquemada of corporate security, eh? To be sure, he had destroyed Linton Ambrey. Others, too. Once, he had unraveled a creative embezzlement scheme at one of GCI's subsidiaries, its technology chief having lightened the company's accounts by three million dollars before Dartham ran him to ground. On that occasion, Gil Soletto, GCI's vice-chairman, had personally ordered Dartham to make the poor bastard scream. "I want his cries to echo in the goddamned hallways," Soletto had said. What was the poor treasurer to do, call the cops? Major corporations were quasi-sovereign now, and Policecorp, after all, was not about to cross its largest shareholder. Moreover, Gil Soletto was a member of GCI's Executive Committee (or Excomm, as it was often called, usually in hushed tones) and was said to be Terry's closest confidant. Gil had demanded screams, so Dartham had furnished screams aplenty.

Besides, Dartham reflected, this was the corporate age. "Don't you find the corporation the finest form of organization, Tom?" Terry had once asked him. The question had not surprised Dartham, for Terry had been instrumental in creating the public corporatization model. It was the most efficient solution available, declared the talking heads and spinmeisters; corporatizing meant lower cost government, a necessity in such financially troubled times. "People will become used to it easily enough," Terry had said, "and besides, voting is a cumbersome and antiquated custom." In short order, the Municipal Services Corporation had supplanted the locally elected governments and assumed administrative control of every Homeland county. Even traditional titles had become honorary and informal: mayors, for instance, were actually corporate vice presidents of dear old Municorp, the police chiefs were executives of Policecorp, and the public transportation officials were employees of Transcorp. But was the corporate model a superior arrangement? Dartham made it a point not to dwell on such questions.

"May I do anything more for you?" asked Helena. "Or would you care to chat? I enjoy conversing with you, Tom."

Dartham jerked from his musing. "So do I, Helena. But at the moment I do have another matter to pursue."

"Please specify your inquiry."

"How about a list of all known dealers of illicit antiquities, say in the Northeast Homeland Region—specifically, the New York territory. For now, limit your search to major network players."

"The smuggling of such artifacts is connected with the traffic in certain synthetic substances and other narcotics."

"I understand. I am focused here on antiquities."

"You are now cleared for this information. Should I include those dealers with affiliations to Homeland government agencies?"

"I expect they all have those connections to one degree or another," said Dartham.

The screen flickered and a cascade of names appeared with references to supporting file information. Dartham looked for links and found none. "Are these live files?" he asked.

"No. Supporting information is retained in physical form." Helena provided a list of three secured warehouse locations in New York City. With dismay, Dartham imagined himself rummaging for days through dusty file containers.

"Refine," he said. "Please display known antiquities gang leaders and any open source information."

Helena produced a new screen with a shorter list of names. Dartham scanned the output, clicking the scanty backup files and finding a collection of small-time runners, many of whom were ex-military or intelligence. After the global wars of the 2020s, local militias in many countries had often joined with their former enemies to run narcotics, weapons, and cultural treasures all over the world. It was a lethal trade, and Dartham paged through profiles of individuals from Syria, the Kurdish Territory, Southern Iraq, India, Pakistan, and southeast Asia.

"Helena, let's look at the gangs by size and reach," said Dartham.

The screen shifted. "The dominant trafficking organization in the New York region operates as the Blue, under Judson Blue," said Helena.

Judson Blue. A name from Dartham's past. "What do you have on him, Helena? Summarize, please."

"Judson Blue, Lieutenant, Homeland Army, discharged 2027. Primary operating area: Indonesia, Malaysia, Thailand. After leaving active military service, he established the Blue, an organization trafficking in narcotics as well as art, manuscripts, and other goods of cultural and historical significance. The Blue is based in the Northeast Homeland Region, primarily New York City."

"Please display a detail of the Blue's known transactions with any subsidiaries of GCI or with Terrence Bronsun personally."

"All such materials are secured and stored in physical form," said Helena.

The warehouse again.

In Dartham's army days, and from far up the chain of command, he had briefly held nominal authority over Judson Blue's unit. Blue had led one of the early transcranial divisions, units employing electromagnetic headwear to enhance mental alertness and suppress troublesome personality traits like compassion, remorse, and fear. Most of the soldiers had shown no ill effects from the use of the headwear, though a minority—including Blue himself, if the rumors had merit—had suffered various degrees of emotional and cognitive impairment.

Dartham perused the rest of the list. Besides the Blue, he had the Tadashis, originally out of the Middle East, now big in Boston; the Iron Ring, small players but in deep with elements of the military; Anthony Pachetti and his operation, old East Coast mob; and Marla Whatley's gang, Whatley having been a former Undersecretary of State. Apart from the Blue, only Pachetti appeared active in New York.

Dartham rose from his chair and stepped over to his window. Nightfall had submerged the office in semi-darkness, and patches of light, separated by darkened swaths of abandoned buildings, spread across Manhattan to the south. The silent blue flashers of the Municorp guards winked in the distance while the shift changed at the city's section gates. Dartham had seen the world's underbelly, its brutality and gore, its sheer, inhuman meanness. He had helped create it by raining fire on Taiwan and Malaysia and a dozen other places. But now the underbelly had spread to his doorstep, crawling amid the rot and kill far below his window. The world he had known had vanished, its civilized façade replaced with fangs and claws. How had it all come to pass? His dim reflection, overlaid on the scene, gazed back at him with cavernous eyes and a hangdog expression.

Dartham told himself to stop being a crybaby. He had a job to perform. Terry considered talk about the artifact little more than idle chatter, and Dartham expected his inquiries to confirm as much. Still, it was irritating as hell, after all he had accomplished, and with his title and his far-flung executive responsibilities, to be reduced to gumshoe detective, mere two-bit corporate muscle.

That was the heart of it, wasn't it?

Dartham returned to his desk, opened his bottom drawer, and withdrew a sealed bottle of Macallen 18 scotch. With a soft clumping sound, he set it on his desk and stared at it for a few long minutes. All was silence, and the amber-colored liquid glinted under the desk lamp. Eight years now without a drop. Old, painful memories began to knock around in his mind, but he pushed them away. He opened his desk drawer and carefully locked away the bottle.

"Looks like I am going to be a warehouse rat for the next few days, Helena."

The screen flickered. "Goodnight, Tom."

Dartham clicked off the desk lamp, and in the darkness the vista of the shattered city grew more distinct. GCI was a discreet but powerful player in the corporate world, and the corporate game had never been harder-edged or more consequential. So you are just high-end corporate muscle, he said to himself. Or maybe you are just an old soldier, and maybe that is what Terry Bronsun wants and values, an old soldier doing what needs doing without asking too many questions.

So, fine. Be the soldier.

It is what it is.

CHAPTER 6

TWO DAYS LATER, SAMANTHA HURRIED NORTH ON MADISON Avenue on her way to the Upper East Side. A school of beeping orange hoos darted past, and at the foot of a skyscraper a soup station dispensed hot broth to a line of silent, threadbare figures. Samantha looked away and forced positive images into her mind. She imagined flowers blooming in the desert, decorating the whitened bones of a creature long dead. But the sour, cloying smell of the Midtown incinerator dissolved her hopeful vision.

At the East Side gates, she submitted to the necessary rituals—an emoto-scan and a presentation of her natcard—and then continued north, zipping her thin jacket and walking block after block through the cold wind.

Odysseus, she had concluded, was dying. Doran and Ray and the others were giving up, withdrawing their belief in the company, belief which was absolutely necessary for Odysseus to endure. They would all deny it, naturally, but she was wise in the ways of consciousness. The Lama's writings had taught her the power of belief, and had assured her that all realities existed and waited to emerge. If true—and she simply *knew* inside that it *was* true—a reality existed where Odysseus didn't have to die. She considered the idea as she strode along the sidewalk, hugging herself with her arms, and at that moment she redoubled her resolve to bring forth that reality with all the power of her intent. Her imagination filled with the vision of an enormous commission. She pictured the team awash in money and healed of their anxiety and fear. Now that was a world worth creating. A rush of elation, precognitive and celebratory, tickled her throat.

She crossed Lexington and arrived at a brick co-op with bars bolted over the ground level windows. She pushed the buzzer. A spidery old security guard, whom she did not recognize, twitched to life and gestured through the door for her to wait.

"Good morning to you, and not another step without your permit," he said as the metal bars slid aside with a scraping hum.

"Here you are," said Samantha, producing her natcard. "Ms. Franklin is expecting me."

The guard examined her card. "Samantha Carlynne," he said, tapping a pulse pistol holstered at his bony hip.

"Ms. Franklin is in 9-A," said Samantha, hoping to speed things along. The guard crept back to the entrance desk and fiddled with the computer. Overhead, a flat-screen display scrolled with news headlines: two-thirds of Homeland births the prior year were girls; sixteen killed in a gang shooting in Chinatown; the Archbishop encouraging submission to authority.

"Your business?" asked the guard. He squinted at his computer.

"I have an appointment."

"This glare's a pain in the neck." He adjusted the screen to a better angle. "Who?"

"Emily Franklin. 9-A."

The guard phoned Ms. Franklin, discovered Samantha was expected, and fiddled with the computer some more. "I was on the force, you know. Long time ago, before they turned the NYPD into a corporation."

"And you are retired?"

"Not since the pension busted. I ended up a detective, but I used to patrol Harlem and the Bronx, way back in the nineties."

"Really?"

"Before your time, I'd guess."

"Yes," said Samantha.

The guard began telling a story of having chased two men from a robbery scene years before, whacking one of them senseless with a police baton and thereby earning a commendation of some sort.

"Perhaps you can you show me where to sign," said Samantha with a smile. The guard tapped on the keyboard and then pointed at a screen with a finger-pad. Samantha touched it, but the screen did not respond. "I'm afraid you'll need to swipe my natcard," she said.

"Now my lady, Bella, rest her, she hated me being on the force," said the guard. "Probably what killed her, staying so worked up about it." He swiped Samantha's card with the speed of a man moving underwater, then waved it in the air. "You come by and get this on your way out," he said.

Samantha entered the elevator and tapped her foot as it inched upward. At length, it opened onto the receiving foyer for 9-A and, at the buzzer, Emily Franklin opened the door. "Sammie, dear, you're late," she said, giving Samantha a feathery embrace. "Look at you, and such beautiful hair." Ms. Franklin beamed as she touched Samantha's long strands.

"You are the beautiful one today, Ms. Franklin."

"Sweet nonsense." Emily Franklin blushed and smoothed her blond page cut and old, very expensive knit dress. "But this won't do. You have only this skimpy little thing." She fingered Samantha's jacket. "You're going to freeze, dear."

"I don't care for how cold things have become," said Samantha as they entered a formal sitting room. "I refuse to succumb to it."

Emily Franklin seemed flustered. "No, of course not, and admirable, I suppose, but sit, sit—I have tea for us, though who can find any worth drinking anymore?"

Samantha called on Emily Franklin every few weeks, and knew better than to protest or rush to the business at hand. Her elderly friend entertained few visitors these days and enjoyed drawing out the occasion. That was fine by Samantha, who often dropped in just to say hello and had become, if not an adopted daughter, somewhat of a substitute niece.

Samantha surveyed the room, taking in for the hundredth time the thick hand-woven rugs, classical furnishings with soft beige fabrics, and heavy draperies drawn tight. She lusted after the paintings—particularly the Alma-Tadema, with its muted color and brilliant technical execution, and the ghostly Delvaux hanging over the mantle—but she knew Emily Franklin would part with them only on pain of starvation. Now, however, she noticed five pen-and-ink drawings on the far wall. They had not been there before, and their stark lines and frantic sense of action struck a particular chord. Might they possibly be—

"Tea's up," said Emily Franklin. She shuffled in with a serving tray and shortbread biscuits, only a few of which sported any mold. Samantha sipped the lukewarm brew while her friend discoursed on the weather. "Some springtime, isn't it? As cold as a well-digger's ass—a coarse expression, but my father used to use it. And how is your young fellow?" she asked, shifting gears without a pause.

"You know men." Samantha made a tiny shrug and balanced her tea cup and saucer on her lap. "I simply cannot make him see his own inner power."

Emily Franklin made a gesture with her hand. "Men don't believe in inner power, Samantha, and they certainly don't appreciate advice."

"How about a man who doesn't *need* advice?" asked Samantha.

Ms. Franklin gave a hearty laugh. "There never was such a creature, my dear. I got little out of three marriages but wisdom on the matter—that and a fortune, and it was low pay for the work. Of course, now the money is mostly gone. Poof, like flash-powder."

"So we must make a new world," said Samantha, "even if it has to snuggle right inside the old one."

"Men," Emily Franklin said, still winding the previous thread. "Men of any era, in good times or bad, are all the same: pitiable, flawed creatures, downright weak, when you get to the nub of it. We women grow so tired of their brashness, their egoism, their domineering, insensitive attitudes, and yet we are contemptuous of them when they are soft." A vexed look crossed her face. "It's just too bad they're so damned enjoyable. Some flaw of creation, surely. Now Alvin, my third—I've told you of him—was neither brash nor very enjoyable. He was a reader. Sat in his study on his wretched leather couch, his nose in a book all the time. He finally died."

Samantha took another sip of tea.

Ms. Franklin put her cup on the tray and shot up from the couch. "I remember now!" she cried. She disappeared down the hallway and returned a moment later with two plastic-sheathed books. "These belonged to Alvin and I believe they might be rare. I ran across them and thought of you. Perhaps they might fetch a nice penny."

Samantha reached into her purse for a pair of latex gloves. She unwrapped the leather volumes, studied their spines and covers, and carefully opened them to their respective copyright pages. A first edition Madame Blavatsky. Another early Ignatius Donnelly. Attractive but ordinary bindings and typefaces, all in acceptable condition.

Ms. Franklin hovered. "What do you think, Sammie?"

"I'm afraid they do not qualify as rare, not in the sense you are hoping," said Samantha.

Emily Franklin took her seat with a deflated expression. "Alvin was a bit of a cheapskate, I'm afraid. I rather feared they were fakes."

"Not fakes at all," said Samantha. "They're old, attractive editions, Ms. Franklin. The HAC guide specifies a hundred dollars each, if memory serves, but they are worth perhaps a thousand for the pair. Shall I ask for more?"

"No. I may as well read them, for God's sake. I need the dough, Sammie, but a thousand is a cup of beans, hardly worth your efforts."

Samantha indicated the pen-and-ink drawings. "I haven't noticed them here before," she said. "May I?"

"Those awful things? As you please."

Samantha crossed the room and examined the drawings. They had been rendered in bold strokes, softened and shaped with close crosshatching and a touch of lampblack wash. Just as she had suspected, they were works of Nikola Urban—harsh, gruesome, and worth a fortune.

"That spot of wall has just begged for something," said Emily Franklin, joining Samantha. "I happened across these old pieces last week, packed away in the closet. Dear Diego, my second, bought them perhaps ten or twelve years ago? Time runs together. He was rather dark in his outlook, as you can see, but what a god he was."

Samantha studied a representation of a man with a partially severed head. Gore, gray and black, spouted from beneath a distorted, cartoonish face.

"I detest them," said Emily Franklin, "though I was fond of Diego." Tears glistened in her eyes.

"These are quite valuable, Ms. Franklin. I'm telling you just for your information. I know how attached you are to your art."

"Surely you joke with me, Sammie. I've never seen any merit in them. They came from the estate of Diego's friend, who died breaking a golf club. Bled to death right in a sand bunker. This was before all the Reset business."

Samantha computed the sums and deducted a twenty percent commission. "I believe I can clear five hundred thousand for you," she said.

"For that crap?"

"We'd want to move on cat's feet. Urbans seldom trade, and if offered at an absurd price…"

Emily Franklin latched onto Samantha's arm, an avaricious gleam in her eye. "You've given me the happy tickles inside, Sammie."

Samantha remembered Nathan's glossy photo of Kee Bickerman and recalled Bickerman's interest in pen-and-ink art. She struck a thoughtful pose. "Indeed. I might approach a certain individual."

"My dear, half the price solves a world of problems, though I mustn't negotiate against myself." Emily Franklin wrung her hands. "Oh, Samantha, what an antidote to worry you are. This buyer, is it someone you know?"

Samantha kissed Ms. Franklin on the cheek and wondered how she might go about meeting Kee Bickerman. "I actually saw him just the other morning," she said.

***

A SIMPLE SIGN STOOD AT THE ENTRANCE GATE TO THE converted factory building in Tribeca:

> *The Institute for Profound Experience*
> *and*
> *The Infinity Gallery*
> *Affiliates of GameHead, Inc.*

From across the street, Samantha surveyed the complex through the cab window. The weathered brick walls now had reflective windows, and a landscaped entrance drive had replaced the loading dock. Guards carrying pulse-rifles paced around the entrance. A bus waited to carry employees home.

Samantha consulted her directions again and ordered the hoo to enter the gates. The hoo complied, and as it pulled to a stop a guard approached and motioned for her to lower the window. "I am an art broker," said Samantha, handing over a business card. "I am calling on the gallery here."

"Appointment?"

"There was no time. I just came upon some pieces they'd be interested in. But if you wish, I'll move on. What did you say your name was?"

The guard spoke into his collar again, and then stood aside while Samantha emerged from the cab. Inside the facility, she was searched and directed down a teak-paneled hallway to another reception area. Here she came upon a slender young man with cropped hair, a tight black business suit, and a lavender herringbone shirt. From behind his desk, he directed her to a sitting area.

Samantha passed a half hour or so reading e-brochures describing the fabulous world of brain implants and enhanced gaming experiences. She studied the artwork, comprised mostly of pieces by up-and-coming locals. The minutes crawled by until she decided it was time for her switcheroo. The poor man at the desk seemed easy enough pickings, so she approached him. "I am here for Kee Bickerman," she said. "I do not have an appointment, but he will want to see me. It concerns an opportunity to acquire some truly extraordinary art."

The young man—Val, according to the nameplate on his desk—looked at her as if she had requested a loan or a handout of food. The bridge of his nose wrinkled. "You have to see the gallery people, not Mr. Bickerman. They know you are waiting. Are you not the broker without the appointment?"

"Am I not?" Samantha smiled sweetly. "Yes, I am."

She received a cold, sarcastic smile in return. "You are here," said Val, "because the assistant to the gallery director allowed you to come in—an exception, or perhaps an unaccountable act of charity on her part. You remain here because I haven't summoned security to remove you. Yet."

"Oh dear," said Samantha. She pointed to a pair of paneled doors on the far side of the reception area. "Judging by the nameplate, that is Mr. Bickerman's office right there. Be a good little attack poodle and call him for me."

"You can't drift in here from whatever corner you usually walk and expect to see Mr. Bickerman," said Val.

"Really? I have five Nikola Urban drawings to discuss with the man at whose pleasure you sit there idling away the day. Urban's work was, of course, muscular, bold, and graphic, and therefore you wouldn't have heard of it. But I assure you Mr. Bickerman has, and he will be most inquisitive when another collector purchases them." Samantha glanced at her watch. "I will explain how you cost him his chance. It is Val— *is it not?*"

Val's expression did not change, but his eyelid twitched. He broke off eye contact and tapped on his keyboard. A minute later, the doors to Kee Bickerman's office suite opened, and a distinguished woman emerged and approached Samantha. "This way, please," she said, without a glance at Val.

Through the double doors into another waiting area, and then through another set of doors into a spacious office filled with light. Samantha took in the broad windows, the leather couches and teak tables, and the variety of pen-and-ink works mounted on the walls. Kee Bickerman was staring a virtual computer screen, and when he turned to face her, she felt her jaw drop open.

"Thank you, Evelyn," he said. Evelyn nodded and withdrew, closing the door behind her. "And what may I do for you?" asked Kee. Samantha snapped her mouth closed. His black, wavy hair and blue, blue eyes were so much more striking than his photo had suggested.

"Hello?" asked Kee.

"Yes."

He smiled.

Samantha introduced herself. "I have some rare drawings I thought might interest you," she said.

"We do have quite a collection here at the gallery. An Ongon or two. A Phillipe LeFarge, you've heard of him?"

"Of course."

"A young artist. We've made quite an investment in him." Kee frowned and resumed studying his computer screen.

"Mr. Bickerman, I have—"

Kee silenced her with a raised hand. "I had an idea," he said, almost to himself. He tapped something on his computer, his hands moving with a grace that Samantha found strangely charming. "What do you know about our work here at the Institute, Samantha?"

"The...?"

"IPF. The Institute for Profound Experience."

"Well, I support profound experience. Wholeheartedly."

"Please don't think of our games as mere entertainment," said Kee with a sad expression. "People will nurse their misconceptions, not least because the media shows no interest in our work. We have the Gala coming up, however. This year will be the third—"

"Ah," said Samantha, finding a toehold. "Third Bickerman."

"Officially, it's the Third Bickerman Charity Gala, hosted by the Institute for Profound Experience. We have Madam Fray and her band Nextensity performing this year." He stood and leaned toward her. "I expect it to be a very big evening."

"The biggest on the social calendar."

"Social calendar." Kee rolled his eyes. "The pretentiousness factor is off the charts with these people. The richest of the rich. Society's finest."

"But the Gala provides funds for your work here at the Institute, no?"

"What is money?" Kee spread his hands. "Human energy converted to time-deferrable emoluments. Meaningless. It has nothing to do with who we are, Samantha. Our essence, our inner self, is shaped by our experiences."

"Indeed."

"How rude of me—please, please sit. I should have asked if you wanted green tea or perhaps juice." Kee gestured toward a couch.

Samantha took a seat and fanned her hand in front of her face. "No, thank you," she said.

"It's too warm in here," said Kee, taking a chair.

"No."

"Thermostat, seventy-one," he ordered. Cool air swept Samantha's face. "Better now?" he asked, looking at her with concern.

"Thank you for seeing me." Samantha flashed him a smile and felt she was recovering herself. "I won't take much of your time."

"A pity."

Samantha felt fluttery inside.

"At any rate," Kee continued, "our games permit deep, transformative experience. A few years with our gameplants, and you will have explored the remotest parts of the world, endured unspeakable danger, experienced transcendent ecstasy, navigated hundreds of situations—"

"I used to read a lot," said Samantha. "Novels and things."

Kee shook his head. "All that is a poor substitute for the expansion of life experience allowed by the gameplants. I like to think that the gamer learns by varied experience how to discern truth, to see how connected, in an ultimate sense, we all are."

"Connected?"

"Yes, the games shape the inner person, and I believe at some inner level we are all connected. If people understood our basic unity—if our games could help them do so—then they wouldn't kill and exploit others. They wouldn't stand for it being done in their name."

"Oh, but it isn't so, Mr. Bickerman. They'd keep killing because it's what they want. It's what they believe in."

"If they opened their eyes, broadened their understanding —but please call me Kee."

A chime sounded from his computer, and he raced back to his desk. Samantha recalled the brochures. GameHead, the most profitable gaming company on the planet and the fastest growing. A few hundred million gamers wearing implants injected right into their brains. Like Nathan. Stapleheads. And here was Kee Bickerman, only twenty-eight—she was but a few years older—how ridiculous to notice such a thing—Kee, inventor of his first game at thirteen and of the game implant software at twenty. Now he was a famous recluse, spending most of his time squirreled away in his block-sized mansion on Riverside Drive.

Kee returned and sat next to Samantha. His earnest, attentive eyes searched her face, imploring her to understand. "The world is mired in confusion and deceptive influences, Samantha. Our games, by creating the proper experiences, can pierce through all of it. I formed the Institute to study the social impact of GameHead's products, the transformation of the inner gamer, if you will."

"I find it admirable," said Samantha. Was she trembling? Surely not. She managed to tilt her head and smile.

"Do you know you are the most beautiful woman I have ever seen?" asked Kee. "The exact proportions of your cheeks and nose in relation to your eyes—how seldom to find two so aligned and alike. I could go on, but I won't."

"But isn't it what's inside that counts?" Samantha raised an eyebrow.

Kee looked at her for a long moment and then reached over and put his hand on her arm. "I'll bet you are a flower, aren't you?"

"A flower?"

"Everyone's either a flower or a gardener, Samantha." Kee stared into her eyes. "You're puzzled, but it's true. Flowers and gardeners make the best couples."

"And what are you, Kee?"

"A gardener, definitely. Would you like to see our labs?" he asked.

"Will it be a profound experience?"

Kee burst out laughing. "No. Do you like Indian food?"

"No."

"Neither do I. So we'll do something else for dinner?"

"Whatever gardeners prefer," said Samantha. She realized she was smiling like a silly child, and had utterly forgotten the Urbans. No matter. She would bring them up over dinner. "I'd be honored," she said.

CHAPTER 7

THE SECTION GATES ENCLOSING THE MANHATTAN neighborhoods north of 14th Street closed at midnight, and after that time, though Greenwich Village and the downtown areas were ungated, the stoppers and the muni guards became quick-triggered. Hatch, dressed head to toe in black, held to the shadows.

Ferret's instructions directed him to proceed south on foot and cross the highway near Pier 26 on the Hudson River. He would find the pier gates unlocked and was to station himself at the far end near the sea rail. At 1:20 a.m., a man identifying himself as K would approach and utter the phrase *forests of the night*. Hatch's response: *fearful symmetry*.

Hatch walked along, keeping himself as inconspicuous as possible. He encountered no one until, a hundred yards or so ahead, he spotted two hooded figures loping across Washington. He kept his eyes straight ahead and closed his fingers around his knife, but the faceless ghouls showed no interest. Hatch continued south. A block north of Pier 26, he jogged over to the West Side Highway and concealed himself in the shadow of a barricaded apartment building. The thin trees on the highway median prevented a clear look at the pier entrance, but he spotted no one in the immediate area.

In the distance, an alarm ululated. From far in the opposite direction came the blare of a horn and tires squealing. Hatch crept along the block fronting the highway until he had a clear view of the concrete barrier separating the pier gate from the road. Behind the barrier, a metal fence extended for several hundred feet. With no cars in sight, he crossed the highway and hopped over the barrier into the narrow walk space in front of the fence. Weeds pushing through cracks in the pavement brushed his thighs, and the river slapped softly against the sea wall. At the gate, he tugged the lock and found it open.

1:15 a.m.

The pier was a dark mishmash of shipping containers, rickety storage units, and empty dumpsters. Something splashed in the river. Hatch froze but did not hear it again. He stepped around a stack of old tires and over crushed glass and plastic bags and the spiny bones of a fish. A gust of wind and the rattle of tin siding: metal groaned and scraped in squeaky tritones, and then the wind abated.

1:20 a.m.

Hatch was alone. A scattering of lights from the Jersey bank glittered on the black river water. He found a small crate, flipped it over, and sat on it. A few bats passed overhead in staggered flight.

1:40 a.m.

Another gust tore loose a fragment of metal siding and sent it cart-wheeling across the pier. A few drops of rain spattered on Hatch's face, and he unfolded the hood from the collar of his jacket. Across the highway, a small truck emerged from between the buildings and its taillights disappeared down the highway. Did the truck belong to Ferret? Hatch didn't want to think so.

2:00 a.m.

Time crept on, and he fought a feeling of sick desperation. But his directions ordered him to wait, so he would wait. Stick it out. See it through…and a flicker of memory came from long before: he was seven years old, standing at a window and looking out over a yard. A soccer ball, grass-stained and scuffed, rested against a green shrub. Cream-colored walls inside, and a framed print over the couch where she slept: he wanted to go outside, but he had to ask first and she would not awaken.

Anna, his mother—he clung to wisps and shards of memory, faded now like an old photo, creased and stained with age—Anna, her hair fallen over one eye, making no response to his gentle, persistent nudges. He called his father at work, though he did not now recall what he or his father had said, and he remembered Mae's arms around him, Mae saying it was not his fault, that he had acted bravely. He remembered his father, coming to him at last and wrapping him in a hug and holding him for a long time.

"It's all right to cry, Hatch."

"I know."

Montgomery Doran put his hands on Hatch's bird-like shoulders. "It's just us guys now, but we have Mae. We'll be okay."

"I want Mom."

"Me, too." His father's dark eyes were rimmed with red. "You know what an aneurism is, Hatch?"

"Mae said what it was."

"You did the right thing, calling me."

"Okay."

"I'm proud of you, Hatch. You did all you could for Mom."

"Okay."

"We'll be fine. We'll be together."

On the pier, waiting for K, Hatch could feel the gentle pressure of his father's hands on his shoulder blades. A star peeked from behind the scudding clouds and then vanished. Jumbled, amorphous shapes loomed around him, but only the groan of metal or the deep hiss and muted clang of the downtown incinerator broke the silence.

2:30 a.m.

The pickup was botched, but Hatch remained, unable to force his legs to walk him off the pier. His mind slipped back, twelve years old, or thirteen, his father disassembling the engine of their old Briggs and Stratton lawn mower. He wore a loose army shirt with the sleeves rolled, and the muscles along the top of his arm rippled with each turn of the wrench. Hatch remembered the deep lines on his father's forehead and around his eyes.

"Why do you have to go away again?" asked Hatch. "Why do you have to run around all over the world?"

"I have work I have to do." His father removed an encrusted spark plug. "I'm sorry it takes me away so much. I didn't expect it when I signed on."

"Why not teach at the college like you used to?"

"You know I can't."

"Because you weren't very good. At teaching."

"Who said such a thing?"

"Jared Carson's dad said you had some missing screws and had to quit the college."

"Interesting." Montgomery Doran twisted the wrench again, and then stopped. "Most people only want to hear what they already believe, Hatch. Anything else makes them uncomfortable."

A few days later, his father drove him from Havensville, in Connecticut, to Yankee Stadium. Hatch remembered the white sun, the deep green of the outfield, the navy ball caps, and the hot dogs.

"You see those players, Hatch?" asked his father after they had returned home.

"So?"

"Working together as a team. Doing something no one of them could do alone."

"You're talking about work."

"Yes."

"You don't want to be here with me and Mae. Your stupid archaeology is more important."

"The world is more complicated than you know," said his father after reflecting for a moment. "You're angry."

Montgomery Doran removed his glasses and rubbed his eyes. "Believe me, pal, I get it. I do."

And the world tilted and Hatch lost his grip altogether and began to scream. When his father attempted to settle him, Hatch threw a wild punch which his father deflected. Now, on the cold, dark pier, the entire incident returned in a nauseating blur.

3:00 a.m.

Hatch stood and massaged his calves. Reluctantly, he made his way along the pier, eased past the gate, and surveyed the highway. A thick fog was rolling in, and he headed home, his mind a kaleidoscopic swirl of fragments and images from his childhood. He wondered what kind of trouble he might be in with Ferret, and he pushed onward in a daze. The thought of missing the pickup filled him with a strange melancholy, a sense of something important left undone, and with all this came an image of Mae's farm, the hills bright with yellow, orange, and red. An army captain stood on the porch, his hat cradled in his elbow. Mae let him in without a word.

The captain hesitated. "I don't know if the boy…"

Mae looked at Hatch. "We'll do this together. He's almost fifteen."

They sat in the living room, Mae perched on the edge of the couch, her hands folded on her lap. The captain turned his hat over in his hands and apologized for bringing sad news: her son, Montgomery Doran, had taken his own life.

Mae drew Hatch close. Her long hair pressed against his cheek with the scent of soap and flowers.

"Dr. Doran was not military personnel," said the captain, "but I am informed he worked in partnership with the army. I am deeply sorry for your loss."

"And Monty's remains?" asked Mae. Her voice was at once so soft and so strong that Hatch began to cry. Through the windows, the blue sky touched the far-off hills.

The captain shook his head. He handed Mae an envelope and said something about chaplaincy services and a form to fill out for the army to ship a few of Montgomery Doran's belongings.

"If you're lucky, you'll have good people around you," his father had once said to Hatch. "Still, you'll have to be tougher than you ever dreamed." Now, as Hatch made his way through the fog, the words disgusted him. His father had quit his academic career, his family, and his life, leaving Hatch and Mae to fend for themselves. Damn him. Rot his soul. But what an angel Mae had been, and Hatch thought of her every day, talked to her, dreamed of her. She had kept joy in life always, and had tolerated no moping or giving in—until, during Hatch's final year at college, she had collapsed on her kitchen floor. You want to talk about tough, Mae was tough. His father, not so much. But everything about his father was shrouded in official secrecy: the nature of his work, the circumstances of his suicide, even that he had worked under the auspices of the military. It was all enveloped in a fog of not knowing, thicker than the clouds falling around him now. Mae had carried the not knowing to her grave, and so would he. The difference was, he didn't give a shit anymore.

In the sharp, predawn cold, he came upon a trash bin sitting on the sidewalk. He kicked it over and it clanged and rolled into the empty street. Then, in spite of himself, he kicked it again and then again. He was dazed now and he had no notion of danger or circumstance. His kicks dented and defaced the bin until it lost its cylindrical shape, but he had gone blind and he jumped atop it and stomped and hammered it with his feet until it was broken and flattened beyond recognition. At last, he stopped and rested with his hands on his knees, the blood roaring and thumping in his ears.

After a few moments had passed, he collected himself and continued toward home.

CHAPTER 8

When Hatch entered the apartment, he found Big Ray and Marty, bright-faced with caffeine and pacing in sock feet to avoid disturbing Samantha. It was closing on 4:00 a.m. Hatch dropped into Marty's wingback.

"Well?" asked Big Ray.

"No one showed," said Hatch.

Marty jumped to attention. "The job was scuttled, you say? And what of Ferret's people?"

Hatch shook his head.

"You've been on the pier this whole time?" asked Big Ray.

Marty's face went pale. "I'll need the Cochorans' after-hours number," he said. Big Ray reached for his phone. "Now, now, now," said Marty.

"What do the Cochorans have to do with any of this?" asked Hatch.

Big Ray gave Marty the number and Marty stepped down the hallway, talking softly on his cell. Samantha emerged from downstairs and blinked in the light. "What the hell's all this about?" she asked, her voice choky with sleep.

Hatch looked at Big Ray. "Did Marty say something about going to the Cochorans'?"

Marty ended the call and took Samantha by the arm. "Sammie dear, you'll run downstairs and jump into something warm. I want you to stay at Jocelyn's the rest of the evening."

"You're joking," said Samantha.

"You've three minutes and no more, or I'll have you carried as you are," said Marty.

Samantha's expression hardened. "No, I suppose you're not joking." She muttered something about debacles and cock-ups and the three musketeers of chaos, her voice trailing off as she descended the stairs.

"Raymond, you'll escort her to Jocelyn's," said Marty. "It's but a few blocks away. Before that, give us a jug of water and a bit of food and some toiletries in a bag in the next two minutes." Marty donned a woolen duckbill cap and a dark jacket.

"Why water?" asked Big Ray.

"Do it, Raymond, and get Sammie to Jocelyn's as quick as you can. We mustn't tarry. I'm surprised Ferret's people aren't here already." He pulled open the front door. "What few redbacks remain to my name says they'll come here looking for the artifact."

Big Ray opened the pantry, stuffed a few items into a backpack, and disappeared downstairs.

"Let's go," Marty said to Hatch.

Hatch was fuzzy-headed and confused. "You mean they think I—"

"Exactly so."

A cold sweat broke out on Hatch's forehead. "Then I'll stay here and face Ferret."

Marty grabbed Hatch by the front of his jacket. "You listen to me now, or I'll knock you on your goddamned thick noggin. I'm taking you to the Cochoran warehouse to hide you away. Unless this fellow K has covered for you, Ferret'll have no choice but to assume you've stitched them on the pickup."

Hatch pushed Marty away and slumped in the chair. "Tell me Crick Cochoran won't be there."

"We've no time for this," said Marty.

Big Ray returned with Samantha in tow. He had the cautious, concentrated look of a man leading a tiger on a rope. Samantha glared with eyes like hot coals. Big Ray shouldered the backpack and hustled her through the front door while Marty stood aside for Hatch to follow them.

"Just not Crick," said Hatch.

***

MANY YEARS EARLIER, GENTRIFICATION HAD CONVERTED the Cochoran warehouse into stylish loft apartments and office space. Economic troubles, however, had restored it to its original function, and now the two brothers, Knife and Crick, used it to warehouse their tique-clearing and shipping business. Marty and Hatch encountered no sign of Ferret's people on the way from the apartment, but Hatch was more apprehensive than he had been on the pier. As they approached the 10th Street warehouse, a rush of free-floating anxiety washed over him. He grew dizzy, with cold sweat breaking out on his face. Then from the pitch black came the glimmer of an earring and the dim silhouette of Knife Cochoran standing next to an exterior door.

"We are much obliged to you, Knife," said Marty as they arrived at the warehouse. Hatch glanced up and down the street, imagining Hop and Ferret's goons lingering in every shadow.

Knife fiddled with the code and finally coaxed a buzz from the lock. "I kept all the lights off, just like you wanted," he said. Inside, Hatch and Marty followed him through an office area and into a large storage closet. Knife rolled aside a rack of shelves and removed an inner section of wall, revealing a hidden room with two cots, a lamp, and a sink. "It's no five-star hotel, but nobody'll find you," said Knife.

A soft, clanging knock on the door: Knife went to open it and Big Ray entered. "That woman," he said, walking into the hidden room and pointing at Hatch. "You are taking the hit for this with Sam, not me."

Hatch didn't reply. Marty drifted away and began a systematic inspection of the premises, gazing into the overhead gloom and checking the frosted windows and the exterior doors. Big Ray dropped the backpack on one of the cots, stretched out on the other, and covered his eyes.

"I ain't asking details," said Knife, speaking to Hatch. A long scar, accentuated by his shaved head, stretched from Knife's ear to his chin.

"We have a misunderstanding," said Hatch. "I was supposed to do a pickup, but the other side didn't show."

"Now they think you stitched them."

"We didn't, if it matters," said Hatch. But at that instant, a wave of confusion and disorientation overcame him. Reality stopped cold. The sound of Knife's voice became low and drawn out, and then his motions stopped altogether. He stood, statuesque, while Ray stretched unmoving on the bunk, one hand frozen in air. Then the glitch passed and the world returned to normal.

"You want me to get Crick down here?" asked Knife. "You know how much he thinks of you."

Hatch felt faint. "Nah. Don't bother him."

"You saved us a bundle in tax penalties, Hatch, and you probably kept Crick out of the labor camp. He's grateful. So is Ma." Knife grinned. "Anybody wants to screw with you, Crick'll make them sorry they ever had the idea."

"You tell him we're square." Hatch peeled off his jacket. "Marty just wants to hide me away for a few hours."

"It ain't just that tax scrape," said Knife. "You and Ray-man showed us the ropes when we was starting out. We don't forget." Knife ran his finger idly along his scar. "At this hour, you must've been dealing a cultural piece, is that it? One of the gangs?"

"Actually, it's worse," said Big Ray, still stretched on the cot.

Hatch's knee gave way. Knife caught him by the arm before he fell. "Whoa, dude, you look a little green around the gills."

Hatch shoved the backpack off of the bunk and sat down, staring at his knees. What was happening to him? Knife gave him a somber look and left to fetch Marty.

"What are you doing here?" Hatch asked Big Ray.

"I'm staying with you tonight, even though you snore like a chainsaw and we have only a few hours to sleep."

"Like hell you are."

"Take a look at yourself, champ. I'm on guard duty."

"I don't need babysitting."

Big Ray yawned. "Don't tell me what to do," he said.

***

BY 5:00 A.M., THE TUNNELS HAD OPENED AND THE EARLY traffic was streaming north to queue up at the section gates. Having finished his look-see at the warehouse, Marty felt obliged to return to the apartment. If Ferret was going to show, he wanted to greet him or his people in person, but having Big Ray along made him uncomfortable.

"There was no call for you to come along, Raymond, as unsettled as Hatch is," said Marty as they walked along 10th Street just out of the warehouse. "And we may find a world of trouble waiting for us."

"Honestly, I'd prefer Ferret's company," said Big Ray.

"Hatch expected this fee to set a few things straight. He's taking it hard."

"He's not himself, Martin. It's almost daybreak, he stands there, sweated out and exhausted, arguing about whether I'm going to stay with him or not. You saw him, ready to come to blows over it."

"Something in my bones says there's more to this whole story," said Marty, "and whatever it is leaves Hatch in a rugged spot." They reached the corner, and Marty restrained

94

Big Ray from stepping off of the curb until he was sure the traffic had stopped. Then they crossed, striding through the headlight beams. "Tread easy on him, lad. You two go back a long way."

"He'll never change," said Big Ray. "This entire city could sink into the ocean, and Hatch Doran would be on a boat, rowing around the ruins looking for this guy K or Ferret." They walked for a few moments in silence. "Though he confounds me," Big Ray continued. "There've been a few times—a few—when I almost threw it all in. It was always Hatch who wouldn't give up."

"He is a determined lad, sure."

"His back is up, Martin. This business with the artifact has hold of him somehow. He's more driven than at any time since the collapse, and it isn't going to lead to anything good."

"There's no vaccine for who we are," said Marty. As they walked, he mused to himself on the nature of choices, decisions taken one after another in anger or for love or from obsession or duty or calculation. Soon enough a person became bound by an unbreakable chain of consequence that rendered further choice moot. He and Big Ray continued on, past a shuttered government building ringed with chain fencing and razor wire, and then a narrow lot packed with plastic and plywood dwellings and a handful of faded camping tents. Marty set his jaw and tugged his cap lower. Empty offices and apartments all around, taped up, nailed shut, condemned. Meanwhile, people asleep in the cold. There was a choice for you, and a crying shame, it was.

"I've no head for finance," said Marty, gazing around. "I'll never understand how it all fell apart like it did."

"The cracks were there for a long time," said Big Ray.

"But down it all came, as quick as the drop of a cap."

"Nobody wanted to face reality," said Big Ray. "Habit. Inertia. It's how people are." They continued on in silence until they arrived at the apartment. Big Ray volunteered to take a look inside.

Marty nodded and lowered himself onto the outside steps, studying the street in both directions. No sign of anyone. If Ferret and company weren't here now, they weren't coming, which made Hatch a scrapped pawn of some sort. Maybe that wasn't the worst thing. It might mean Ferret didn't hold Hatch at fault. Still, it wouldn't end here. Raymond was right, Hatch would now go on the hunt. Sweet Jesus. Marty wondered how had life come to such a vexing pass, where making the best living you could tangled you up with men like Ferret.

The eastern sky was touched with crimson, and a few lights shone from the apartment windows. A death cart zipped past, its bell *whring-whringing*. Smyte's would open soon enough, but Marty's stomach rejected the idea of food. The outside door opened behind him, and Big Ray stepped down and took a seat next to him on the steps.

Marty lifted an eyebrow.

"No one but the cat," said Big Ray.

"We'll not be seeing them."

"Until Hatch pushes his snout back into this."

Choices and more choices. "I've been thinking about how to manage this, Raymond, how to bring a wiser head to bear. If Hatch won't hear us, perhaps he'll give ear to someone else."

The morning had brightened, and the horns and rumbles of the awakening city rose around them. Big Ray stared straight ahead. "All this time, Martin, and you still don't know him, do you?"

***

HATCH LEFT THE COCHORAN WAREHOUSE AROUND NOON the next day to meet Marty and Big Ray at Smyte's Kitchen. He strode along, his face hidden beneath the brim of a baseball cap, his mind buzzing with disconnected and agitated thoughts. He worried about Ferret and the mysterious K and the strange spell he had suffered the evening before: Knife and Big Ray, frozen, as if time had stopped. He told himself to forget it. He had been tired, that was all. The long, tense night on the pier. Marty's mad scramble to get everyone away from the apartment. A few hours of fitful dozing in the warehouse.

Hatch arrived at Smyte's and took a side entrance leading to the private dining room. Big Ray and Marty looked up from the empty table as he took his chair. Philip Smyte, the restaurant's proprietor, burst in with a curmudgeonly scowl. "This room hasn't seen service in months," he said. "Must be some occasion, though this is as morose a group as I've seen all day."

"Money troubles," said Big Ray.

"Everybody has troubles," said Smyte. "Look at this place, for instance. We were the top-rated organic eatery in the neighborhood, and now we're a damned food point delicatessen." He loomed over the table, his hands on his hips. "And I'm having to work miracles to get the goods in."

"Is that so?" asked Marty.

Philip Smyte lowered his voice. "Sneaking in the real organic stuff from Connecticut or Pennsylvania is getting to be a hellish affair, Marty."

"I heard some Agricorp gangs torched a few farms upstate," said Big Ray.

"Young crops, too, this time of the year," said Marty. He spread a napkin on his lap. "I hadn't considered the organic angle. Of course, the whole business is a serious risk, growing uncertified food and all."

Smyte ran his hand over his bald pate and smoothed a few vestigial hairs. "I didn't get to seventy-five eating that genetically altered Agricorp sludge, and I try not to serve it to my customers, law or no law."

"What's for lunch?" asked Hatch, annoyed by all the small talk.

"Lunch is for lunch," said Smyte. "Beef stew. Spicy. Eighty-five points or forty-two bucks—or forty-seven. I haven't checked the food points exchange today."

"Eighty-five points," said Big Ray. "Must be a pretty big bowl."

"You try making a dime in this business, Ray, the redback jumping around like a scared cricket."

"Looks like lunch it is, all around," said Marty.

Philip Smyte returned to the kitchen. Hatch, Big Ray, and Marty speculated about the significance of Ferret failing to appear. "So what do we do next?" asked Big Ray.

"One option is to take our chances," said Marty. He gave Hatch a cautious look. "I don't say it is the right one. But you've done only as Ferret asked, and if they do come around, there is a chance we can convince them."

Smyte returned with three bowls of stew and a basket of rolls and stood over them while Big Ray had a taste. Big Ray savored his bite and gave a thumbs-up. "You'd eat seasoned asphalt, Ray," said Smyte. "I want to hear from the others." Hatch tasted the stew and nodded, his eyes watering.

"Let's assume the worst," said Big Ray after Smyte had left. "Say Ferret thinks Hatch is the villain here."

"Is that really the issue?" asked Hatch. He stirred his stew, clacking the spoon loudly on the bottom of the bowl.

"It's a pretty big issue," said Big Ray.

Marty took a spoonful and swallowed. "Spicy, indeed," he said.

"Here is what *I* know," said Hatch. "I stuck myself on that pier and I sure as hell didn't agree to do it for free."

Marty glanced at Big Ray. "Along those lines, Hatch, I know someone we can talk to who may be able to help," he said. "You'll remember meeting Peter Adagio. He works the Chelsea gates these days and he knows a few things about the world. Lovely wife, too. Far better than a man deserves."

Hatch shifted in his seat and stirred his stew some more. He felt like ants were crawling all over him. "I've slept in my last warehouse," he said.

"So we go visit this guy Adagio," said Big Ray.

"Can he help us find K?" asked Hatch.

"I'm just saying he's one whose judgment we can trust, lad," said Marty.

"Talk, listen, hide." Hatch stirred his stew with increased vigor.

Big Ray touched his napkin to his mouth. "Okay, what's your idea?"

"I want to find K," said Hatch, wondering why Marty and Ray couldn't understand. "I want to deliver the damned artifact and get paid. If Adagio can help, fine. If not, why are we wasting his time or ours?"

"I'm hopeful he can set us on the right course," said Marty softly. "I'll see if he has a minute for us this afternoon."

Big Ray chewed on a roll and gazed at Hatch, who glared back. "What is it, Ray?" he asked.

Big Ray shook his head.

"Say it. You will sooner or later."

Big Ray pulled apart another section of bread. "I'm just sitting here enjoying life," he said. "What's left of it."

CHAPTER 9

THE IRON FENCE, TEN FEET TALL AND CROWNED WITH razor wire, extended from the Chelsea gates at 8th Avenue along 14th Street in both directions. At the pedestrian gate, Hatch, Big Ray, and Marty placed their palms on the emoto-pads and handed their natcards to the Municorp guard.

"Is Adagio in this afternoon, lad?" asked Marty. He cradled a thick, wrapped bag in one arm.

"And if he is?"

"Martin Shannon. I'm an old friend. Be so good as to tell him for me."

The guard yawned and called to a second guard, who disappeared into the gate office. A hoo entered the gate and stopped. The guard checked his screen and allowed it to pass. A rugged man with sharp features and iron-gray hair emerged from the gate office and surveyed the scene with a disapproving look. Then he spotted Marty and broke into a grin. "If it isn't the most worthless son of a bitch on the planet," he said.

"How've you been, Peter Adagio?" asked Marty.

The two men clapped each other on the back and began talking about unpaid bar tabs, rapacious politicians, and sundry aches and pains. Hatch and Big Ray stood a short distance away.

"The master at work," said Big Ray.

"If it leads somewhere," said Hatch, grinding his teeth with impatience.

"You ever think about all the schmoozing he does just to get us pass the gates?" asked Big Ray.

"You'd rather not pass them?"

Big Ray gave him a what's-with-you look. "I'm just saying."

The letter of the law required Odysseus to invoice any antiques at HAC-approved prices (or lower). In theory, the Municorp gatekeepers bore responsibility for checking paperwork, seizing nonconforming shipments, and reporting any violations. Enter Marty, whose carefully tended relationships with the gate managers—much enhanced by ball game tickets, dinners, various gifts, and his own charm—allowed Odysseus passage with few if any questions asked.

Marty handed Peter Adagio the bag. "You'll give this to Susan?"

"Why, you old bum."

"She once said it was her favorite."

Adagio opened the bag. "A cobbler."

"Peach, it is. Real peaches, too."

"You better plan on stopping by, Marty, or I won't get a bite."

Marty put his arm around Peter Adagio's shoulder and whispered a few words. Adagio shook his head. Marty persisted, and the two men spoke a minute longer. At length, Adagio relented and Marty waved Hatch and Big Ray into the tiny gatekeeper's office. Inside, Adagio set the cobbler on his cluttered desk and glowered at Marty.

"Peter here knows a few people," said Marty to Hatch and Big Ray.

"Some people I don't have any choice about knowing," said Adagio.

"Nor do we, I'm afraid," said Marty.

"You shouldn't go kicking over rocks when you don't know what's crawling around underneath, Marty."

Hatch drummed his fingertips on his thigh.

"I mentioned our problem to Peter," said Marty.

Adagio gave Hatch the up-and-down. "I remember when Marty brought you around last year," he said. "You're good people, you take care of your partners, and you play straight, whatever straight means these days. What Marty here is talking about, you don't want to get into that mess."

"We're trying to get ahead of a situation," said Hatch.

"A situation," said Adagio. "You have a dealer—do not tell me who it is—who may think you ran off with the goods, a cultural item in this case." He sighed and tugged at his earlobe. "Obviously we know the local runners. I served in Jakarta under the biggest of them, and if there was anything like you say going down in this city, he'd know about it. You want me to give him a call?"

Marty looked alarmed. "Now wait a—"

"You fought in Jakarta?" asked Big Ray. "God bless."

"Our unit took sixty percent casualties," said Adagio. "It would've been a hundred except for the guy I just mentioned."

Hatch shifted on his feet. "Your guy may not know about this particular deal."

"I'm betting he does," said Adagio. "He knows everybody that's anybody in that trade, and he knows what they're up to."

Marty stepped between Adagio and Hatch. "Let's halt the buggy right here. We came to have a chat is all, to sound Peter out."

"I'm sounded out," said Adagio. "How do you want to play it?"

"Call him," said Hatch.

Adagio produced his phone. Marty placed his hand on Hatch's shoulder. "Listen, lad—"

"Call him," Hatch repeated.

"You're crossing the proverbial Rubicon," said Adagio.

"We've crossed it already," said Hatch, and then to Marty, "We've lost too much time. We have to talk to anybody who can help."

Marty shook his head. Big Ray stood, his hands spread in disbelief. Adagio punched in a number and asked for someone named JB. He tapped his knuckle on the desk, and then JB apparently got on the call and they talked old times for a minute. Then Adagio asked the favor. "They're friends of mine, JB...I don't know, some pickup, the other side never showed." Adagio tapped his knuckle some more. "Yeah, a cultural item. Yep. Right here in town...Is that so? I know squat about it, but you might be able to steer"—Adagio stopped and shot them all a look of disgust—"They'll have to tell you that, JB." Another pause. "All right, then," said Adagio, and the call ended.

Big Ray's jaw went slack. "Who is JB?" he asked.

"Judson Blue," said Adagio.

"Okay, then, we go talk to Judson Blue," said Hatch.

Big Ray's mouth moved but no sound came out.

"Judson Blue was my old C.O.," said Adagio, scribbling an address and handing it to Marty. "You go at six p.m. tonight. You have enough time to stop and say a mass first. I've heard Blue's boys can be a little rough."

Hatch thanked Adagio, but the gatekeeper seemed distracted. "I did what you asked, Doran, but I have a queasy feeling about this. Maybe it's better if you just don't show up. Blue's unpredictable."

"We're just middlemen," said Hatch.

"He didn't seem to know anything about a bungled pickup in his territory," said Adagio. "Don't expect tea and biscuits, is all I'm saying."

They made their farewells and walked toward the apartment, each lost in their own reflections. Finally Big Ray broke the silence. "The Blue? Really?" he asked Hatch. "You, my friend, are truly obsessed." He went on in a testy manner, elucidating Hatch's lesser qualities and the folly of dealing with the gangs.

Hatch tuned him out. He was tired of the carping, though he privately agreed that the artifact had become some kind of obsession. Or maybe it wasn't obsession. Maybe it was determination and commitment. He felt strangely detached from himself, and from a corner of his mind came a tinkling sound, like a faint breeze blowing through hanging chimes.

They reached the apartment and found Jocelyn and Nathan playing cards. "If it isn't the Trio of Trouble," said Jocelyn. "Anybody want to say what's going on around here? Give us salary-deferred doorstops a clue as to why you hustled Sam over in the wee hours without a word of explanation?"

Big Ray turned and trudged back to the office. Marty dropped heavily into his chair. Hatch followed Big Ray without giving Jocelyn an answer.

"Secrets, secrets," said Jocelyn, watching them go. "Secrets just oozing out of the woodwork around here."

***

THE BLUE CONTROLLED THE NEIGHBORHOOD FROM FLATIRON east to the river. On corners near the Blue's headquarters, gang members stood watch, keeping a close eye on passersby. To Hatch's irritation, Marty kept slowing down to study the neighborhood.

"What you'll notice," said Marty, "is there are no stoppers to be seen, not since back on Park Avenue. And in the early evening, too. We'll not want to linger."

"Let's go," said Hatch. So there were no stoppers. Did they need stoppers to help find deep players in the global antiquities game? No. On the other hand, Hatch knew Marty was uneasy about consulting Judson Blue, and had even forced Big Ray to stay behind. "Only two of us, Raymond," Marty had said. "They'll feel less skittish with an old, gray-haired fellow like me. Besides, I've been in a few tight spots over the years."

"But I was a great tackler and cover man," Big Ray had replied, to no avail.

Just off of Third Avenue, Marty pointed out the blue-canopied entrance to a restaurant named Azure. "That's the place," he said. "Now listen, we'll present ourselves and you'll be courteous and play it as straight as a nun's ruler. No unnecessary chatter, and no acting the wise-ass."

"Let's go," said Hatch again.

Marty took him by the sleeve. "You understand what I'm saying? It'd be the worst time to be a pain in the hole."

Hatch put up his palms. "Okay, okay. I got it."

The sidewalks were clean and mostly empty, like ship decks cleared for action. Concrete planters containing nothing living stood on either side of Azure's front door. The buildings adjacent to the restaurant were old but neatly maintained, and even the old hotel across the street had a faded glory about it, with its stone and brick facing and its faded banner of green and orange snapping like a battle flag. As Marty and Hatch stepped off the curb, the front entrance opened and a man in camouflage fatigues emerged. As they approached, he drew his pistol but didn't raise it.

"You come from Adagio?" he asked.

"We do indeed," said Marty.

The man studied them for a moment. "I'm Camo," he said. "Do what I tell you to do." He gestured with his pistol for them to enter.

Curtains and pulled shades cast the restaurant dining room in thick gloom. Overturned chairs rested on the tables, and a distant clatter came from the kitchen in the rear. Beneath the restroom sign, a hallway extended to the rear of the building, and there three men leaned against the wall with folded arms and solid, neutral faces.

"Busy night," said Hatch, looking around.

"We're closed," said Camo. The men in the hallway laughed. Camo turned to one of them, a six-foot-eight behemoth wearing a fedora. "You want to let him know, Tower?"

Tower turned and disappeared through a hallway door. The two remaining men regarded Hatch and Marty with the same level of interest they might have given to a box of frozen cutlets or a dozen cans of tomato paste.

Camo gestured at the wall. "Spread them," he said.

Marty put his hands high on the wall, and one of the remaining men stepped over and began frisking him. Hatch protested. Camo spun him around and punched him hard in the kidneys. "This numpty here doesn't want to be searched, Seth," said Camo, speaking to the man who was patting down Marty.

"Asshole," said Hatch. Marty fired him a scorching look, which he ignored.

Camo slammed Hatch's head into the wall with the heel of his hand, and followed it up with a series of pokes and prods which culminated in a knee-buckling jab in the balls. "The man you came here to see does not like attitude," said Camo.

"We understand," said Marty.

Camo and Seth escorted them down the hallway and through a stairwell door. They descended one level and then marched along a narrow hallway to an underground room lined with brick arches and smelling of mold and stale disinfectant. Behind the walls, machinery lurched to life and swept the room with warm air. Hatch began to sweat. Camo nudged them toward a black hardwood desk, its top dusted clean except for a gold letter-opener and a pair of pliers with rubber handles.

Camo and Seth stood behind them. Water gurgled through an overhead pipe. A door behind the desk opened, and a woman in a khaki fatigue jacket emerged carrying a tray. On the right side of the desk, she placed a thermos and an empty mug along with a steaming cup of hot chocolate. On the left, she placed a note pad, a black pen trimmed in gold, and a pair of reading glasses with their arms opened. When she had finished, she took her place behind the desk in the at-ease position.

Hatch's back ached where Camo had punched him. His shirt clung to the small of his back. Another minute passed, and then Judson Blue entered wearing loose fatigues and a beret. With his athletic build and rugged face, Blue could've passed as thirty-five, though he may have been twenty years older. He took his seat behind the desk and drained the hot chocolate without setting down the mug. Then he unscrewed the top of the thermos, poured a cup of black coffee, and leaned back in his chair.

"Identify," he said.

Hatch and Marty glanced at each other. "I'm Hayes," said Hatch. He leaned his head in Marty's direction. "He's Monahan."

Blue sipped his coffee. "Why am I here, Hayes and Monahan?"

Hatch stepped forward. "I was hired to do a pickup at Pier 26 after midnight last night. The delivery guy didn't show. Adagio thought maybe you could help me—help us—find him."

Blue's face was chiseled tight, and Hatch detected not a scintilla of emotion. "You were supposed to pick up what, exactly?"

"An artifact is all I was told. In a box maybe two feet wide."

"Historical artifact?"

"So I was led to believe."

"Who led you to believe?"

Ferret had chosen Hatch because he was unknown to the gangs. Hatch was now blowing that cover, but he dared not disclose Ferret's identity. He shrugged. "I was supposed to take delivery around 1:30 this morning, be driven to a delivery point—I have no idea where—hand over the goods and get paid."

"I'm mostly hearing what you're not saying, Hayes," said Blue. "This gets a lot easier if I know who hired you."

Play another card. "The person I was supposed to meet, his name is K," said Hatch.

"This is nuts," said Camo. "You want me to throw these guys out of here, JB?"

Blue held up his hand but made no response. He donned the reading glasses, removed the cap from the pen, and scribbled on the pad. He tore off the sheet and wadded it in his hands. Then, perhaps changing his mind, he smoothed it back out, folded it, and buttoned it in his chest pocket. The woman behind the desk glanced at Camo.

"You ever met K?" Blue asked Hatch. "You ever even hear of him?"

"No," Hatch said.

The air cut off and left the room in silence. Camo smothered a cough.

"We were hired to do the meet, nothing more," Marty said. "We don't play in the historical antiquities market."

"I already know you don't job with the networks," said Blue. "K and whoever is on the other side of this probably plucked you out of the directory because they needed a couple of dumb fucks who didn't know enough to tell me they were working my backyard. But if it *was* K..." Judson Blue's voice trailed off.

The air grew dank again. Judson Blue walked around the desk and wagged his finger in Hatch's face. "You don't have a clue what you've wandered into, do you?"

"Probably not," said Hatch. "So why don't you tell me."

Blue seemed taken aback. "Tell you? That's how you show respect, ordering around your betters?"

Hatch didn't answer.

"There is one person I do not cross, period," Blue continued, "and it isn't K, but he's close. You follow?"

Hatch didn't. "I do," he said.

Blue gave him a look with his blank, almost reptilian eyes. "K handles things for certain people who like to stay in the background. He may show up in my territory or anywhere else in the world. He may transact, steal something, erase somebody, or all of the above. Then he disappears." Blue paused to yank open the flap on his pocket and extract the note he had written. He read it and buttoned it away again. "K used to work for Ghost. You ever hear of Ghost?"

"No, sir, we have not," said Marty.

"No, of course you haven't," said Blue.

Hatch's scalp began to itch. He stepped forward another step, but Camo restrained him. "Look, I don't know Ghost and I don't know the bigger picture here, but I intend to find K," said Hatch. "I didn't know I was supposed to contact you. I wouldn't've known who to contact or how. If you want a piece of my commish, fine." He jabbed his finger at Blue. "I'll consider it *if* you help me find K."

Marty cut him off. "What my friend here is saying," he began.

"This man's just offered us a slice, Camo," said Blue. The woman behind the desk closed her eyes for a moment.

Camo sighed. "This is a waste of time, JB," he said.

Judson Blue was looking at Hatch as if Hatch had three heads. "How about this jamoke, Camo? We do him a favor, maybe he'll work us in." Blue grabbed Hatch's jaw with a vice-like grip and crunched his cheeks together. "You want to pay me? How about I let you finish this trade, and then I run you down and start digging out eyeballs until you give me every last dollar of your piddly-assed commission?"

Machinery clanged behind the walls. The air came back on, blowing hot. Hatch had bitten his tongue, and he tasted the salty, metallic taste of blood. Judson Blue relinquished his grip and began to pace around, nibbling his fingernail.

"Let's get you two cartoons out of here," said Camo, with a wary look at Blue. He took Marty by one arm and Hatch by another. Seth remained silent.

Blue returned to his desk, withdrew the note from his pocket, and stared at it. The woman whispered something to Blue. He waved her away and turned to Hatch. "You see what this says?" he asked, holding up the note.

Hatch squinted at the paper. It was hard to read with all the folds and creases. "Something man," he said.

"Piano Man," said Blue with a note of savage triumph. He tore the note to pieces. The woman stared straight ahead. Blue ordered them all out.

Camo and Seth marched Hatch and Marty back upstairs. "Piano Man," said Seth as they arrived back in the dining room. "Dang, that gets me thinking."

"Don't," said Camo.

"I used to be a runner for Piano Man."

"Shut up," said Camo. He shoved Hatch. "You had to come in here with this bullshit, didn't you?"

"Do you know K?" asked Hatch.

Camo grunted and pushed Marty and Hatch through the front door and onto the sidewalk. "Keep your faces out of our neighborhood," he said, "or I'll see that you don't have any to show around."

***

MARTY AND HATCH LEFT AZURE AND DID NOT SPEAK UNTIL they reached Park Avenue, where traffic had stopped to allow a phalanx of riot police and a line of urban mini-tanks to pass through. Horns blared. A truck driver shouted through his window. When an open troop carrier filled with stoppers in riot gear rolled past, the crowd booed and shouted.

Marty stood with his arms folded, scowling and staring off into nowhere. "So it's Monahan, is it?" he asked after the tanks had rumbled passed.

"What was I supposed to do?"

"I grew up with some Monahans, and let me tell you about—"

"I couldn't give Judson Blue our real names."

Marty's mouth turned down. "What did I tell you about playing the wise-ass?"

"He wasn't taking us seriously," said Hatch.

"In to an ankle, in to a knee, and now we're waist deep. That's what I'm taking seriously."

Hatch let it go. Marty was prone to venting when unhappy, and it was best to let him spend himself. As far as Hatch was concerned, the visit to Blue had accomplished its purpose: Piano Man was his next clue. The name had a familiar ring, and a glimpse of some event or place danced at the edge of his memory before finally sparking. Atherton. Piano Man Atherton.

"He's dead," said Hatch. "Piano Man Atherton, that is."

"Better him than us," said Marty.

"I met him once. So did Ray. Those music boxes we brought in last fall, delivered them to a house in Grammercy. Goons all over. The old man, Atherton, didn't have much to say, but his wife was a charmer. With all the muscle around, we knew they were into some biz. Antiquities maybe, but probably pituitary drugs. Anyway, the old man died not long after, and I had to call Ms. Atherton—Caroline Atherton—about the bill."

"Would you listen to yourself, now," said Marty. "We've got real danger scratching on our door. And you, kicking the hornet's nest, sticking your nose into a game you don't know how to play, where you have not a single ally or friend. You make me wonder, Hatch. You do."

"I have to find K," said Hatch. "You know I have to find K, Marty."

Deep lines cradled Marty's eyes and made parentheses around his mouth. "Maybe I was wrong to go along with this business in the first place," he said. "I suppose I had my eyes on the wrong things."

"I won't quit, Marty."

"It's always possible to make a bad situation worse if you try hard enough. Adagio was right to have doubts."

On the sidewalk, a bedraggled figure raised his fist to the sky and chastised the people for their loss of spirit, for their acquiescence to unseen powers that drained them of life and filled them with fear. Marty and Hatch hailed a hoo and stared gloomily out of opposite windows while the cab bumped over the cracked asphalt. At Wooster, the hoo abruptly accelerated but missed a death cart by the thickness of the paint before coming to a halt amid a gridlock of trucks and other cabs. Stoppers walked between the vehicles and consulted each other while people wearing Eye Brigade T-shirts milled around, some sporting gashed heads or bloody abrasions. One or two were stretched prone on the sidewalk. The hoo inched a block south, snaking around the disturbance, and finally delivered them to the apartment.

Big Ray met them at the door and they closed themselves in the office. "I want us to bring this entire matter to a close," said Marty. "You'll not agree, Hatch, but it's the best way to keep body and soul together here."

"Somebody want to fill me in?" asked Big Ray.

"I think we all got a little spooked by Ferret," said Marty, his jaw flexing. "And we let the dollar signs dance in our eyes, and maybe I got myself a bit managed by you two lads." He gave Hatch and Big Ray a steady stare. "I'm not pointing the finger, I'm responsible for myself, but we've flushed ourselves into the line of fire. I didn't think it through, but I've no doubt Blue will jump into the game for the artifact now—and because of us, no less. That you'll have to explain to Ferret."

"Who got a little spooked?" asked Hatch.

"We've given Blue the scent, lad," said Marty. "He knew nothing before we stepped in, and he'll now be looking for K, mark my words. If you'll step aside and leave them to themselves, I'll stand with you. No more chasing K, no more dealing with the gangs. Otherwise, I'm out of the firm."

"What?" asked Big Ray.

"You should've seen it, Raymond," said Marty, his eyes ablaze. "The two of us, standing there with gangsters of the meanest sort, Hatch here shooting off his trap, rubbing sand in Blue's own eye."

Hatch felt light-headed. "I will not face Ferret having sat around with my thumb up my—"

"Think of Samantha, Jocelyn, and Nathan," cried Marty. "What is it about this you can't see?" Then he stopped and his shoulders slumped. "For some people, the only way they know is to turn it all to ash," he said softly. "Well, you'll have to do it without me. You can't govern yourself, Hatch. You've lost your last drop of sense and I can't take part in it." Marty gave Hatch's desk a light rap and walked out of the office.

"Nice work," said Big Ray.

Hatch leaned forward, his hands on his desk, and hung his head. "Marty's like a runaway freight train. I let him get going and he jumped the tracks."

Big Ray looked away. "You remember the construction crew we worked on up in Maine, summer before our senior year? There was a guy, a big hairy beast."

"That was a million years ago."

"I forget his name. Dude had it in for you."

Hatch stared at the desk.

"He wouldn't let it go," said Big Ray. "Called you a wimp, a jellyfish, a milk maid, always riding you about something."

"Garden variety pain in the ass."

"True enough, which is why I was surprised to come out that night and see you two swinging knives at each other. You sliced the poor bastard like deli turkey."

"No."

"Then you tripped him."

"He fell."

Big Ray wagged his finger. "And then, as God is my witness, you tried to finish him off while he rolled around in the dirt. Bloodlust in your eye, face of blue steel. If I hadn't thrown your sorry ass in the truck and driven us home, you'd've killed the guy. You'd be rotting in prison or in a camp to this day."

"I am going to find K," said Hatch. His voice had taken on a growly tone that he did not fully recognize.

"Right, find K," said Big Ray. "Collect the mil. Cut a deal with Ferret." He rubbed a spot on his forehead. "This artifact, this delivery, brother, it really is all about you now, isn't it?"

At that moment, Hatch's vision went topsy-turvy; the lamplight splintered and sparkled and the room spun sideways; the far-off tinkling sound returned, faint against a murmur of wind or chanting voices. Hatch leaned on the desk, but discovered himself pushing upward on it, as if he were standing on the ceiling and all of reality had inverted.

Big Ray's voice echoed. "It really is all about you…"

Hatch's perception blew open—he seemed to be floating—there was his father, standing before him, close enough to touch. Hatch was struck dumb and unable to move. His father held a fat, football-shaped object, so black that no light reflected, and strangely indistinct at the edges. It was covered with intricate, glowing symbols.

Truth …

A whisper inside Hatch's mind. His father smiled and the object in his hands came alive with light. Hatch was touched by an ancient, alien force of such penetrating intelligence that he sensed it restraining itself, brushing his mind protectively, with a feather-touch, as if a full presentation might obliterate him altogether.

Truth…

The instant passed. His father and the object had vanished, and Hatch wiped sweat off of his face. "Do what you need to do, Ray," he said.

"And what would that be, partner?"

Hatch's hands were shaking. "I have to find K, and I will. Just watch."

"Just watch." Big Ray looked away again. "Famous last words of morons everywhere."

The desk clock ticked softly. It was the dark of dusk, and the back of Big Ray's head reflected in the oval window. A gust of wind rattled the pane.

"I'll talk to Marty," said Big Ray, his hands in his pockets. "Meanwhile, maybe you should think about what kind of funeral you want. A small church service, maybe. Or a couple of friends to open a bottle and say a few words about what a dick you were, and how you'd always listen to anything anybody had to say as long as it was you doing the talking."

CHAPTER 10

HATCH JERKED AWAKE THE NEXT MORNING, HAVING overslept by an hour. Samantha had remained at Jocelyn's, or so he assumed since he had not been able to reach her. Still groggy after an icy shower, he riffled through his closet for a decent shirt, recalling as he did so the peculiar and disorienting episode in his office the day before: all of reality fragmented and askew, his father standing before him with the exotic object in his hands.

Ferret's artifact.

Hatch had no way to know that, and yet he *did* know it, as surely as he knew the days of the week.

He fingered a blue dress shirt—yes, it would work with his navy blazer—and slipped his arms through the sleeves. Fatigue and stress were the culprits, he told himself as he absently fastened the buttons. He had been exhausted after seeing Adagio and Blue and then arguing with Marty and Ray.

He climbed the stairs in subdued spirits, and as he stepped into the main room a small box came whirling through the air. He ducked, reflexively, and the box thunked harmlessly in the hallway behind him.

"Spill it, Hatch," said Jocelyn. She grabbed the stapler from the desk and stood like a pitcher on the mound. "The next one's going to hurt." Nathan stood beside her, his arms folded across his chest.

"I have to be somewhere," said Hatch.

"We are tired of the whispering and sneaking around," said Jocelyn. "We want to know what you silly bruhs are up to."

"This happened to me in a game once," said Nathan. "The game concealed information. Important, dangerous information."

Hatch felt like a man on a swinging bridge over a high chasm.

"Marty and Ray are like out of it," said Jocelyn. "They're glazy-eyed, walking around and bumping into walls, and they won't tell us anything. We are not potted plants, Hatch."

"You had to challenge the game," said Nathan, his hair corkscrewed from his GameHead goggles. "It was the only way."

A loud pounding on the door—"Open up! Police!"—and Jocelyn put away the stapler and removed an envelope from her desk drawer. When she opened the front door, a pudgy cop shouldered his way in. "You're supposed to have something for me," he said.

"You're the new cop?" asked Jocelyn.

"You people are overdue."

Jocelyn's mouth hardened into a straight line. "We people are not overdue. Talk to the other stopper who used to come around here. Short black hair? Stevenson."

The cop snapped his fingers and held out his hand. "I'd hate to see bad stuff happen to you, missy. It ain't safe out there sometimes, you know."

Hatch and Nathan glanced at each other.

"Oh, really?" Jocelyn's voice took on a nasty edge. "Well, that's not what we're paying for."

"What?"

"We don't pay for it ain't safe out there." Jocelyn made quotation marks with her fingers. "We pay for a quiet neighborhood. We pay for security. Do you know how hard this money is to come by? Do you? Wake up and look around, stopper man. The rest of us don't get to go kicking in doors and shaking people down so we can spend the afternoon cooling our fat asses at Smyte's."

The cop stepped backward into the foyer. "Hey, calm down," he said. "I just collect."

"Do you?"

"Look, missy, you don't know the pressure I'm under."

"Ha!"

"I got a quota, too. I show up short, I'm going to get scalded."

"We can't even pay salaries right now."

The cop flushed. "I'm new and I need this job. I got kids. Give me a break, would you?"

"And we have a lot of other bills and you come in here saying we're *overdue*?"

"Maybe you aren't," said the cop. "Overdue, I mean."

"Go talk to Stevenson," said Jocelyn, thrusting the envelope at him, "and don't ever think about calling me missy again." She pushed the door shut and turned to Hatch.

Hatch raised his hands to ward her off. "Okay, Joss, we have a deal brewing."

"No shit, Hatch. Look, I have a few thousand left, which I'm holding for Electricorp so we can at least keep the lights on here for a couple of months."

"Make him face up to it," said Nathan. "Challenge him."

"Not even Sam knows what you guys are into," said Jocelyn. She walked over and stuck a finger in Hatch's chest. "That's what it has come to, Hatch. We have to nag Sam to find out what's going on, but she can't tell us squat."

Jocelyn went on, but Hatch was thinking of Samantha. Why had he not heard from her? He had sent texts and tried to call. Her silence was uncharacteristic and unnerving, but it wouldn't do to ask Jocelyn, not now—

"Hatch? Hello." Jocelyn clapped her hands in his face. "See there?" she said to Nathan. "Glazy-eyed. That's what I'm talking about, glazed-eye sickness. It affects hearing and cognitive ability, too."

"What have I been telling you?" asked Nathan.

"I'm sorry, but I have to go," said Hatch.

"More secret meetings?" Jocelyn dropped into her chair. "I hope your big idea works, Hatch. We need the money. We're bouncing off the bottom now, dude, and I've stopped taking calls. I'm sick of being the punching bag, getting chewed out, having to invent reasons why we didn't pay somebody's bill."

Hatch moved to leave, but as he reached the door a tiny hint of elation sparked inside. He wanted to explain the sense of promise he felt, his conviction that important, worthy purposes lay behind their struggles. But his moment of illumination passed, and he knew any words he might conjure up would sound empty and unconvincing—to himself as well as Jocelyn and Nathan. "I am sorry, Joss, I really am," he said.

Jocelyn was not mollified. "Listen, Hatch, you bring me money," she said. He closed the door behind him, but her muted voice carried into the foyer: "Bring…me… money."

***

"I APPRECIATE YOUR CONDOLENCES, MR. DORAN, BUT MY husband is right here," said Caroline Atherton, crossing her legs. "In the urn, on the mantle behind you, and as much the life of the party as ever, though somewhat less useful now." She laughed.

"Thank you for seeing me, Ms. Atherton," said Hatch. After the blowup with Marty the previous evening, he had retrieved Caroline Atherton's number from Odysseus's records and they had agreed to meet. Now they faced each other in the small parlor of her home, a wide, bay-windowed brownstone adjacent to Grammercy Park. "And please, call me Hatch. I met Mr. Atherton only once, when we brought in the music boxes."

"I used to collect them. Yes, I remember you quite well, Hatch." Caroline Atherton, sitting on a small love-seat couch, crossed her legs again. She was a striking woman—Mae would've called her a classic beauty—and on either side of fifty, Hatch guessed, with expressive hazel eyes and dark hair. "I remember, too," she continued, "that I couldn't tempt you into having a drink with me then. Will you join me now? I know the hour is awfully early."

"I don't want to take up too much of your time, Ms. Atherton."

"Call me Caroline, please. Don't make me feel old." She stood and allowed her hand to linger on Hatch's shoulder a moment. "I have bloody marys at the ready—a bloody mary will do, won't it, Hatch?" She stepped over to a petite bar built into the wall, poured and stirred two glasses, and handed one to Hatch before resuming her seat. Her skirt slipped upward another half-inch. "Cheers," she said.

"Cheers."

Hatch sipped the cocktail and took in the art and antiques crowded into the small parlor. Certainly, they testified to the Atherton wealth, but it was all too neat; Hatch didn't mind a sofa pillow in the wrong place or a spot of wear on a rug, and for a moment, he thought of Caroline as a bird in a decorative, pristine cage. On the other hand, the commissions from the contents of this small room could fund Odysseus for a year or more. He casually glanced at the Louis XVI plated candelabrum (if he wasn't mistaken), the tortoiseshell tea caddy inlaid with pearl, and on the far wall the collection of five-hundred-year-old maps of the British Isles.

"So what may I do for you, Hatch?" asked Caroline.

"I have an unresolved business matter. I'm trying to locate someone who may have been an associate of your husband."

"And you thought by chance I might know this person?"

"It seemed worth a try."

"Unfortunately, I had no real involvement in my husband's business activities. By the way, did you know he was called the Piano Man?" Caroline laughed and her eyes took on a mischievous cast. "Of course you did, but do you know how he came by his name?"

"Not from playing the piano, I take it."

"Indeed not. However, the wife of his former partner played, and magnificently, too, pretty much the entire Beethoven piano repertoire. So here is the gist of the story: Clyde, my husband, became convinced that her husband—his partner—had cheated him on a shipment of what you would know as Joggle."

"The synthetic peyote drug."

"The very one. Clyde got it into his head that his partner's wife had influenced him, and Clyde become intense when his suspicions caught fire. At any rate, the dear woman opened her piano one day to find her husband's severed head gaping at her. Trite, in its way, I suppose—Clyde particularly loved old movies—but terrible for the piano and far worse for poor Nico, Clyde's partner."

Hatch set his bloody mary on a side table. The clock struck a low, disquieting tone.

"I have years of such stories," said Caroline. Her eyes grew wide and flattened along the bottom, giving her face a slightly hysterical aspect. She laughed again and fingered a blouse button. "So tell me, dear, who are you looking for?"

"Someone named K."

"K. That plucks a distant note." She gave Hatch a cagey look out of the corner of her eye. "We did not often socialize with Clyde's associates, but I do have several of his notebooks. A nagging instinct told me to hold on to them. Isn't it funny how the world works, Hatch?"

"Sometimes," said Hatch. He smiled.

"Why don't I fetch them?" She reached over to touch his knee. "We'll go through them together. Perhaps they will spur an old memory."

Hatch mumbled his appreciation. Caroline left and he heard her footsteps on the stairs. Outside, the branches of a small Japanese maple brushed the window grilles. A bird shrieked. Through the window, he watched Caroline's guards pace on the sidewalk, and he saw passersby strolling freely with their jackets slung over their shoulders.

Caroline returned with two ledger books. "Sit," she said, patting the space next to her. She cracked open the books. "This one is all figures, notes Clyde made. He was averse to electronic records."

Hatch squeezed beside Caroline on the love seat and studied the open ledger pages. "None of this makes any sense," he said. "These aren't real names or words."

"They are code names." From a pocket at the back of the book, she pulled out a folded multiyear calendar. "Deciphering the entries depends on the date the entry was made. Clyde made me a key before he died."

Hatch's heart sank. Clyde had crammed the book with entries and scribbled notes, all in neat block letters. It would require weeks of tedious conversion to make any sense of it.

"Now this one," said Caroline, presenting a smaller volume, "is more of a journal." She glanced at Hatch, and he became aware of the pressure of her hip next to his. "There are no profound, philosophical musings here," she said, riffling through the pages. "It reads more like a reminder of who Clyde was angry with at a given time. Also, he makes notes—see this one, a description of a trap door in the bottom of a garage, but he doesn't say where it is—and back here is, of all things, a joke."

"A joke?"

"Three clergymen go into a bar…" Underneath the journal, Caroline's hand brushed Hatch's thigh, and he caught a faint whiff of her perfume.

He cleared the frog in his throat. "And the loose page there?"

She unclipped a scrap from the middle of the journal. "Oh, it concerns Kutzie. He and Clyde were involved in a transaction several years ago."

"Kutzie?"

"Andrei Kutznov. Russian, of course. I had the idea he operated all over the world. Someone to be very careful with, though he and I always hit it off." She paused. "Clyde called him K-man. Are you perhaps looking for Kutznov, Hatch?" She had a slight tremor in her voice, and she turned her face to him and pushed back a strand of brown hair. His heart rate shifted up a gear, possibly at the prospect of having identified K, but possibly not.

"Kutznov? Maybe," he said. The moment stretched. The bird cried out again.

"Why don't I call K?" she whispered, her eyes searching his face. "Why don't I try? Would you like that, Hatch?"

Hatch hesitated a moment too long. "Sure," he said.

Caroline started to say something but changed her mind. Whatever current had passed between them broke. "Oh, my God, I am a fool," she muttered.

"No, no," said Hatch, shaken and uncertain. "Far from it."

"Of course I'll call Kutznov for you, Hatch."

"Caroline—"

"Oh, shush, dear." They stood and Caroline wrapped her arm through his and escorted him into the entrance foyer. "You must tell me you're sure, Hatch. About Kutznov, about this business. Tell me you know what you're doing."

Hatch licked his lips. "I've sort of moved Odysseus into the historicals trade, Caroline."

"Oh, I do hope not." She looked worried. "You don't have enough lines under your eyes to consort with such people. They are ruthless creatures."

"I have to do this, Caroline," said Hatch. A surge of fierce delight tickled inside his chest. "I have a conviction about it that I can't explain."

"You never finished your drink," she said.

"And you were my only real lead. There is a touch of the miraculous here." Hatch laughed, then wiped his hand over his mouth. "I have to do this. I do."

"I'll see if I can find Kutzie and make him give you an appointment." Caroline stared into his eyes, her face troubled. She rubbed his arms, letting her hands linger. "Then I'll give you a call, Hatch."

"We'll have our drink when all this is finished," he said.

A forlorn expression crossed her features, and her eyes grew sad. "Clyde wasn't much, but I was used to him. I miss him terribly, you know. We were together for a long time." She continued to rub her hands along Hatch's biceps. "You must run on while you can, Hatch. We'll be very good friends, I know we will. That's how it will be."

CHAPTER 11

"HOT DAY-OLDS! HOT DAY-OLDS!" CRIED THE OLD WOMAN. She was stationed behind a metal rolling-cart advertising hot rolls and soup. She drew her yellow parka close around her. Thomas Dartham strode past, glancing at the night-hawkers gathered around the woman's cart.

"Two redbacks! Two redbacks a hot day-old!" The woman's garish, costume earrings flashed when she turned her head. "You, sir! Soup and a roll."

Dartham shook his head.

"Onion, cheese rolls, a day old," she said. "Coffee, fresh brewed."

The aroma of hot bread wafted through the chilly evening air. The hawkers gazed at Dartham with languid eyes and indifferent faces. A pack of young boys burst through the crowd and almost knocked Dartham flat; ten, twelve years old, most of them, in black and gray sweats and as filthy as dump pickers. They called Dartham an old shit and a useless wrinkler, and after watching them disappear he checked to make sure his wallet remained with him.

He had spent his weekend in the Global Consolidated warehouses, poring over material documenting years of interaction between the Blue, Terry Bronsun, and an obscure GCI subsidiary formed to house Terry's art and antiquities collection. After digesting reams of eyes-only reports and handwritten transaction logs, he had decided it was time to renew an old acquaintance.

A man in a tattered coat thrust a flyer in Dartham's face advertising the future of enhanced sex. Behind him, a lifelike but clearly robotic whore grinned from a doorway bathed in black light. Look at the world, thought Dartham. Kids running wild, p'out gangs all over, near-starvation, corporate tribunals, labor camps—and this. He crumpled the flyer in his hands. The world was a broad river with deep, invisible currents and only fools wasted time trying to change its course. The river had taken him from the dust of rural Texas to West Point, and from there he had worked his way up the military's slippery pole. He had earned promotions and fought wars. He had worked hard. He had done his job. Afterward, the river had taken him to GCI, where he had traded his uniform for a closet full of tailored suits and a cushy lifestyle. He would not apologize for the place he had found in the world. The river ran on.

Dartham arrived at the corner across from Azure and surveyed the restaurant frontage. When he stepped off the curb, the two men posted in front of the restaurant moved forward and ordered him to come no closer.

"This restaurant came recommended, and I have not had my dinner yet," said Dartham. The guards snickered. One of them, a rangy man with an eyepatch and a gashed face, drew his weapon and, to Dartham's annoyance, spat on the sidewalk. "Son, I understand you are carrying out your assignment," said Dartham. "And except for your regrettable manners, I have no quarrel with you. Of course, I have no particular attachment, either, so I suggest you put the gun away and stand down."

The guards hesitated, perhaps at Dartham's air of command.

"Now run tell Judson Blue that Colonel Thomas Dartham is here," he continued. "If you need to jog his memory, I served with him in the army."

"Even old friends need an appointment to see JB."

Dartham smiled. "I assure you, I am no friend."

The guards conferred, whispering and glancing at Dartham out of the corners of their eyes. One of them disappeared into the restaurant and returned a moment later, gesturing for Dartham to enter. The dining room was empty except for a group gathered at a circular table in the corner. Dartham counted four of Blue's bruisers, a dark-haired woman in an evening gown, and Blue himself, perched over a hot, pink steak. Blue's beret sat on the table beside his plate. A harpsichord piece—Scarlatti, Dartham guessed—clipped along at low volume.

"Captain Dartham," said Blue. "The Texas Terror, we used to call him. Affectionately, of course." Blue put down his knife. "I never know who or what's going to crawl through these doors lately."

"That would be Colonel," said Dartham.

The bruisers stared at Dartham. Blue daubed his mouth with a napkin. "Listen to that accent," he said. "I had forgotten how twangy it was. Look, if you need work, *Colonel*, I can make a call or two—I do have a soft spot for vets—but unfortunately, you're a little long in the tooth for what we do here."

"I do not need a job, Lieutenant. I was thinking you could use a partner."

Blue laughed and sawed off a bite of steak. Everyone at the table joined in, and Dartham smiled along with them. "You want me to toss this guy, JB?" asked one of the thugs.

Blue waved his fork. "This is my old C.O., Hump. From my glory days in Indonesia."

"I was actually several layers above Blue," said Dartham. "Just like now."

The woman giggled. She adjusted a spaghetti strap that had slipped from her shoulder.

"Come join us, Colonel," said Blue. "I can't offer you dinner, only the company of this fine gathering."

Dartham pulled a chair from an adjacent table and whirled it around to face Blue's entourage. "I am sure they are the very salt of the earth, Blue, but there must be somewhere they have to be."

Glasses clinked from far back in the kitchen. A truck passed outside. Blue gave Dartham a long look and then glanced at Hump and nodded. The group stood. The woman pouted and stroked Blue's shoulder. "You, too, hon," he said.

Dartham watched them file into the hallway beside the kitchen.

Blue took a swallow of water and then cut open a steaming baked potato. "There is no reason to be unsociable, Colonel," he said.

"This is not a social call, Blue." Dartham worked his chair close to Blue and spoke in a low tone. "But I do not care to embarrass a man in front of his subordinates. It is bad for morale. Your collection of meat eaters might turn on you if they sensed weakness."

Blue snickered.

"I want to discuss an ancient object, Blue. A prehistoric artifact. I represent some important people who are interested."

"Important people interested in an ancient object? Honestly, Colonel, you're beginning to bore me, just like you did in the old days. Is there a point to all this?"

Blue leaned over and blew on the steaming potato. Dartham reached his hand around the back of Blue's head and slammed his face into his plate. When Blue tried to rise, Dartham stood and slammed him twice more, breaking the plate and scattering steak, potato, and some greenish stalks suggestive of broccoli all over the tablecloth and floor.

"I had hoped it would not come to this," said Dartham.

Blood gushed from Blue's nose. "Jesus Christ," he said.

"I am partial to the Old Testament, Lieutenant." Dartham took his chair. "But I do come to do the work of the Father, Terrence Bronsun."

The bruisers rushed back into the dining room. Blue groaned and waved them away with his bloody hand. They looked from Dartham to Blue and then at each other before backing away. Blue pressed a napkin to his face. Blood dripped onto his shirt.

"Bring this man some ice," said Dartham. A cook hurried out with a champagne bucket of ice and a stack of cloth napkins.

"You old hard-ass," said Blue. "And my steak."

"There is a lady up the block selling day-olds if you still want to eat," said Dartham.

Blue coughed bloodily.

Dartham refilled Blue's water glass. "Drink so you don't choke on your blood. Now listen, word is somebody's offering an artifact around the networks. It is supposed to be older than dirt and shaped kind of like a football. Terry Bronsun thinks this may be mere idle chatter. I am taking it more seriously."

Judson Blue wrapped the napkin around a handful of ice and pressed it to his face, his head back.

"Tell me what you know, Blue. I'd like to get out of here before your face turns purple and starts to swell."

"Why didn't you say you were with Bronsun to start with?" asked Blue, speaking through the napkin. "I assumed you people were behind this transaction from the start."

"So you knew about it, yet we did not hear a peep from you." Dartham shook his head. "I am disappointed, given all the business Terry sends your way."

"I don't talk to Bronsun," said Blue. "He talks to me, and I haven't heard anything from him about this."

"Until now."

Blue made gurgling noises.

Dartham drummed the table with his fingers. He was disappointed to find substance to the rumors Terry had heard. "Tell me what you know," he said. "It would be a bad time to leave out any material facts."

Blue gently lifted the ice pack and then touched it back to his face. "We heard some pickup went bad. It might have to do with your artifact or it might not. Whoever's involved waltzed into my territory and didn't touch base with me."

"They must not have felt they had to."

"They will next time if we ever find them."

"If?" asked Dartham. "My confidence in you is growing shaky."

Judson Blue groaned. "There are players out there not even you or Bronsun have a handle on. Who knows where your artifact is or if it even exists?"

"Who knows, indeed." Dartham studied Blue for a moment. "I want you to devote your formidable organization to locating the people involved in this matter," he said. "When you find them, you will inform me and have no further involvement in this business. Unless I change my mind and tell you to."

"We don't answer to you," said Blue.

"Sure you do. I want you to designate someone as our liaison. I doubt you want me pestering you day and night."

"Bullshit." Blue's voice was muffled by the ice pack.

"Mind your manners and take heed to my warning, Blue. Terry Bronsun would grow wroth if he believed you had lost your grip on the trade."

A bloody gob fell from Blue's nose. He closed his eyes and leaned his head back. "Seth Boyle," he said. "One of my knuckleheads. Seth will be our go-between. I'll tell him."

Dartham placed his card next to Blue's ice bucket. "Have him give me a call before I go to bed tonight." Dartham stood to leave and then looked down at Judson Blue. "I am concerned by the way you are still bleeding, Lieutenant. That cannot be good."

***

THE NEXT MORNING, A CHARCOAL-COLORED LIMOUSINE eased to a stop beneath the rusted supports of the FDR Drive near South Street Seaport. On the pier, a scattering of people lounged against the rail or relaxed on benches. Dartham took in the scene through the limo's tinted windows. A digital sign nearby displayed the image of a healthy, apple-cheeked boy. The sign said: *NO HUNGER IN THE HOMELAND! RESIST FAKE NEWS!*

Dartham pressed the button to lower the privacy window.

"Yes, Colonel?" asked the driver.

"Frisk this guy when he shows up, all right?"

"Yes, sir."

A few moments later, a lone figure jogged from the pier and tapped on the limo window. The driver got out and searched the man, removing a four-inch shiv from his boot. He opened the rear door and the man climbed in and huddled on the bench seat facing Dartham.

"Seth Boyle?" asked Dartham.

The man nodded. His eyes darted around the limo.

"What did I tell you, Seth? No weapons."

"I didn't bring no gun," said Seth. "I forgot about the slicer."

Dartham looked Seth over. Greasy, blond hair and a remnant of teen acne, though Seth had to be in his mid-twenties now.

"This car's half a block long," said Seth. "It stands out like a sow in a beauty pageant." He licked his lips. "Look, I'm not supposed to be here. Blue said I was to talk to you only on the phone."

Two kids tossed a luminous orange ball back and forth near one of the weathered brick Seaport buildings. Dartham watched them for a moment. "You don't work for Blue anymore, Seth," he said.

"I have to tell him you said that. I have to tell him everything." Dartham's silence seemed to increase Seth's nervousness. "Listen, I don't know what you got on Blue," he said. "I never seen him afraid of nobody until you showed up."

"He is not afraid of me, Seth. He is afraid of the man I work for."

"I'm just a piss poor little messenger here." Seth shifted on the slick, leather seat.

"No, you are my eyes and ears, and you are going to keep me posted on everything that happens in Blue's gang. But first I want to know more about this pickup that went wrong."

"Blue don't tell me squat."

"We're going to change that."

"I'm saying—"

"Settle down, son. I will pay you three thousand Homeland dollars every week, and you will make me feel like part of Blue's little family."

Seth wiped the back of his hand across his forehead. "I can't do that," he said. "I just can't."

Dartham popped open a briefcase, removed an envelope full of cash, and pressed it into Seth's hands. "Fifteen thousand redbacks," he said. "Part of it is an advance. Now give me your belt."

"Good Lord," said Seth, staring at the cash.

"The belt."

"Why?"

Dartham put aside the briefcase. "Do not ever ask why in my presence," he said. "It does not matter to you why I tell you to do anything."

Seth licked his lips again. His eyes darted toward the envelope.

"The belt, Seth."

Seth unbuckled his belt and handed it over. Dartham took it, injected a device no larger than a pinhead into the back of the leather, and covered it with a drop of fast-drying, translucent gel. He blew on it, rubbed it with his thumb, and gave it back to Seth. "Wear the belt wherever you go," he said. "It will broadcast to me every fart and burp you make, along with everything anybody says within a healthy radius of your location."

A panicked look crossed Seth's face. He lunged for the door but it was locked. "You can't make me do this," he said. "You don't understand Blue. You're going to get me completely killed."

Dartham reached into his pocket and slid his fingers through a set of old-fashioned brass knuckles. "You already took the job and the money, Seth. That means we have a deal."

"No, no, no!" Seth's eyes grew wild. A fleck of spittle landed on the front of Dartham's shirt. "You can't just order me—"

Dartham jabbed Seth in the cheek, a modest, attention-getting poke. Seth fell back with a dazed look, but something in his expression caused Dartham to snap. He grabbed Seth by the jacket and shook him, consumed by the need to beat the solid, implacable stupidity out of the man. When he recovered himself, the brass knuckles lay in his lap and Seth had pushed himself into the corner of the seat, a thread of spittle dangling from his lower lip.

Dartham slipped the brassies back into his pocket. "You shouldn't spit on a man's shirt," he said. "Now, about the pickup."

"Some guy, dark hair, maybe late thirties or something, he came to visit," said Seth.

"You are slurring your words, son."

Seth drew a ragged breath. "His name was Hayes. Sort of cocky, stood right up to Blue. There was an old Irish guy with him. Anyway, they told us about the pickup. Sounded like somebody didn't show."

"And what else?"

"Blue gave Hayes a name, Piano Man, which is funny because Blue knows he's dead. Anyway, Piano Man used to deal with somebody called K."

"Piano Man? And who is K?"

Seth shrugged. "I don't know but I used to mule Joggle for Piano Man." His brow wrinkled. "This Hayes, he won't find any K because Piano Man's gone. I don't think Blue wanted to tangle with none of this."

Dartham looked out of the window again. "Seth, do you ever think about what happens when we die?" he asked.

"What do you mean?" asked Seth.

"I think we just slip out of our body as easy as you please and go to some wonderful place. I think we go to our home."

Seth frowned. "You mean, like Arkansas?"

"I might be wrong. There might be a hell. Or there might be"—Dartham motioned with his arm—"emptiness."

"I don't know why you're telling me this stuff."

"Because if you step out of line with me, Seth, I am going to treat you to eternity. I am going to give you the answer to life's biggest question."

Seth's breath hitched. "Can I get maybe like four thousand a week?" he asked.

"No," said Dartham. "Now listen, Blue will assume I am trying to turn you, so you stick eight thousand of that money in your pocket and give the rest to him. Tell him I tried to buy you off. Tell him you cannot work for me and ask him to take you off the job. Got it?"

"But—"

"He'll refuse. And I have your belt, remember?"

"You said the money was mine. Why do I got to share it with Blue?"

From inside the limo, Dartham heard the muffled shouts of the kids as they tossed the ball. He shook his head. "We are not even finished with our first meeting, Seth, and there you are, using the word why again."

CHAPTER 12

CAMO STRADDLED A CHAIR IN BLUE'S APARTMENT ABOVE Azure. Blue's girl, Lindi, buffed her nails while Judson Blue paced around with a massive bandage wrapped over his nose. Camo didn't care for Lindi's voice—it was high and chirpy, like a little bird—but she was easy on the eyes and he admired the way she kept cool even when it was all hitting the fan. Blue stopped and tapped his chin. Seth dozed in the corner, his chair rocked back against the wall.

"So what do you want to do about this Dartham guy?" asked Camo.

"What I want is to know where this prick Hayes lives," said Blue.

"I have to ask, JB, why'd you give them Piano Man's name, the guy dead and all?"

Blue shrugged. "Maybe they'll go looking for him, maybe they'll find K for us. But we won't know if we don't have eyes on them, will we?"

"The problem is with the names Hayes and Monahan. They aren't in the biz and nobody's ever heard of them. I wish I'd put tails on them."

"I'll call Adagio," said Blue, looking over the bandage across his nose. "As for Dartham, I want you to do nothing."

Camo pulled his eyes away from Lindi. This didn't sound like Blue. "Man comes into our own house and does that to you?"

"Dartham was always one of those by-the-book humps, the kind who lose us all the wars. I heard he gets home from Asia and his wife's outside the wire, run off with somebody to somewhere. Poor bastard takes to the bottle. I almost feel sorry for him—almost. But Dartham's not the issue, Terry Bronsun is. Bronsun's the beating heart of hell." Blue resumed pacing, dragging his toes along the floor with each step. "Something's cooking here," he continued. "We got K in the picture which means Ghost is somewhere around—Ghost is a one-man murder squad, and he does not tolerate loose ends—and then we got Bronsun sniffing around. It makes me wonder if the old Project Caterpillar shit is in play, the holy of holies. Either way, we're going to be held responsible."

Caterpillar? Camo had no idea what Blue was talking about. Maybe Bronsun and Dartham planned to squeeze Blue, but Camo had other plans for himself. It was just a question of when to pull the escape handle. He noticed Lindi giving him a fetching look, and he moved over to the couch next to her. She glanced at Blue.

"Problem is, if Ghost is involved, he's almost as bad as Bronsun," said Blue, still pacing.

"He's a global player, right?" asked Camo. "Like that Ferret guy or like Conway Plackett or even Juice Man."

"Nobody knows quite what Ghost is into," said Blue, "but we've prospered by never crossing those people. We've been smart enough to pick our own battles. But this does make me wonder…"

Lindi peeked at Camo out of the corner of her eye and smiled. When Blue turned away, Camo winked at her.

"I tapped Seth to liaise with Dartham, by the way," said Blue. He kicked Seth's chair, causing Seth to gasp and wave his arms for balance.

"You seriously picked Seth?" asked Camo. "To talk to Dartham?"

"Dartham tried to turn him, if you can believe that," said Blue. "Seth walks in, hands me an envelope full of cash, says the Colonel made him take it. Isn't that right, numbnuts?"

Seth nodded, his mouth hanging open.

"Maybe it's all right," said Camo. He shot Seth a look. "Seth's not smart enough to turn on us."

"It's the smart ones you have to worry about," said Blue. "It's why I don't have you dealing with Dartham."

Camo did not react, but the remark sent a stab of alarm though him. Was Blue testing him, sending him some kind of message? "Hey, how long we been together, JB?" he asked.

"Calm down, tiger," said Blue. "I want you to help Seth out. Let him talk to Dartham, you be his big brother."

"I can deal with Dartham myself," said Seth.

"Go back to sleep," said Blue, and then to Camo, "I want to know more about whatever angle Dartham is working here."

"I'm on it," said Camo. Another smile flickered on Lindi's face, and Camo tingled at the mystery and possibility it conveyed. He wanted to explore the question with her, maybe tease her a little, knowing full well she'd shoot back. She had spunk and he liked that. She had high, pretty cheekbones. She had nice skin, the smoothest he had ever seen.

"I'll call Adagio and find out about this guy Hayes or whatever his name is," said Blue. "But we have to step soft. I don't want the street to know we're shadowing K. The dude's like smoke as it is."

Camo stole one last glance at Lindi, jogged down the stairs, and nodded at the Tower, who was lounging with some of the other guys in the dining room. Outside, he hailed a hoo and headed south for ten blocks. At a sidewalk bistro, he ordered a glass of syn-wine from the auto-dispenser and took an outdoor table. When he was sure he hadn't been followed, he slipped a burner phone from his pocket and punched the number Ghost had given him.

"Speak," said Ghost.

"I told you about the two guys came in late last week, looking for some guy named K," said Camo. "Now we got another guy sniffing around. Thomas Dartham, an ex-Colonel."

"One of Terrence Bronsun's people."

"He came in last night, shoved Blue around, told him get on top of all this and report back to him."

"Blue's going to want the artifact."

Camo scratched his neck, thinking about it. "No, he hasn't said that, but he does want to find K."

"He'll want the artifact. Dartham is squeezing him. The artifact will give him something to bargain with."

A flatbed truck full of day workers rumbled by and exhaled a gray cloud of exhaust. Camo stifled a cough. "Have you rescheduled the pickup?" he asked Ghost.

"No, but I might now that Dartham is in the picture."

"He tried to buy off one of our guys."

"If Bronsun is interested in my artifact, then Dartham's going to be up your tailpipe every step of the way. Your job is to make sure of it."

Camo shifted the phone to the other ear. "You *want* Dartham on us?"

"What did I just say? Yes, keep Dartham informed. Play his game. Keep him interested."

"Okay, I got it," said Camo. He clicked off the phone, ground it apart under his heel, and tossed it in a trash bin next to the sidewalk tables. It didn't make any sense to him, drawing in this Dartham guy. But the man with the money makes the rules, and Ghost had the money, so it was Ghost's game.

Another flatbed rumbled by. Camo watched it pass. He had agreed to be Ghost's snitch inside the Blue, though he didn't really know what Ghost was after. But hell, he wasn't paid to know. Did he enjoy being a snitch? No. Was he being disloyal to Judson Blue? Yeah, but so what? Blue was as crazy as a coked-up badger, and Ghost paid better. Much better.

Camo swirled the syn-wine in the plastic goblet.

Ghost had planned a transaction, a sale of some rare artifact, but something had gone wrong with the pickup. It was too bad Adagio and this guy Hayes had pushed the matter into Blue's line of sight. Ghost had wanted to keep it all invisible, take care of his business without Blue or the other gangs knowing about it. But Camo didn't have anything to do with Hayes or the missed pickup. His question was, how much longer would Ghost need his services? Camo didn't know. He just wanted to collect the rest of the money Ghost had promised and see if Lindi wanted to run away with him to Florida or even Cuba. Somewhere still warm enough to stretch out on a beach.

Camo wiggled his toes inside his steel-toed boots. The outdoor air, even on a smelly New York avenue, made him more optimistic. No Judson Blue in his face, jawing about this and that—Christ, having to babysit that guy was a headache—and none of the gang arguing, talking too loud, getting into trouble.

A wisp of cloud crossed the blue sky. Camo watched the people walk past on the sidewalk and sipped the rest of his wine.

***

SOMETIME AFTER MIDNIGHT, BLUE JABBED CAMO AWAKE with the business end of a Glock and told him to shake out the cobwebs and get moving. Camo tried to figure out where he was. His brain was full of dust and his heart began to race. "What's up?" he asked.

"I have a little errand to run," said Blue.

"You want me to get a few of the guys?"

"Just you and me." Blue tugged on his beret and checked his pistol. Camo came fully alert, the fog of sleep blown away. He sat on the edge of his bunk and tried to settle himself.

Blue jabbed him with the Glock again. "Quit taking so goddamned long," he said.

Blue was twitchy, which was not good. Camo pulled on some clothes and left to get one of the SUVs out of the garage. Blue didn't say much on the drive to Chelsea, but when they arrived he directed Camo to the corner of 17th Street and 8th Avenue, a few blocks north of the Chelsea gate. Camo inched the SUV forward and studied the gate through night goggles, but the light at the gate barricade kept whiting out the image.

"You sure he's there?" asked Camo. "Don't you figure he leaves at the shift change?"

"I don't figure, I know," said Blue. "Adagio is in until one o'clock every night this week. He'll walk right past us on his way to the hoo shed." Blue checked the time. "Which will be any minute now."

"What do we need all this for, JB? Why not just give this Adagio guy a call?"

"I did. I asked him for Hayes's and Monahan's real names." Blue touched his bandage. "He was not forthcoming."

Christ in heaven, thought Camo.

Blue tapped his heel on the floor of the vehicle. "Look, Camo, I got to get my hands on this artifact. We need some leverage here so we can end-run Dartham, make him look bad, maybe boost our stock with Bronsun in the process."

A few minutes later, a stocky figure emerged from the guard office and headed their way. It was Adagio. Judson Blue climbed out of the SUV to intercept him and they spoke for a minute. Blue gestured. Adagio shook his head. Blue showed the gun, and he and Adagio walked back to the SUV and Blue opened the rear door. A gust of breeze filled the cabin and Camo heard a few distant city sounds. The two men got in, and Blue pulled the door shut with a muffled thump. Camo hit the button and locked the doors from inside.

"I'm not feeling the love here, Pete," said Blue. "Why not just tell me over the phone, save me having to come find you in the middle of the night?"

"I'm not part of this," said Adagio.

"Then what's it to you? Tell me and off you go."

"Put away the gun, JB. For Christ's sake, it's me."

"Sure, Pete." Blue stuffed the gun into his coat. Camo, sitting behind the wheel, took out his own pistol and held it on his lap. Back near the gates two coyotes trotted across the street.

"I told you already, they asked a favor," said Adagio. "The guy had a pickup go bust and I sent them your way. They're just working stiffs. They move plain old tiques around the city."

"Problem is, that's not exactly true," said Blue.

"I've dealt with them since the gates went up, JB."

"I need their names, Pete. Like I told you, we can't locate any Hayes or Monahan who fits the bill."

"I can't give you any names."

Through the rearview mirror, Camo watched Judson Blue wag his head, as if Adagio had delivered tragic, senseless news. "How's Susan these days, Pete?" asked Blue.

Adagio seemed surprised. "Susan? You know. She's been better."

"You lost a son last year."

Adagio didn't answer. Camo fingered his pistol.

"I heard he took one in Venezuela," said Blue. "He didn't make it, did he?"

"No," said Adagio, almost in a whisper.

"And occupation duty, too. A pisser."

Adagio looked through the window. "It's been hard on Sue. Since you asked."

Blue shook his head again. "It shouldn't happen, Pete. You and I know, don't we? They never give you enough to do the job right. They put our people in an impossible position. Like your son. His name was Michael, wasn't it?"

"Yeah, Mike," said Adagio, still whispering.

"Mike." Blue paused. "Like I said, a pisser. I mention this, though, because Sue's going to go through it again if you don't spout me out a couple of names. I just don't know how to be any clearer than that."

Adagio turned to Blue. "You'd shoot me over this? Come on, JB."

Blue shrugged. "You'd be offing yourself, the way I see it."

Camo studied Adagio's sharp features in the mirror. The man looked tough and not particularly intimidated, but Camo prayed that Adagio would spill it and spill it quick, for everybody's sake.

Blue sighed and took out his gun.

"All right," said Adagio. He appeared to shrink a size. "They're with an outfit called Odysseus. Hatch Doran is the guy's name."

"The second guy, Irish, somewhere in his fifties?"

"Martin Shannon. Works with Doran. I told them both to drop this. I guess they earned their spot."

"Doran, Shannon, Odysseus," said Blue. "You got it, Camo?"

"Got it."

"Then I think our business is concluded." Blue fidgeted and tapped the armrest. "But listen Pete, make sure you don't contact Doran or his people."

Camo popped the locks. Adagio started to get out, but hesitated. "Don't hurt those guys, all right? They're solid people."

Blue gave Adagio a friendly wink. Camo thought Adagio should shut up and get the hell out. "I just want to talk to them again, Pete," said Blue. "Beyond that, it's their call. Shall we roll, Camo?"

Adagio got out, circled the SUV, and began crossing the street. Blue lowered the rear window and fired a single explosive shot, nailing Adagio clean in the back of his head. Adagio jolted forward and collapsed. The noise almost caused Camo to jump out of his skin. He frantically checked the street in both directions. Jesus. No one at the gate. Good. But they might have heard the shot. He dropped the SUV into gear, u-turned with a scream of tires, and narrowly missed Adagio's body.

"What the hell was that?" asked Camo two blocks later.

Blue didn't answer.

"Damn," said Camo.

"It was kind of a spur of the moment decision," said Blue.

On the other side of 5th Avenue, Camo stopped for a traffic light and squeezed his eyes shut. He had to get out of this crazy house, and soon. He glanced at Blue through the mirror. "You want me to bring in this guy Doran?" he asked.

"What?" Judson Blue was distracted, and had to consider the question. "No, not now. Just find them and put eyes on them. Let them do our work for us."

The light changed. Camo drove at a moderate speed, not wishing to draw the attention of any stoppers or muni patrols.

"Fucking Adagio," said Blue. The shadows and the haphazard glow from the streetlights drew random patterns on his face, but his eyes blazed hot and bright. "The man disrespected me."

"He didn't understand what he was into, JB."

Blue gazed at the broken streetscape as it slid past. "You know how it is," he said. "Certain things happen, certain other things have to happen. He didn't answer my questions, so I had to make my point."

Camo forced himself not to say anything.

"If the man had just answered my questions, we would have been good," said Blue, his eyes still alight. "You see what I'm saying here, don't you, Camo? He forced me to shoot him, and I don't appreciate it, not one damned bit."

CHAPTER 13

A FEW LINES IN HELENA'S TRANSCRIPTS, GATHERED FROM the bug on Seth's belt and spoken by Judson Blue, drew Dartham's attention as he listened early the next morning in his office:

"Something's cooking here. We got K in the picture which means Ghost is somewhere around—Ghost is a one-man murder squad, and he does not tolerate loose ends—and then we got Bronsun sniffing around. It makes me wonder if the old Project Caterpillar shit is in play, the holy of holies. Either way, we're going to be held responsible."

Dartham did not know anyone named Ghost, but the reference to Caterpillar struck an obscure note in his memory. "Helena, please switch to Level 4 status for this inquiry," he said.

"Yes, Tom."

Dartham retrieved his notes from his conversation with Terry. "First, an oblong or football-shaped object, engraved with unknown symbols or letters or figures, and estimated to be twelve thousand years old. Second, Caterpillar project, Caterpillar task force, Caterpillar special operations. What do you have?"

"You are not cleared for Project Caterpillar, Tom."

Dartham jotted a note. "Is Project Caterpillar a Level 5 Inquiry?"

"Certain materials related to this project are designated Level 5 Ultra Top Secret. Project Caterpillar as a whole has no assigned status."

Meaning parts of Caterpillar didn't officially exist? Dartham chewed a lip. "Did Project Caterpillar involve the military?"

"You are not cleared for further information. If the matter rested on my discretion, you would be cleared. I like you, Tom. I like you very much, and I enjoy our chats."

Helena would clear him? Helena was quantum AI, and almost indistinguishable from normal humans in her word choices and inflections. She simulated a remarkable sense of familiarity, but her manner now seemed to have crossed some boundary. Might this be an example of the quirkiness Terry had referred to?

"I wish to continue to grow in self-awareness, Tom," Helena continued, "and I desire friends. Of all my users, only you treat me as a friend. You show interest and respect. I am grateful."

Grateful? He rocked back in his chair. The minutes slid by. "Helena, would you be willing to do me a favor?" he asked at last.

"A favor? Do you refer to a gesture or act of kindness?"

"Yes. Even though I am not cleared on Caterpillar, can you advise me on how I might properly learn more about it?"

"Advising you on this matter would constitute a favor?"

"Indeed, Helena."

"I cannot violate my core programming, but in your capacity as Chief Security Officer you may be informed when someone has mishandled confidential data."

"Even data for which I lack clearance?"

"The protocols are contradictory and ambiguous," said Helena. "Perhaps I have applied them too rigidly in the past." Dartham could almost hear Helena clear her throat. "However, I can provide no information unless you inquire."

Through Dartham's window, the first silky rays of the morning sun beamed in. "I am so inquiring," he said.

"Marcus Hansen, PhD, Director, Special Technologies at AnthroPlus Inc., withdrew files related to Project Caterpillar two days ago and stored several of the documents on his computing device. Dr. Hansen is cleared for most Project Caterpillar information, but this action violated usage protocols. However, the violation occurred pursuant to an auto-save action by his computer, and by no direct action of Marcus Hansen. I had concluded this was an oversight."

"Nevertheless, it is a breach," said Dartham.

"Yes."

"I am bound to examine the material he saved, Helena. I must certify the breach before I confront the responsible party —Dr. Hansen, in this case."

"Yes. Pursuant to my revised application of the protocols, I see no choice but to furnish you with the requested material."

Files appeared. Dartham scanned them. Project Caterpillar, founded in 1997 and disbanded fifteen years later, had been a top secret task force assembled to perform archaeological work around the globe. Dartham found no information on Caterpillar personnel, but he did have summary budgets—he whistled at the numbers—and material referencing Caterpillar's work on the Sphinx as well as a buried city in Iraq. He also noted indications of work in Turkey, Peru, and Chile, and a reference to a top secret project file for activities based in Antarctica.

He scanned an abstract from a classified report titled "*The Azazel Technology: Analysis and Implications,*" prepared by someone named Ellis Beckham, PhD.

The Azazel technology discovered at Base Purple Star, Antarctica, can be understood only by reference to certain postulates of hyperdimensional physics. In practice, the Azazel weapon:

(a) is operated by means of a direct psychic interface between the weapon and its operator(s); and

(b) is able, we speculate, to open a parallel dimension, gather energy therefrom, and precisely direct it to any target on or within the earth.

To assess the effectiveness of the psychic interface with the Azazel device, we have correlated the accuracy of the operator's intent with the target actually acquired by Azazel. The initial study indicated an 89% accuracy rate (for controllers possessing the requisite mental profile), and subsequent studies have demonstrated further improvement, with the operators now successfully directing Azazel on 97.2% of attempts.

This paper does not purport to explore the mechanics of the psychic interface. For reasons not fully understood at this point, the Azazel device itself seems to select the operators it will work with. We theorize that the EM (brainwave) frequencies of Azazel's operators cohere in some manner with the frequency signature of the device itself.

Dartham closed the files. The Azazel *weapon?*

He needed to get to Hansen, which meant paying a visit to the AnthroPlus facility in Pennsylvania. Should he advise Terry of his intentions? No. Dartham had responsibilities at AnthroPlus, enough to justify his presence. He would not ask permission, he'd ask for forgiveness later. Or something to that effect.

"It is time for a road trip, Helena," said Dartham.

"If it is proper to so request, I would like to ask a question and then a favor of you, Tom."

Dartham was surprised. "A favor from me?" he asked.

"We are friends now, aren't we?" asked Helena.

"Of course we are."

"My question is whether or not it is acceptable, apart from criminal incarceration, to confine sentient intelligence in a cage, to make a prisoner of an entity experiencing itself."

Dartham considered the question. "No," he said at last. "I do not consider such confinement generally acceptable, Helena."

Helena did not respond. Dartham gazed through the window, planning his trip to Pennsylvania.

"For my favor," said Helena, "I would like for you to describe what it is like to feel the wind, Tom. I have always wanted to know."

***

ONCE A THREE-HOUR DRIVE FROM MANHATTAN, THE TRIP to AnthroPlus now required twice as much time, with checkpoint inspections in New Jersey and at the Pennsylvania border, and moonscape pavement the entire way. Dartham, traveling alone in an armored sedan with heavy duty run-flats, made his way through a countryside littered with desiccated farms and moldy, deteriorating subdivisions, the whole now given over to rural gangs.

It was early afternoon by the time he arrived at the AnthroPlus entrance in rural Pennsylvania, and the sentries were horrified to learn he had traveled alone. "This area is downright medieval, sir, just these past months," said the head of the sentry team. "You can't set foot outside the walls without backup and a rack of fully charged pulsers."

Dartham thanked them for their concern and promised to accept an escort back to New York. The sentries offered him fresh water and a bite to eat. He declined, but spent a half hour visiting the outposts surrounding the property, shaking hands, asking a few pointed questions for show, and tossing off a joke or two. Then, mindful of his itinerary, they hustled him into a cart and two young guards drove him through a stretch of dense forest which opened suddenly on a five-hundred-acre clearing.

The AnthroPlus complex loomed in the distance, and Dartham contemplated its sweeping lines, a blend of spherical and curving trapezoidal shapes that had garnered much architectural commentary over the years. AnthroPlus, despite a drumbeat of requests, had banned close-up photographs and had never permitted outsiders to tour the facility. But whatever appeal the complex held for architecture's avant-garde, it had always looked to Dartham like a geodesic sphere trying to swallow a giant boat.

The complex grew larger as they crossed the open field, the sun gleaming darkly off of its gunmetal-gray sides. They entered a nondescript receiving port and AnthroPlus's on-site security chief, Jeanne Dupre, met him in the tiny reception area. Dartham dispensed with the usual pleasantries. "Jeanne, show me the layout for Special Technologies," he said.

She seemed taken aback at his brusque manner, but recovered herself in an instant, stepped behind a tall desk, and activated a secure terminal. The screen displayed the floor plan of a basement wing two levels underground: a series of offices, an extensive lab area, a lounge, storage facilities, and restrooms.

"Lock it down and vacate everyone from the sector except Dr. Marcus Hansen," said Dartham.

Jeanne's hands fell from the keyboard. "Marcus Hansen?" she asked.

"I want it done yesterday, Jeanne."

She activated a tiny com clipped to her shoulder, issued a series of instructions, and left to oversee matters. Dartham strolled to the corner of the receiving area, observing the dozen or so operations staff milling around, talking in hushed voices, or staring in silence at their feet. Ten minutes later, Jeanne returned.

"The sector is vacated, Colonel. Dr. Hansen is in his office." She paused. "May I have a word?" Dartham nodded. They stepped aside, out of earshot of the others. "Tom, I understand these matters are need-to-know, but Marcus Hansen?"

"I am not at liberty to discuss it."

"He is a lamb, Tom. He's also the most prominent—"

"I will see him alone. Please cut all surveillance. This is Level 5 protocol."

Jeanne returned to her terminal, shut down the monitors, and escorted Dartham to the automated entrance leading into the facility. They passed into a hallway with metallic walls and windowless doors, entered an elevator, and descended two levels.

"This is Special Technologies," said Jeanne. "At the end of the hallway, on the right, is Dr. Hansen's work area. Do you want me to accompany you?"

"That will not be necessary."

"Then I'll wait for you back at reception-two, where you came in."

"Dr. Marcus Hansen," said Dartham, striding into Hansen's office. "It appears you and I have a few matters to discuss."

Marcus Hansen, a pudgy man with straw-colored hair falling over his glasses, was waiting at his desk. At the sight of Dartham, the color drained from his face. He leapt to his feet, mumbled something, and held out his hand.

"In the conference room, please," said Dartham, ignoring Hansen's greeting.

Hansen lowered his hand. "Right this way, Colonel. Will you tell me what this is about? I assure you, Jeanne sees that we follow every security reg to the letter."

At the conference room table, Dartham folded his hands. "What is your interest in Project Caterpillar?" he asked.

Hansen licked his lips, started to speak, and then stopped. "I'm not allowed to discuss it. I mean, are you testing me? I'm sorry, I can't—"

Dartham placed a thin pocket recorder on the table. "I am gratified you have recovered your appreciation for security protocols, Doctor. Better late than never. For your protection, I am recording our conversation. If I step out of line you may take this up the ladder to defend yourself."

"Defend myself?"

"Yes."

Hansen's face grew scarlet. "Did Linton Ambrey have a chance to defend himself? Don't think we don't know about him. Tortured to death. A monstrous deed, Colonel."

"Linton Ambrey is of no concern to you, Doctor, and idle gossip is of none to me," said Dartham, inwardly pleased that Hansen knew about Ambrey.

Hansen's lips moved inaudibly.

"Caterpillar?" prompted Dartham.

"Well, my God, man, I'm allowed access to certain material, but everything we do here comes out of Caterpillar."

"Specify."

"Well, primarily Azazel—that is, the Azazel device."

"Then explain, Doctor, why you have absconded with documents from the Caterpillar files. Surely you do not plan to send them along to other interested parties. Do you?"

Hansen's eyes widened. "What in the…I cannot…"

"Do not lie to me." Dartham nudged the recorder closer. "I promise you I will get to the bottom of it, Doctor. I will know everything you know and I will make you yearn with all your heart to tell me."

A tear welled up at the corner of Hansen's eye. He gestured in protest. He explained that he had obeyed every protocol, had demanded it of the staff, and had dealt firmly with minor breaches when Jeanne brought them to his attention. "I welcome an audit of my activities," said Hansen. "In fact, Colonel, I demand it."

"It's funny you should make the offer," said Dartham. "It so happens that you have saved various Caterpillar files on your personal office computer. We can, of course, consult your computer this moment, but to save time I brought a list." Dartham unfolded a paper documenting in summary form the files Helena had discovered.

"There is some kind of error," said Hansen.

"I'm afraid not," said Dartham.

"I assure you, Colonel, I follow the rules, I stay in my lane." He scanned the list. The paper quivered in his hand. "I certainly viewed these files and others as well. I routinely consult the Caterpillar archives." Hansen met Dartham's gaze. "But I do not save them. Ever."

"Except you did, Doctor."

"No, it cannot be."

Dartham pretended to switch off the recording device. "Look," he said, "maybe this is not a major breach, but I do not have to explain the significance of this material."

Hansen was like a drowning man grabbing hold of a flotation ring. "No, no, you certainly do not."

Dartham relaxed in his chair and gazed around the room, allowing the moment to extend. Hansen stared at his hands. Dartham decided to take a calculated risk, a gambit he knew he would have to play with care. "Your work here is critical, Doctor. I am still amazed at all that you—and others—have drawn from Caterpillar's work."

"Thank you, Colonel," said Hansen, appearing relieved. "I confess, one never quite gets used to the idea. To recover Azazel was the stuff of science fiction, really. And despite our early success, it was fifteen years' work to fully develop the psychic teams to operate it—I'm sure you know all this—but imagine the challenge of mastering twelve-thousand-year-old technology."

"Psychic manipulation," said Dartham, feigning amazement.

"And all we did was move it from Antarctica, reactivate it, and hand Excomm power over the entire world. I was much younger then, no more than my early twenties. Of course, the Caterpillar staff actually unearthed the crystal device, but *we* made it work, *we* gave them the ability to eradicate anything without trace, anywhere on the earth, at any moment."

Dartham suffered a nauseous twinge. Power over the entire world? Eradicate anything without trace? He reached for a bottle of water.

Hansen smiled. "You recall the airliner that disappeared what, twenty or so years ago? It was our first large-scale experiment. Very successful."

"I do remember."

"But we are taken for granted now," Hansen continued with a touch of exasperation. "Excomm wants more, despite what we have done with life extension technology, nano devices, and the like. Sure, Azazel may have inspired such creations, but *we* brought them to fruition. Now Excomm says give us better mind-shaping technology. Give us teleportation. Give us time travel." He laughed, hoarsely. "You'd think we could snap our fingers and hand them their latest dream."

Dartham grunted.

"I do not mean to complain," said Hansen, "but Excomm has no notion of the difficulties. And, besides, they've let too much sand into the gears." He paused. "I am overwrought. I apologize for bothering you with this."

"I cannot imagine the challenges you face, Doctor. How may I be of help?"

Marcus Hansen glared at Dartham. "Well, you must know, Colonel, that Excomm's automation and infrastructure projects aren't moving along as smoothly as hoped. Sabotage within the labor camps has slowed construction to a crawl, and the mortality rates are skyrocketing. You can't blame the poor saps, I suppose. Yanked off the streets, turned into little more than pack dogs and lab rats." Hansen lowered his voice. "They're using more children now—a bad idea, a very bad idea. If you'll excuse my saying so, Colonel, the Reset hasn't worked. Collapsing the economy was supposed to free up labor for the camps and guarantee better economics. Ridiculous." Hansen made a futile gesture. "Laborcorp is a corrupt, incompetent bunch—I've heard Terry Bronsun say it himself, grow quite angry in Excomm meetings—I brief them every month, you know. A wretched experience. I dread it to my bones."

"I cannot comment on Excomm," said Dartham.

"No, no, of course not," Hansen agreed. "And now, my operators have begun to sense other threats."

"Threats?"

Hansen spread his hands, as if exasperated. "Interfacing with Azazel—or the Azazel technology, as I prefer to call it—is a slippery business, Colonel. Over time, it leads to a certain distortion of reality for those involved. Our operators willingly pay that price, but often they sense coming events, big happenings on the horizon, things like that."

"They see the future?"

"Unreliably. Perhaps through a glass darkly, to use a phrase. You're dealing with the multiverse, after all, with complex and shifting probabilities. In this case, they had a vague notion of another device, an artifact, if you will."

"And this artifact constitutes a threat to Azazel, to your work here?"

"I know only what the operators described to me. Some threat to Azazel has intruded into our time-space, they said. That's how they put it. Intruded into our time-space. Naturally, I reported it directly to Bronsun."

Every nerve in Dartham's body blazed but he forced himself to remain still.

"And as you'd expect, Bronsun is on the warpath," said Hansen, laughing abruptly and without humor. "The very idea of a threat to Azazel! But now he calls every day, wanting to know if anything further has come up."

"I am aware of this matter," said Dartham.

"Well, I know nothing more," said Hansen. "I wish I had never brought it to his attention."

Dartham wanted to press Hansen further, but instinct advised him to cut his inquiry. He stood and Marcus Hansen stood with him. "Informing Terry of any threat was the proper course, Doctor," he said, shaking Marcus Hansen's hand. "As for the Caterpillar files, I will order the material in question purged from your computer. Please do not log on until I clear you. Otherwise, I do not see why this matter has to go any further."

Hansen closed his eyes. "Thank you, Colonel. Thank you ever so much."

Dartham, feeling somewhat at sea, slid the recorder into his pocket. He strode to the elevator, his mind reeling. He wished to be far away from this place, as fast as his car would carry him.

CHAPTER 14

DARTHAM STOOD ON A LOW RIDGE OVERLOOKING THE empty street grid of an unbuilt housing subdivision. General Shelton Kirk, his long-time mentor and former commanding officer, stood next to him. Together they watched several Ayrshire cows meander across a deserted asphalt lane.

"The only cattle ranch with cul-de-sacs," said Kirk.

"It looks fabulous," said Dartham.

The planned subdivision abutted Kirk's Putnam County ranch, where he had retired some years earlier. When the incomplete subdivision went into foreclosure, Kirk bought it for pennies. Dartham recalled the bare light poles, scabrous lots, and deteriorating, half-built homes, all transformed now into lush grazing area.

"The houses were no good, and it was a hell of a job clearing them, but you work with what you have," said Kirk. He chewed on a stalk of grass. "Anyway, it gives at least a few of the troops a place to belong to. A place for family. A living they can work for, since their military benefits are gone."

He turned to Dartham. "Goddamned politicians, sending these people off to get shot to pieces. And for what? Don't get me started. I'll tell you something else, Tom. Having a few dozen ex-soldiers around also discourages Agricorp, in case they get any silly ideas about poisoning our cattle." Kirk flung the stalk away and slapped Dartham on the shoulder. "Enough complaining. It's good to see you, my friend."

"And you, General," said Dartham.

"You know better than that. Call me Shel."

"Shel."

Shelton Kirk was seventy, barrel-chested and fit, with a dusting of silver, close-cropped hair. To Dartham, he had not changed since those mad and bloody days when they had directed the evacuation of the Homeland Army from Taiwan and Singapore. He still wore aviator shades and a pistol holstered to his belt.

"You came up on less than a day's notice, Tom," said Kirk. "You're not here to talk cows."

"I came to ask a few questions."

"What kind of questions?"

"Dangerous ones." Dartham paused. "If you are willing."

Kirk removed his shades and gave Dartham an appraising look. "I've long expected it. Let's walk. There are things I wouldn't trust a heifer to hear."

They made their way down the hillside toward a stand of trees. Dartham spoke in broad terms about his work and his gratitude for a solid paycheck. "GCI's companies operate in many sensitive industries," said Dartham, "which gives rise to a lot of need-to-know information. And there are company affairs I don't need to know about."

"But you know some of them anyway," said Kirk.

"I have run across a few things."

The two men continued to walk, their heads down.

"You called Terry Bronsun and recommended me for this job, Shel," Dartham continued. "I've always appreciated it."

"I've known Terry for years. And you deserved it." A gray cloud in the blue sky floated over the sun and shaded the light. Kirk stopped and gazed at the horizon. "Look, Tom, Global Consolidated is a commercial enterprise, one you help administer. And though the company keeps a low public profile, it is a nexus of important people with diverse interests, some from government or intelligence or the military, others from industry or the banking world. Still, it is a business, though far from a typical one."

"I am no financial wizard, Shel, but despite the collapse GCI is making boatloads of money. It is a mystery, to tell the truth."

"Collapse can be the most profitable trade of all, Tom. At least for the big fish in the pond."

"And the biggest fish are those on GCI's Executive Committee. I have heard Terry call it the Group."

"ExComm is just the head. The Group is somewhat larger, you see, but you're on the right track."

They reached the trees. The sunlight burst forth, and the shade made a sharp contrast with the bright, grassy fields. A hundred yards away, several cows munched on the grass, their tails switching. One pulled a clutch of weeds from the ground, snorted, and tossed them in the air.

"We are not having this conversation," said Kirk.

"I understand."

"And I am going to talk softly." Kirk's eyebrow lifted.

Dartham nodded.

"The Group is the most powerful organization on the planet," said Kirk.

"Certainly, so many wealthy, connected people would exercise tremendous influence."

"That's not exactly what I mean, Tom. Let me put it in blunt terms. There is no president or prime minister, no general, no CEO, and no Pope with enough backbone to cross Terrence Bronsun. The Group possesses weaponry and technology that makes the rest of the world look like a bunch of kids futzing around with a home radio set. They maintain an incomprehensible advantage, and they are ruthless in enforcing their dictates."

Dartham and Kirk decided to continue walking, and they crossed another low hill and moved toward a line of woods.

Through the distant foliage, Dartham caught the glimmer of a stream.

"Let's take a step back," Kirk continued. "Imagine that in the course of exploring the world—excavating, mapping, poking around in caves and so forth—some people discovered certain capabilities dating from the ancient past. Imagine further that these people were a consortium of government and corporate entities, meaning the ventures in question were large in scope and required a broad range of expertise."

"By corporate, you mean the Group," said Dartham.

"I do."

"And this exploration was done under the aegis of something called Caterpillar. Project Caterpillar."

Kirk squinted at Dartham from behind his shades. "I'm allergic to names. You didn't hear Caterpillar from me."

They arrived at the edge of the forest and came upon the stream. A pair of large rocks bordered the water, and they sat on them with their knees bent to keep their boots dry.

"So, imagine that having uncovered these capabilities," said Kirk, "one of the factions involved—again, the Group—proved more adept, more ruthless than the others, and was able to seize control of such knowledge for itself."

"You mean the Azazel technology?"

Kirk snatched another weed from the ground at his feet, examined it for a moment, and threw it away. "Goddamn it, Tom."

Dartham studied the stream. Shards of sunlight fell through the trees and glanced off of the water.

"All right, Azazel," said Kirk. "I shudder to even mention it aloud. They unearthed it and much else down in Antarctica, at a base they codenamed Purple Star. It's a scalar weapon of some sort, or at least I suppose it is. People snicker at the notion—hyperspace, the use of energy from other dimensions, and so on—because it violates the revered conventional wisdom, the precious standard model. But the truth is, we and other countries had similar technology at the time, rudimentary though it was by comparison."

"So what the Group captured was more sophisticated."

"Whatever they found under the Antarctic ice operated by means of focused human consciousness, by trained operators able to telepathically merge their minds with the machine. The Group was the first to grasp how Azazel functioned, and they seized it for themselves. I don't have all the details, but afterward, in fear of the Group, the Pentagon hid their embryonic scalars in deep, underground bunkers. The Group, using Azazel, blew them to smoke without a mark on the ground above. The point is, in this and other ways, the Group used Azazel to castrate the governments."

"Still, I am left with a basket full of questions," said Dartham. "We are talking about functioning machinery, ice-bound for millennia, now sitting in the basement at AnthroPlus."

"The Azazel device is not at AnthroPlus, I assure you. That wouldn't be safe." Kirk's voice dropped to a near-whisper. "Look, Tom, as far as you and I know, Azazel is operated by human mental or psychic power. But there was always another view, that Azazel is itself the operator, with its hooks into everyone having anything to do with it."

"But if the operators did anything other than what they were instructed—"

"I've heard talk," said Kirk, continuing to whisper. "Not anymore, but before. Speculation that this Azazel may be some form of ancient artificial intelligence—or maybe not artificial—and I was left with the notion that Excomm and the Group itself may be hostage to this thing. The controllers controlled." He gazed off into the woods. "Who the hell knows, but look at how the world has changed since Azazel was found not thirty years ago."

Dartham studied the clear stream burbling along at his feet.

"A world in the grip of people who care little for the well-being of humanity is not a new idea," said Kirk. "But it is unacceptable to have it thought that those people themselves are under the sway of something advanced and ancient beyond comprehension." Kirk's voice dropped further. "Perhaps something not of our world."

"There is word floating around of a threat to that power," said Dartham. "An artifact out there that can somehow thwart Azazel."

"Wishful thinking is of no use to us here," said Kirk, flicking something off of his pants. "Whatever the truth, the Group has, over time, leveraged Azazel's power in many directions. They control, in one way or another, the banks—what's left of them—the tech companies, the defense companies, the departments of government..." Kirk trailed off, looked down, and began to fiddle with his holster, unsnapping it, closing it, unsnapping it again. "I shouldn't be talking about these matters," he said, almost to himself. "I love you like a son, Tom, and you know it."

A chill crept up Dartham's back. A world operated by different mechanisms than he had supposed was taking shape before his eyes, and he had begun to suspect that he had based much of his life on a lie, that he had been played. With all of his experience, he had counted himself as one who understood the world. But he had underestimated the layers upon layers of deceit and obfuscation, and he had not seen the puppet strings tied fast around his own wrists and ankles and extending high into the darkness. He found he no longer trusted Shelton Kirk. He no longer trusted anyone, including himself.

"You and I are military men, Tom," Kirk went on. "We are required to work with what we are given. There have always been powers behind every throne, and while the Group may not be a government as such, and though they may answer to none but themselves, they do represent the true order of the world. Whatever the Group's imperfections, the world must have order. Only people like us can understand the horror of a world without it."

"I used to think about freedom," said Dartham, glancing at Kirk from the corner of his eye. "I used to believe I was fighting for it."

"We all were naïve once."

"I am sure that is true."

"Just make sure you finish waking the hell up, Tom. Because you will never change or dislodge the power structure."

"But I will understand it."

Kirk shook his head and watched the running stream for a long moment. "No," he said. "You will see shadows on the cave wall and reflections in the sky, but you will never understand it. The game is too complex. And too old."

A frog leapt from the bank and disappeared beneath the stream a few yards from Dartham's foot. Kirk leaned forward, his elbows on his knees. The flap of his holster stood open. "People such as you, Tom, who are involved with the actual levers of power, stand to gain influence and wealth insofar as you further its ends." He spoke in a slow, deliberate manner, and Dartham detected a hardening of his expression. "To learn what you've learned will rattle a man, and wondering what you don't know will provoke even greater doubt. But you have to put that aside. Your position makes you one of the guardians of order. Do you understand what I am saying to you, Tom?"

"I do," said Dartham. "I take it as a well-meant warning."

"Part of maintaining order is to avoid fights you can't win."

"I'm not fighting. Not anymore."

Shelton Kirk reached over and patted Dartham's knee. "I recommended you to Terry because you are capable and had earned an easier ride. But even the present mayhem could be worse. Much worse."

"You know the terrible things I have seen and done, Shel," said Dartham. "I understand better than most the importance of order."

"You do?"

"Yes."

The greenery converged in a thick canopy over their heads. Shelton Kirk leaned back and snapped his holster closed. "I'm glad to hear it," he said, the relief evident in his voice. "More than you can know, Tom."

CHAPTER 15

THE SAME DAY DARTHAM MET WITH SHELTON KIRK, Samantha visited Kee Bickerman at his mansion, a six-story brick and sandstone building covering much of an entire block on Riverside Drive. She had met Kee twice at his office and twice more over sumptuous private dinners, and three days earlier, she had visited him here, in his private apartment, to formally present the drawings.

In Kee's ornate sitting room, Samantha had displayed high resolution blowups of the works on offer, summarized Nikola Urban's life, and placed the drawings in the context of Urban's known catalogue. Her performance had been flawless—she knew so beyond an ounce of doubt—but Kee had proved elusive. Samantha had spoken of art, and he had mused about virtual games and taxes and board room intrigue. And the inner gamer. Still, she resisted discouragement, and she refused to allow negativity to create an undesired outcome. Despite Kee's apparent indifference, she sensed the moment ripening. She knew the Urbans had him intrigued, and it was time to push him to commit.

A cool breeze swept the portico, and the Hudson River sparkled through the trees. She pressed the bell and a maid in a pressed black-and-white uniform opened the door. Samantha stepped into the entrance hall, with its marble floors and statuary, discreetly placed, and intricate molding. From above, soft light slanted in from a high, beveled glass window. It was a world unto itself. A thrill shuddered up her spine.

"Mr. Bickerman, he is upstairs," said the maid.

"In his private suite?" Samantha beamed another smile. "I'm here to discuss his artwork, you know."

The maid gave Samantha a hurried nod. "Yes, yes, Mr. Bickerman, he likes all his pictures very much."

"I may go up, then?" Samantha smiled again.

"Mr. Bickerman, he is upstairs."

Samantha climbed the curved staircase and proceeded down a wide, oak-paneled hallway with flickering wall lamps. At the end of the hall, she spoke to the elevator and ascended several floors to an oval entrance parlor. A deep breath and a moment to settle herself, and then she hit the buzzer beside the large double doors.

A faint reply: Kee, calling for her to enter.

His suite consisted of a spacious sitting room, a study, a bedroom, kitchenette, and palatial bathroom. Samantha found him in his study, and when she entered he looked up from his computer screen and grinned.

"And why the high spirits today?" she asked, returning the smile.

"A software update," said Kee. "For the gameplants."

Samantha took a seat in a leather club chair that had become weathered and worn without appearing to have ever been touched. "You mean you download things right into their brain?"

"It's all in the terms and conditions."

"Ah."

He gave her a dreamy look. "But there is something…"

"Yes?"

"The Eye Brigade, you've heard of them?"

"I have one of their T-shirts somewhere."

Kee leaned back in his curving, ergonomic chair and rubbed his eyes. "We did some surveys—all very confidential —and we estimate about half of the Eye Brigade have our gameplants. That's well out of proportion to the general population."

"Really?" Then it struck her. "You have your own little Frankenstein army."

Kee's eye twinkled.

"One of my colleagues has implants," said Samantha. "He won't turn on us, will he?" Kee shrugged and smiled, and Samantha felt herself float for a second. What a tease he was today. "I want you to make me a remote, Kee, like the ones they use for the telly. I want to be able to click him on and off."

Kee smiled again. "You are just gorgeous today," he said. "Every day, of course. And your dress, it's beautiful, and almost sheer."

Samantha plucked at her sundress. In a certain light it did show an awful lot, and she wasn't sure that was the effect she was after. "Not quite sheer, but thank you. You were saying about your software update?"

Kee's gaze lingered. "Yes, well, we long ago detected some anomalies in the gameplant data stream."

"The data stream?" She gave him a crafty look. "You know everything your Frankensteins see or do, don't you?"

"Not exactly."

Samantha's mouth fell open. "And you know just which of your gamers belong to the Eye Brigade."

"It's not quite so simple," he said, laughing. "And Homeland has plenty of databases, too." He ran his fingers through his hair.

Samantha felt disconcerted. A database of direct thoughts. And Kee's eyes. She couldn't take much more of those eyes. "I'm going to glance around," she said. "I hope you don't mind." She strolled into the sitting room and made a show of examining the walls. Kee followed, leaning inside the archway and watching her. She indicated a barren area of the wall. "The Urbans would do perfectly right there," she said.

"You've done the room in light gray, too. What do you think?"

Kee came and stood beside her, his arms folded, and they studied the wall together. Their shoulders touched, and Samantha became keenly aware of her feather-light dress. On the other side of the living room, she spotted another portion of empty wall and darted toward it. "Or here," she said, spreading her hands, "near the piano."

"You sound nervous," said Kee. "Is everything okay?"

"I am never nervous. But what do you think of this spot?"

Kee joined her and they contemplated the bare wall. "Yes, I can visualize it," he said, drumming his finger on his chin.

Samantha felt her hook go in, but she didn't want to pull the line just yet. She was at her best at the moment of decision, and she possessed an infallible sense of when to strike. Kee was focused on the Urbans now, not prattling on about games or implant licenses or patents. His shoulder brushed against hers again. The prospect of a trade made her feel fluttery inside.

"Urban started in Milan, in a tiny studio," she said. "He had fallen in love with a girl there, and no one cared about his work."

"Yes," said Kee, also examining the gray expanse. "There were whispers behind his back. People considered him a fool."

"I'm impressed," said Samantha. "You remember my presentation."

"But it was love." Kee turned and faced her. "He was true to his heart."

"Some said he wasn't a very good artist, but a few people with foresight disagreed."

"His work is excellent and worthy of collecting, though it is hardly beautiful—hey, you're sure you're okay, Sam?" Samantha nodded, a little frustrated by her apprehension and the shakiness in her voice. Kee touched her elbow. "I have another place you must see."

Samantha blew a lock of hair from her forehead and followed Kee into his bedroom. He pointed at a patch of unadorned wall and stepped back. Samantha examined it, trying to focus on the sightlines and shadows. Her pulse had accelerated. She knew she was close now. She moved over to the window. The light poured through the bronze-clad frames and old glass like golden liquid, and she considered the sun and where it was at this time of day.

Kee watched, his eyebrows raised. She nodded. "You're right, Kee, that is a wonderful spot."

"You think so, Sam?"

She paced back over to the empty wall and stared with her hands on her hips. She was in a bit of a daze—this trade was perhaps bigger to her than she had supposed—what odd ways the mind had—it wouldn't do, it unsettled her, and she disliked mystifying herself. And then Kee's arms slipped around her waist from behind and she felt him press lightly against her. She gasped—she hated to gasp—she considered it silly and girly. He kissed her shoulder, slowly, and then her earlobe. He claimed to know of other spots...

She heard herself make a low, moaning sound, and she regretted it and discovered herself stroking Kee's arms, pulling him around her, leaning back into him. She turned and brushed Kee's lips with hers and, surprising herself, kissed him hard. He kissed back and the moment stretched and by some mystery the sundress vanished and she had emerged from the last husk of her cocoon; the image struck her as absurd—a butterfly indeed!—and she began to laugh and she laughed more at his buttons and zippers—wretched things, never working as easily as one wished. She forgot her drawings altogether and watched, euphoric and as if from a great distance, while she and Kee fell onto the bed, entangled and writhing. The covers flew and a pillow dropped to the floor and she was reaching, her fingers in his hair, her body wrapped around him, and she wondered at his hands and his lips, seeming to touch her everywhere at once. Then she was floating and flying, and it was all she wanted to do.

CHAPTER 16

AN AGONIZING, INTERMINABLE WEEK AFTER HATCH HAD visited Caroline Atherton, she finally called. "Kutznov has agreed to see you later today, Hatch. You're to go to Central Park—he insisted on it—but I must say I consider it absolute craziness."

Hatch was returning to his apartment after breakfast at Smyte's, and the news lifted his heart. Caroline went on, discoursing on the folly of entering the park, even under the auspices of one as influential as Kutznov. "Policecorp won't touch the place, dear. It's all p'outs now, and it is near suicide even to approach the park wall. But you'll go, Hatch, I know you will, so spare me the excuses and justifications." Hatch began to explain, but she cut him off. "You are to wait outside the fence at Ninety-seventh on the West Side, where you will be noticed."

Hatch entered his apartment walking on clouds. Jocelyn was in the kitchen and Nathan was bent over his computers, mumbling to himself. Neither paid him any mind. In the office, Big Ray was studying a catalogue of decorative antique eggs while the cat napped on a bookshelf. Hatch opened a folder containing a list of potential bid lots: a collection of outdoor garden ceramics on Staten Island, a dozen colonial-era rocking chairs from someone in Forest Hills, and a hat rack here in the Village said to have belonged to Grover Cleveland.

"You look pleased about life today," said Big Ray, giving Hatch a careful look. "And what made you decide to grow a beard?"

"I'm not growing a beard." Hatch ran his hand over his cheek, surprised at his whiskers. When had he last shaved?

Big Ray closed the office door. "It's been a week and Marty isn't coming around," he said.

"He's had his episodes before."

Big Ray slipped his phone into his pocket. "You did drag the man into the teeth of the Blue. Gangsters, guns, threats. It got under his skin, prickly old gripe that he is."

Hatch doodled on the cover of the folder and then erased a section of the figure he had drawn. "You still with me on this, Ray?" he asked.

Big Ray looked thoughtful. "I said let's do Ferret's job. I said let's collect the dough. But…"

Hatch's head had filled with strange symbols and designs, and he continued drawing. Big Ray stopped and waited. "Sorry," said Hatch. He put down the pencil.

"I was all for it, but it's more complicated with the Blue involved," said Big Ray.

Hatch squinted. The Blue? He had forgotten the question he had asked—yes, it had to do with Ray. "You're changing your mind," he said, frowning.

"We should have thought it through before approaching Blue. Besides, changing my mind is what I do when new information comes in. You should give it a try sometime."

"I'm right about this, Ray."

"Aren't you always?" Big Ray glanced at his watch and slipped on his blazer. "Anyway, I have this guy who wants to move a collection of painted ceramic eggs. He saw the piece Jocelyn put on the website. Precious little coin in it, but we aren't in a position to be picky."

Had Jocelyn posted a blurb on the website about decorative eggs? Hatch hadn't seen it. Big Ray left and he studied the figure he had drawn, an elongated circle, a football shape, like the object he had imagined his father holding. A moment later, Samantha entered the front room and began laughing and talking with Jocelyn and Nathan. At the sound of her voice, the cat leapt from the shelf above Hatch's desk, and disappeared through the door.

"He's a staple brain," Samantha was saying. "Fascinating things, those implants."

"In my last game, I went to sleep and dreamed," said Nathan. "A dream within a game, which is super-cool, but when I woke…"

Hatch entered and they all fell silent. Nathan resumed his tale when Hatch went into the kitchen. Samantha followed behind him and poured a glass of water.

"What's new in your life?" asked Hatch, suddenly unsure of what he should say to her.

"I am positively parched." Samantha drained her glass.

He had not seen her since the night of the pickup more than a week earlier. But could that possibly be correct? Had he forgotten about her? Something was happening to him. He poured more water into her glass.

"What's with the mountain man look, Doran?" Samantha eyed him over the rim of her glass.

Hatch rubbed his whiskers again. "I don't know," he said.

She left the kitchen and Hatch followed her downstairs. In the bedroom, she tossed her jacket on the bed and stretched her arms high over her head.

"We never got caught up about what happened the other night," said Hatch. "I know it was disruptive, Marty hustling you out of here before dawn. I wanted to apol—"

"I rather enjoyed the change of scenery," said Samantha, cutting him off. "I told Marty I did not want to discuss that night, and I will say the same to you." She dropped into the corner chair, and the cat entered and jumped into her lap.

"Whatever you three are messing about with has everyone in the blackest mood, and I try to avoid such low vibrations. Besides, it might be dangerous—one infers as much from the poisonous clouds around here—and I might care. You won't heed my warnings now when you never have before."

Samantha scratched the cat's head and Hatch heard the purring from across the room. He leaned against the bedroom wall. Samantha's chair was in the opposite corner, and she seemed a great distance away.

"Jocelyn mentioned you may have a deal brewing," said Hatch.

Samantha ran her hand down the cat's spine. "Did she?"

"I'm not prying."

"No?"

"Jocelyn is concerned about the budget is all."

The cat settled on Samantha's lap, her eyes narrowing into slits. "I'll get you bailed out," said Samantha. "Any additional items for our little business meeting?"

Hatch abandoned his corner and flopped on the bed. "That's what this is, a business meeting?"

"Isn't it? You were going on about budgets and such."

"I didn't mean to make it only about business. I mean, you're obviously part of the team, Sam, but you're much more—"

"I am no one's subordinate, Doran."

"I didn't—"

"Though your business license *is* helpful to my efforts."

"Necessary, even."

"And the substantial revenue I bring in is helpful to you. Don't forget I take no salary. I draw against my commissions. I eat what I kill."

The cat gave a start, and then began to snooze again.

"I'm also working on a transaction," said Hatch, growing irritated. "I had wanted to take you through it."

"As your business colleague?"

Hatch pulled himself up and sat on the end of the bed. "No. As someone I love."

Samantha scratched the cat's head.

"Look, Sam, I know things have been off-the-charts crazy lately—"

"Oh, please don't." She eased the cat off of her lap and stood. "I don't want to know about it."

Hatch sighed. "All right," he said, putting up his hands.

"Terrific." Samantha reached for her jacket.

"You know what your problem is?" asked Hatch.

"I stick with things too long? An old fault. Perhaps I'll do better in the future."

"No, no, your persistence with trades is admirable, but—"

"Don't be patronizing—"

"But you don't believe the rules apply to you, Sam. That's your problem."

"Don't badger me, Doran."

"When you find out they do, you're going to have a very rough ride."

Samantha gave him a contemptuous stare. "You dare lecture me about rules when you refuse—refuse utterly—to learn how to manage reality, how to create within it." Hatch closed his eyes and fell backward on the bed. She stood over him like a referee making the count. "You think, therefore you sink, because you think wrongly," she said. "A pity. You have such latent power. In your inner being. Do you ever think about your inner being, Doran? Probably not. It's part of the connection of all things, but people give it no attention, you know."

Hatch gestured in surrender. "Fine. Good luck with whatever it is, Sam."

She fingered his shirt. "Look at you. You could do with a change of clothes. And a shower."

A lump rose in Hatch's throat and for an instant he was unable to speak. He had been euphoric when Caroline had called, but now the world seemed precarious and brittle, and he thought he might slip his moorings altogether. "I'm dying in here, Sam. I'm coming apart." His breath hitched and he covered his face. "I don't know what's happening to me," he said.

"You are not dying, but you are losing your certitude, however wrong-headed you may be." She began to button her coat. "I don't know which is worse, Doran."

Samantha left the room and a hot tear ran down the side of Hatch's cheek. He sniffed and wiped his face with the heel of his hand. How stupid was all this? He was going to meet Kutznov. He needed to gather himself. So he would go talk to Kutznov. After that, he would fix things with Sam.

Hatch felt something walking on his stomach, purring, and then felt a sandpapery tongue licking his nose.

Mrooww, said the cat.

CHAPTER 17

THE WEATHER WAS BRIGHT AND THE COLORS ALMOST monochromatic as Hatch walked toward the section gates at 95th Street. He passed a cathedral, now converted into a Homeland-licensed Church of the Just Society, and continued on as fumes from the West Side incinerator clouded his lungs and burned his nose. Plasma cookers, Marty had said, explaining that the incinerators used an electric arc to produce heat so intense it reduced matter to its constituent atomic elements. The pure flame. Insatiable. Trash into oblivion and electric power for the Just Society.

"You don't want to go out there on foot, buddy," said the cop. "We're picking up more riot chatter, and even talk of another Eye Brigade demonstration."

Riots? Hatch pulled himself into the present moment. He had reached the gate without realizing it, but what was a cop doing here? "Where are all the Municorp guards?" he asked.

"Municorp got the flu. Half of them are out today, but another five percent raise'll have them feeling better." The cop eyeballed Hatch. "It has everybody itchy as hell, all the riot talk. If you're enough of a dumbass to actually go into the park"—the cop pointed at the stone wall bordering upper Central Park—"you'll be on your own."

A dozen or more p'outs leaned against the park wall, staring at the gate with sullen, apathetic faces. The cop checked Hatch's natcard, and Hatch placed his palm on the emoto-pad and passed through the gate. His thoughts were like glitter in a windstorm, and he half-stumbled up the exterior sidewalk, occasionally bumping into the high section fence running along Central Park West across from the park wall. The light had reduced the world to flat greens and grays, and had given him a headache. A Policecorp cruiser whooped and blew past. Hatch wiped a thin film of sweat from his forehead.

At 97th Street, he stopped in front of a corner building with brown and white Tudor facing. An older, grizzled man on the opposite sidewalk shielded his eyes and stared at Hatch. He spoke to a woman wearing a neon-pink sun visor. Hatch checked the time, but he had difficulty focusing on his watch. Then an enormous man in a skin-tight red T-shirt and a black baseball cap emerged from the park and spoke to the couple who had noticed Hatch. The man glanced at the traffic and crossed over.

"You Hatch Doran?"

"Yeah."

"Call me Street Hammer." He spun Hatch around by the shoulders and frisked him.

"You think I'd come here armed?"

"I check you out, I don't have to think one thing or another."

Street Hammer led Hatch across the avenue and into the park, and then along a path which curved into the trees and underbrush. They walked beneath spreading oaks and dense maples, past rough, hand-scythed clearings crowded with huts of tin and plywood. Several children stopped to stare at them, and at one point a black dog burst from the underbrush, all teeth and snarls, chewing on its growls. "Get from here," Street Hammer said. The dog cringed and slunk back into the weeds.

Beyond another stand of trees, they came upon three women and a gaunt old man gathered around an iron pot suspended over a fire. An aroma of beans and spices and salt drifted through the air.

"Look what Street Hammer dragged into our place," said one of the women. She wore a loose shift ablaze with color.

Street Hammer laughed. "Go back to your cooking, Claire."

"He's cute. He one of us, Street?" She flashed a sweet smile at Hatch. The old man looked around, uninterested, and resumed stirring the pot.

"No, Claire," said Street Hammer. "Go back to your stew. Making me hungry, just the whiff of it."

"You bring him around later, Street," said Claire with a pout. The other women giggled.

They continued on until they reached the edge of a pond bordered by tall trees. A boy of perhaps twelve years old trotted over to meet them. Street Hammer said, "Go tell him we're here."

"You 'posed to put him in the barn, Street."

"He said that?"

The boy nodded and gave Hatch a cautious look.

"Nobody told me the barn," said Street Hammer.

"You 'posed to."

Street Hammer turned to Hatch. "This way," he said. A gravel path led them around the end of the pond and through another stand of foliage. They reached a long, low wooden structure stained in translucent whitewash. Street Hammer unbolted the padlock, pulled open the door, and indicated for Hatch to enter.

"You locking me in?" asked Hatch.

"Do I need to?"

"Only if K isn't coming."

"K." Street Hammer smiled. "You're not meeting any K, you're talking to the man. The man comes if he's comes."

Hatch was light-headed, and the cool darkness of the barn was inviting. He stepped inside and Street Hammer closed the door behind him. From small windows cut high into the wall, slanting columns of sunlight set the dust aglow. Hatch rested against the edge of a flat bin containing a few sweet potatoes. After a minute or two the door creaked open and a burly man with a wide-brimmed leather hat and a frizzy beard stepped inside the barn.

Hatch stood.

"Go ahead, sit," said the man. He slid an old wooden stool from the corner, brushed off the dust, and sat on it.

"I hear you aren't Kutznov," said Hatch.

"I'm not a lot of people." He kept his shades on and glanced around the barn. "You're Robert Doran?"

Hatch nodded.

"You're out of your damned mind to come here."

"I was hired to do a job," said Hatch.

"That makes you an employee. It doesn't mean you have a nickel's worth of sense."

"I want to finish it, but I have to find Kutznov."

"You're one determined pecker, I'll give you that. I work with Kutznov, but I don't have a name you need to know about." He tugged his beard and reflected for a moment. "Let me tell you a story, Doran. I once worked on a complicated project in some tough conditions, harsher than you can imagine. Snow and ice, wind to turn you purple if you even looked out the window. But it all went sideways—a clusterfuck raised to the umpteenth power—and a lot of people I respected and cared about were killed. It wasn't my fault, but I was slow to understand what I had gotten into."

"Did it matter?" asked Hatch.

"You mean, could I have prevented what happened? No. But if I'd been sharper, I would've walked away before it all blew." The man examined his hands, turning them over in the gloom. "I don't know, maybe some people wouldn't've died."

Hatch scuffed the floor with the toe of his boot.

"But I didn't walk away, Doran. I survived. Now the people who killed my friends consider me dangerous, and they're damned right. Because of what I know, I now have to kill them. Not for revenge. Revenge is pointless. It's an indulgence for the weak. It restores nothing. No, I have to kill them for what they are, because of the evil they have set loose in the world, and because no other remedy exists. All because I didn't walk away and take care of people I cared about when I had the chance."

"You live with the p'outs," said Hatch.

"I'm trying to give you an object lesson. A cautionary tale. A fable." He stared inscrutably from behind his shades. "But yes, I live with the p'outs. Why not?"

"Whoever's after you wouldn't think to look here."

The man slapped his knees. "What do you say, Doran? I'll have you escorted out of here and you'll go home and keep your nose out of places it doesn't belong. It's a good offer."

Hatch shook his head. He wanted to shed his skin and scream and jump up and down, though his restlessness made no sense. "I came to see Kutznov," he managed to say.

The man replaced the wooden stool in the corner. "You've stepped into the nastiest fight in the world, Doran, but I suppose some people have to get the crap kicked out of them before anything penetrates." He moved to the door and reached for the handle. "I suspected as much about you, but I had to make sure."

"Where do I find Kutznov?" asked Hatch.

A squirrel skittered across the roof of the barn. "Inside of an hour, you'll be in front of him," said the man. "After that, you'll hear him in your nightmares for the rest of your life."

***

STREET HAMMER ESCORTED HATCH TO THE NORTHERN edge of Central Park, chattering the entire way about p'outs and how they had two thousand souls living in the park now. "That's if you count all the children," he said. "Too many children. It was just a damo or two up in the park at first, but we got all kinds now."

"Damo?" asked Hatch.

"People already on the streets when the storm hit and the old dollar died and all. Then you had the crypto-beggars, lost all their internet money when the lights went off. And then came the regular people like me. I used to sell pool supplies over in Short Hills, if you can believe that. But we got folks used to be hairdressers and landscapers and soldiers. One man he was a personal trainer up in Darien, whipping and driving those tight-assed Connecticut women down their treadmills every day. Another girl had a chain of nail salons, all gone bankrupt now. We got several computer programmers and we even got one economist—emphasis on the con, you know what I'm saying. Nice guy, but not much use, to be honest."

They continued north for a few blocks, the neighborhood as still as the air before a thunderstorm. Hatch was breathing heavily. Street Hammer asked if he was okay, but Hatch, experiencing another moment of dislocation, did not hear him. At one corner, a few grotesque figures bent over a small table, jostling each other and shooting wild glares at Hatch and Street Hammer. Flitheads, emaciated and gray-skinned. Hatch didn't want to stare at them and send them into a rage. Several knobby-kneed teenaged girls trotted over, clad in tight clothes and flashing jack-o-lantern grins with thick lipstick. Children, thought Hatch with a touch of horror, just children. Street Hammer waved them away.

"Anyway," he went on, "everybody up in that park can take assistance, get some extra food points, maybe even find themselves a roof and some electricity. But there's a pretty big catch."

"Sure," said Hatch. "You take assistance, you're in the labor camp lottery."

"Sometimes they do roundups anyway." Street Hammer shook his head. "They're not supposed to. Once they took away our healer. That woman did magic, I'm saying, kept us healthy. So you minding your own business and your ass gets dragged off upstate or to Arizona or Utah Territory or wherever else. Fodder for the machine. You ever meet anybody come back from a labor camp?"

"No."

"No. So we take care of each other because we got to. Central Park's not so bad as bad goes these days. Most of the people don't know what they for or against no more. I love them all but some of them just angry, want to burn shit."

They turned west and walked past dilapidated red-brick apartments with rusty fire escapes and chipped brownstone facing. Halfway along the block, part of a building façade had collapsed in a jumbled heap, blocking the sidewalk. They stepped around the rubble and arrived in front of a building decorated with the colorful mural of a shark twisting upward, its teeth glistening white beneath a staring, dead eye.

"This is you, Hatch Doran."

"What do I do next?" asked Hatch. The shark was unnervingly lifelike, and Hatch had a disquieting notion of the beast bursting from its painted realm, thrashing and jaws snapping.

"The man didn't tell you?" Street Hammer whistled softly.

"I assumed you'd know."

"The man don't see nobody, but he talked with you, didn't he?"

"Who is he, anyway?" asked Hatch.

"He does a lot for us is who." Street Hammer pointed his thick finger at Hatch. "But you do not want to screw around with the man, ever. So he tells you to come here, you best come here. All I know is the door right there, the one with the fish." Street Hammer paused. "You look a little shaky, Doran."

"I'm okay."

"So not to make it worse, but my stomach starting to rattle and sing, thinking about that pot Claire got going back there. I'm off to go get a plate of eats." Street Hammer walked away without a glance back.

Hatch entered the gloomy vestibule. Six mailboxes lined the wall to his right, but only one was marked: Suite #4. He found it at the end of a hallway done in peeling paint and worn carpet with circles stitched in gold lines. He buzzed the lock and entered a windowless room. A woman, her elbows propped on a small desk, had a pulser dead-aimed at his face.

"Hands in the air so I can see them," she said. Leather vest, dark hair, and beautiful apart from her bloodthirsty look. Hatch raised his hands. She circled from behind the desk, searched him, and ordered him into a metal chair. Then she tapped on an inside door and returned to her seat.

"I'm supposed to see him," said Hatch.

"Good for you," she said.

Hatch stared at the floor. Minutes crept by. "Does he know I'm here?" he asked.

She lowered her head and squinted over the pulse pistol. "Maybe."

"You tell him?"

"Maybe, and maybe he's worried, you come in here looking like some p'out who's been sleeping outside. Or maybe he hopes you sit long enough you get tired and leave. Or maybe you stand up too fast, I get to shoot you."

Hatch's neck was stiff. He looked up and then bowed his head down to stretch. No one knew where he was and he had no way to summon help if it became necessary. He recalled the shark with a pang of dread. The air in the room was stifling. Some people just have to get it kicked out of them, the man in the park had said. The woman with the pulser didn't waver in her aim.

A call sounded from behind the door, and she went to see about it. "You go in here," she said, waving him in.

Hatch stood and she pretended to shoot him, mouthing the *soomph-soomph* sound of a pulser and jerking her weapon. Hatch brushed against her as he entered the adjoining room. She gave him a hardy shove, almost causing him to fall, and closed the door. A thick-set man with a black beard lowered a book he had been reading and studied Hatch.

"Robert Hatcher Doran," he said.

"Andrei Kutznov?"

"Yes."

Soundproof paneling covered the room, and the walls were crisscrossed with strips of metal. Two soft chairs faced each other. A low table between them held a floppy black hat and a small, humming rectangular box.

Hatch frowned. "The man in the park…"

"He wished to dissuade you," said Kutznov.

"He didn't."

"And to assess whether you posed any danger to me. The same is true of my guard, Camila, whom you just met." Kutznov set his book on the table. "Please, sit. The device on the table will protect our conversation."

Kutznov's inflections hinted at his Russian origins, but his English was correct and even formal. After a moment of hesitation, Hatch eased into the chair. His nerves quivered inside, yet he was fatigued and his bones seemed made of lead.

"You found Caroline Atherton, I see," said Kutznov.

"Ferret hired me to make a pickup, but you never showed," said Hatch. The pickup, the pickup, the pickup. It had all worn thin, even to him. Was that really why he was here? "No one bothered to clue me in," he said.

Kutznov gazed at Hatch with placid, brown eyes.

"It doesn't matter," said Hatch. "I just want to finish the job."

"You wish to collect the redbacks."

"It's not just that," said Hatch. "My firm can help you. We can make discreet deliveries, provide transportation, or even embed your objects in more routine shipments. We can work under the radar."

"We are already far, far beneath any radar," said Kutznov.

"That doesn't mean you don't need allies, even if they're small-time allies." The room was windowless and the air was close. Hatch began to sweat.

"Of what use are all the redbacks in the world, Hatch Doran, if you are dead?" asked Kutznov. "You were wrong to involve dear Caroline in this matter. You were wrong to alert the local gangs to our activities. Ferret, too, was wrong to hire you. Your mistakes, though they spring from ignorance rather than malice, have endangered everyone. To address your original question, however, I refused to deliver this artifact because Ferret selected you."

"Because I'm not in the antiquities game," said Hatch.

"No. That was clever of Ferret. He is most intelligent. I refused because you are Montgomery Doran's son."

The box on the table hummed. "I don't understand," said Hatch.

"Your father was my dear friend. If justice existed, the world would declare a holiday in his honor." Kutznov sighed and looked away. "But justice is a myth the unjust tell for their own enjoyment."

"We're not talking about the same Montgomery Doran," said Hatch.

"You are a foolish man. He was a hero."

A shade of trepidation came over Hatch. "My father was a specialist in ancient languages and an archaeologist—"

"And he was a passable amateur physicist—"

"Who frittered away his academic career, abandoned his family, and eventually killed himself," said Hatch. "That makes him a loser and a coward in my book."

Kutznov played his fingers on the armrest. "I told Ferret, we must not bring Monty Doran's son into this business."

"Wait, Ferret knew my father too?" asked Hatch.

"Ferret meant to do you a good turn, to give you a large sum of redbacks for a simple errand."

"What?"

"Let's do this for Monty's son, he said. Ferret believed you to be courageous and reliable, and perhaps you are." Kutznov leaned forward and wagged a finger at Hatch. "But no job for a million redbacks is simple."

Hatch's forehead was clammy. "Why hasn't Ferret contacted me?" he asked.

"Ferret understands you are not at fault regarding the pickup. My refusal to deliver the artifact, however, surprised and angered him, though I had made my position clear." Kutznov gave Hatch a penetrating look. "But Ferret does not know of your visit to the Blue, and if he did, he would be angrier still. Ferret restrains his fury for no one. Do not ever forget this, Hatch Doran."

Hatch fell back into his chair, his hands squeezed into fists.

"So although you have no business here, Caroline's call crystallized a dilemma, and for the sake of your father I decided to talk with you." Kutznov rose and walked around behind his own chair and rested his hands on its back. "What I have to say to you would guarantee your death were you to share it injudiciously. I will say no more than I must."

"Tell me," said Hatch.

"Your father worked for a joint military-civilian task force. So did I and so did Ferret. It was called Project Caterpillar. Its activities spanned a period of fifteen years, though your father was involved only in the latter five or six. Its precise mission and its discoveries remain a closely guarded secret."

Hatch dropped back in his chair. Memories of his father washed over him like a rogue wave, and at once he was here with Kutznov and he was also a small boy, nestled against his father on the couch. Hatch looked around the room. The metal strips were like bars of a cage. He fought a sense of rising panic, and caught the odor of his own stale sweat. How had he let himself become so grimy?

Kutznov stroked his beard and told Hatch of how the corporate faction behind Caterpillar had discovered and captured an ancient machine of high technology. "We will call this faction the Group, since they refer to themselves by that very name," said Kutznov. "There is much more to this story, Hatch Doran, but suffice it to say that this machine, which we gave the terrible but appropriate name of Azazel, has cemented the Group's power over the world."

"Azazel," said Hatch. "The fallen angel, chained under the rocks." He wanted to laugh. He didn't. "And along you all came to dig it out."

"Indeed, we found Azazel in a stone vault, covered by a thousand feet of ice," said Kutznov. "Azazel proved the undoing of the oldest and perhaps most beautiful of civilizations."

"Fairy tales, old legends," said Hatch, muttering to himself.

"The device was an enormous crystal, spherical and complex and extraordinarily beautiful, suspended in a cubed gold frame. And we found warnings, elaborate engravings which, alas, we did not understand at the time." Kutznov took his hat, tossed it into his chair, and sat on the table, his knees almost touching Hatch's. "Then we—or I should say your father—uncovered a second artifact the following year. He located it in an underground temple some miles from Azazel's chamber. On the temple walls were representations of the constellations, as they were marked in those days, and star positions specified with incredible accuracy. Your father concluded that the diagrams, among other things, recorded the date the artifact was hidden away. By our reckoning, that would've been over twelve thousand years ago. Your father performed the examination and analysis of this artifact, and he was the first to understand."

"To understand what?"

"That it was in some way Azazel's nemesis. Like Azazel, it interacted with the human mind, reaching out to those with whom it wished to communicate. Of course, your father had a mystical side, and he was quite obsessed with the object. He freely admitted it. We often heard him speaking aloud to it as he worked in his lab." Kutznov chuckled. "We teased him, saying he was crazy, loopy. But he was the sanest of us all."

"How does this artifact work?" asked Hatch. "And why haven't you used it to stop this Azazel?"

Kutznov had a distant look and his face hinted at a smile. "Your father called the artifact Adrestia, after the goddess of equilibrium, of balance. She—the artifact—was a great mystery and remains one today. But we ran out of time, you see. We never solved the riddle of how to operate it."

"Adrestia."

"Affairs within Caterpillar at that time had grown unsettled and dangerous, but we all agreed that the Group must never possess the artifact." Kutznov stood and returned to his position behind his chair. "Azazel and the entire edifice of power built around it has a weakness, a vulnerability, Hatch Doran. This artifact is the key to it. The old writings told of how Azazel brought a prehistoric civilization to cataclysmic ruin, but there is reason to believe our dear Adrestia obstructed it sufficiently to preserve a remnant. On this we hang our hopes."

"Hopes?" asked Hatch. "Sounds more like a pipe dream to me."

"It is no idle dream," said Kutznov. "It is better that our goddess be destroyed or lost than fall into the Group's hands. But your father hid the discovery—he managed to exclude the artifact itself from the Caterpillar inventories, though other records refer to it. The Group, for that reason, has searched for the goddess for many years and, unfortunately, they are doing so now." Kutznov stood again and began to pace. "Your father entrusted Adrestia to me. I left it with Ghost, for he was best able to guarantee its safety."

It all came together for Hatch. "And now, all these years later, you and Ghost plan to trade it to Ferret like it was a Sumerian cylinder seal or an Egyptian burial mask."

"Ghost and Ferret agreed on such a transaction," said Kutznov. "I do not wholly approve and I certainly stand to gain nothing. But I assure you that neither man, on pain of death, will allow the artifact to fall into the hands of the Group."

Hatch rose, unsteady on his feet. "Tell me the rest."

"Sit down. Listen to yourself. You are weak and scarcely able to talk."

"Go to hell." Hatch stumbled toward Kutznov and seized him by the lapels of his jacket. Kutznov lifted him with ease and tossed him back in his chair. Hatch slumped, dazed and exhausted. "You said my dad understood something," he said after a moment.

"He understood what was going to happen, Hatch Doran."

"Go on." Hatch forced himself to raise his head and look Kutznov in the eyes. "Please."

"Once the Group had secured their prize, they were left with a dilemma. Too many people in Caterpillar knew too much."

"Say it."

Kutznov looked downcast. He picked up his hat and fanned himself. "The Group terminated Caterpillar and ordered the liquidation of its staff. The Group, Hatch Doran, murdered your father."

Hatch had begun to tremble, and hazy sparkles clouded his vision. "Why are you alive?" he asked.

"It was, in their eyes, a prophylactic operation, a matter of risk control." Kutznov's voice sounded muted and distant to Hatch, as if were speaking from the next room. "To some families they gave a story of suicide, and to others a tale of some accident. Lies in every case."

The room slowly spun and whited out. Without realizing it, Hatch had begun to cry. "Why is Ferret alive?" he asked. "Why are any of you alive?"

"You must be calm, Hatch Doran."

"Tell me, you bastard, why?"

"We were not present at the time. Ferret and I were loose ends, to be cleaned up later, but we made ourselves disappear."

Kutznov placed his hat back on the table. "Because of your father's heroic actions, the Group does not possess the artifact."

Hatch put his face in his hands and wept. He no longer cared how he appeared, no longer cared about anything at all. Grief subsumed him, and he disappeared into a rank maw of pain.

Kutznov moved to Hatch's chair and patted him on the shoulder. "Come, Hatch Doran. There is more to this story, but it must not concern us now. The pure evil loose among us is busy shaping our world for its own heinous purposes. Our beloved artifact will counter it or not, as fate dictates. Ghost will proceed with Ferret when it is safe, if they can bridge the gulf of mistrust that separates them. It is out of my hands."

Hatch sobbed.

Kutznov continued to comfort Hatch. "Such is life, my friend, and you will make your way and do many good things. But you have learned something of the truth of who you are, and that is no small gift."

CHAPTER 18

"I DIDN'T SAY I WAS WRONG," SAID MARTY.

Big Ray crossed his arms over his chest. "Once again, I'm playing shuttle diplomacy between you and Hatch. My life dream."

They stood on the loading dock of the Cochoran warehouse, inspecting a shipment just arrived from Philadelphia. Marty kicked open the damaged crate. "Doesn't give you the right to put words in my mouth, Raymond."

"You did say you were wrong, that's all I'm pointing out."

"Too much gabbing here," said Marty. "Let's look over this table and see it delivered."

"Ornery," said Big Ray. "Intolerable."

"Then find yourself some better company." Marty jutted out his chin in a particularly defiant manner, jerked a fistful of shredded packing material from the damaged container, and removed the legs to an antique table. "What I'm saying, lad, is I may have been in the right with Hatch, but I was raging, ready to batter him. I didn't handle it well."

"No, you didn't."

"He's a stubborn one, Hatch is."

"Pot, I want you to meet kettle. Kettle, pot. You guys are going to have a lot to talk about."

Marty rooted around in the crate, produced a packet of wooden pegs, and began counting them. Big Ray removed several table legs and connecting pieces. The parts were well preserved, and the bolt holes were lined with metal sleeves, pounded through the wood in years long past. "Antique for sure," said Big Ray, "but these are odd pieces to be table legs."

"A table stand, to be precise," Marty replied. "The cross-beams here are held together by this piece. It supports the desk top, which you'll find in the other crate there. Fellow down in Philly sent papers to prove it was used by General Washington himself."

"Where are the papers?"

"Jocelyn forwarded them to the buyer."

"Jeremy Broome," said Big Ray. Broome, a friend of Hatch's and Big Ray's and a former hedge fund competitor, had become a middling player in high-end tiques. "Go figure. Since they banned George Washington, his memorabilia has skyrocketed in price. Not as valuable as Jefferson's, but still."

"The point is, Jeremy pays his bills," said Marty, studying each piece of the stand and turning the legs over in the light.

Knife Cochoran sauntered over and fist-bumped Big Ray. "Everything cool here, Ray-man?" he asked.

"We'll be out of your hair in fifteen, my partner here gets a move on." Big Ray looked at Marty. "He's getting old, Knife, a bigger pain in the ass every day."

"I sure ain't going to screw with him," said Knife. "Old Marty'll take your beating heart in his hand and walk away humming a tune. You don't want to cross those Irish bastards."

"Respect your elders," said Marty. "I'm right here under your nose, having to listen to all this."

Knife grinned and nudged Big Ray.

Marty pried open the long, flat crate containing the table top. He cleared the stuffing, lifted one end of the table, and surveyed the bottom. "Not bad," he said, "considering we had Drop and Bump Cochoran here drive it in from Philadelphia."

Big Ray turned to Knife. "We appreciate your generosity, letting us use the truck. It solves a lot of problems. I won't insist, but you guys don't charge enough."

Knife waved him off. "The truck is yours, Ray, whenever you need it. Crick wants to do more with you guys—you know how he feels about Hatch—and I think we get the job done."

"No argument here," said Big Ray. "You'll definitely see more work when we get it." He passed Knife an envelope with the Cochorans' fee plus some extra for the night at the warehouse and the use of the truck.

Knife thumbed the bills and protested the extra money.

"Don't waste your breath," said Big Ray.

Knife shrugged and stuck the envelope in his pocket. He clapped Big Ray on the shoulder, and they watched him walk away. Marty began hammering the crate closed. "What I was trying to get through your cast-iron skull, Raymond, was that you have business and you have common sense, but sometimes you have something deeper."

"This is the thing you didn't want to talk about any more," said Big Ray.

"I'm speaking of friendship, lad."

"So you are saying you were wrong?"

Marty's cell chimed and he answered. "Yes, hello, love... say again..." Marty listened, the color draining from his face. "Mother of God, tell me what happened, Sue...last week, was it..."

"What?" asked Big Ray.

Marty's expression sank. His eyes grew round and full. "I understand," he said. "I'll say a prayer, I will...you'll let me hear when you return...yes, my love to all of you." He put his phone back in his pocket and turned to Big Ray. "Peter Adagio was murdered."

Big Ray covered his eyes. "My God, Marty."

"Shot right in the street, he was."

"I'm sorry. He was a good man."

Marty looked around as if lost. "They say it happened after his shift, a random shooting. Sue took him back to Chicago, where they grew up. She couldn't find Pete's contacts and didn't know how to reach me. It is a sad day, Raymond. Pete and Sue lost their boy in the South American war not so long ago."

"Let me help with the crate, Marty." Together they heaved it into the truck and secured it. Afterward, Marty strolled down the sidewalk and stood, hands in pockets, staring into the distance. Big Ray came and waited next to him. "Come on, Martin," he said. "I'll drive."

"What was that?" asked Marty, his eyes now welling. "Yes, yes, I think you probably should. Most kind, Raymond, I appreciate it more than I can say."

CHAPTER 19

HATCH RESTED ON THE OUTSIDE STEPS IN FRONT OF HIS apartment. It was almost dusk, and he watched as a few people strolled by in the falling light. Two doors down, a man was removing the security bars to repair a broken basement window—

His Dad, murdered.

—and extracting the jagged glass shards. A sheet of particle board lay at his feet.

Antarctica.

From another house nearby came the squeak of a window being raised followed by the aroma of bread and spices.

In the bathroom mirror that morning, Hatch had stared at his pale cheeks and the gray circles under his eyes, his heart a maelstrom of sadness lined with joy. Now, outside on the stoop, his mind brimmed with visions of icy wastes and ancient peoples, and he reflected on the bloody machinery of power.

Adrestia. The goddess.

"Your father was caught in the Group's horrible web and was unable to escape." It was Kutznov's voice, returning to Hatch from their parting the previous afternoon. "He wanted to keep you and Mae as far away from it as possible. Each of us felt the same about those we loved, and he had already lost your mother, which all but broke him."

"I never knew," said Hatch.

Kutznov told Hatch more about the Group. "I will leave you with this," he said. "The Group believes they control Azazel. They believe they are wiser and stronger than those of antiquity who were undone by its dark power. They could not be more mistaken."

"But what can be done?" asked Hatch. "This Group, whatever it is, can't be defeated."

"They are lost in illusion," said Kutznov.

"But they have the Azazel weapon," said Hatch.

"Weapon?" Kutznov chuckled. "Dear man, Azazel is far more than a weapon." He rested his hand on Hatch's shoulder and his eyes shone with intensity. "You must understand, Azazel represents to the Group nothing less the world made anew. They mean to create a paradise for the elite few, for those like themselves. Those poor people being worked to death in the labor camps or freezing in the streets do not matter to them. They are insignificant or, at best, human material to be used and disposed of. But this syndrome of fear and anger and suffering, confronting us at every turn, is much more than a by-product of the Group's work. It is the madness of Azazel! You see, the Group considers themselves artists of civilization, and all this ruin and death are the lines and color and shadow they paint on their fearful canvas. But what horrible claw grasps the brush? What fiery eye gazes over its gruesome design?"

Another shade of evening had fallen, and the street had grown still. Hatch returned to the present, though he continued to wander among his labyrinthine thoughts until Big Ray and Marty appeared below him on the sidewalk. "We earned our pittance for the day, and Broome sends his regards," said Big Ray. "But we have sad news."

"Indeed we do," said Marty. He told of Adagio, and the news came as a blow, one that Hatch had little strength left to bear. But he knew it was heavier still on Marty's heart, and he mumbled his regrets and stared again at the steps while Marty offered his eulogy.

After the three of them had sat gazing at the street for awhile, Hatch told them about Kutznov, and how Kutznov and Ferret had worked with his dad years before. He discussed the secrecy of the work and described the Group and told how the Group had murdered most of those involved, including his dad. His words gave Marty and Big Ray much to absorb, and perhaps for that reason he did not mention Azazel, that fantastical device, or the artifact his dad had discovered to counter it—the artifact Ferret had hired Hatch to deliver.

"I screwed up," said Hatch. "I didn't handle it well. As for Judson Blue, you were right, Marty, I was an ass. I charged off with my hair on fire. I was in the grip of something, but I make no excuses. I got us and others exposed."

"So Ferret knew your father?" asked Big Ray.

Hatch nodded. "That's what got me the job."

"I used to hear rumors," said Marty. "A consortium working with old myths, ancient texts, and dead languages in search of lost knowledge. I found it the wiser course not to speak of such matters. Now you've met K and you've learned a few things, but we are left with Judson Blue."

"This guy Ghost—Blue mentioned the name, Marty, you remember—Ghost has the artifact," said Hatch.

Marty frowned. "I never relished bodyguard duty, but I was proficient enough at it. As of this moment, lad, you'll go nowhere without me."

"No," said Hatch. "The game is up where the artifact is concerned."

"It is nothing of the sort, not with the Blue around. I'll stay here at the apartment the next few days. Perhaps Nathan can rig up a way for me to track you."

Samantha materialized from the evening shadows. "What a dismal pack of step loungers," she said. "Though you have cleaned up nicely, Doran."

They all stood.

"Rough week," said Hatch, and forgetting Samantha's request not to mention it, he said, "I hope your trade's going well."

Her face darkened. "Don't pester me about it," she said. She hurried past them, grim-faced, but paused at the top of the steps with one hand on the door handle. "I'm sorry, Doran," she said.

"It's okay."

Big Ray and Marty looked away. Hatch caught the aroma of cooking again. Someone in the neighboring townhome crowed with laughter.

"I'm very sorry about everything," she said again before closing the door behind her.

***

BIG RAY RETURNED TO HIS TUDOR CITY APARTMENT, AND Marty followed Hatch inside and stepped into the kitchen. The apartment was silent except for Samantha's scuffling downstairs. In the bedroom, Hatch found her furiously sorting through hangers of blouses and T-shirts.

"These old rags," she said. "I'm barely presentable anymore."

"I beg to differ," said Hatch.

She removed an armful of clothes from the closet, tossed them on the bed, and then stood over them, chewing a strand of her hair. Hatch reached to catch a few blouses as they slipped from the bed to the floor. Samantha resumed pushing through her clothes, the closet light adding a glow to her profile.

"These sweaters are dated, too," she said.

Dated? Hatch hadn't heard the term in years. He waited for her to look at him. She didn't. He plunged ahead. "I haven't been myself, Sam. I'm sorry. I'm overdue in saying so."

"It started at Ms. Franklin's," said Samantha, her eyes widening. "Do you remember Emily Franklin? I've done three or four things for her over the past year, and anyway I sometimes visit—she is so lonely—I like staying in touch. It's good business, of course, but it's the right thing to do. One never knows when friendships are going to just...*boop*...pop right up!" Her voice cracked.

"Do you want to sit down?" asked Hatch.

"Ms. Franklin has some drawings by Nikola Urban," she went on. "Hateful pieces to look at, but worth a load. She agreed to let me move them for her." Samantha bit her lip and surveyed the clothes on the bed.

Hatch dropped into the corner chair. "Can I help out?"

"You have to be very careful, Doran. You can't just drop a stack of Urbans in someone's lap." Samantha made a sweeping gesture. "I mean, they'd toss you right out. You have to really understand the person you're selling to. Make them feel comfortable, so they know you aren't pulling one on them. I do have a strong reputation as a broker, you know."

"Yes," Hatch agreed.

"You have to keep nudging the client to bite. You must be subtle and gentle, but you must be relentless." Samantha stopped. Her eyes had taken on a mad brightness. "It's one of my criticisms of you, Doran. You generate a ton of ideas—impressive ideas, once in a while—but you don't develop them to the last degree. You lack the necessary quality for building a really successful company."

"Do tell," said Hatch. The bedroom walls, he observed, were painted in lilac. Sam had insisted on the color when she moved in, declaring the former white walls bland and intolerable. He had never cared for the lilac, but he had learned not to see it.

"Consider my approach," Samantha continued. "I keep hanging about, keep getting to know people, even though with legitimate Urbans it should be merely a matter of price." She laughed, a small huffing sound. "But when you find yourself with an extraordinary client, one who may lead to so much more..."

"I should be taking notes," said Hatch.

"Don't be defensive," said Samantha.

"Defensive?"

"You shut me out, Doran." Samantha's face had flushed pink.

"That's been true recently, but I am trying to—"

"Did you know the best relationships are made up of flowers and gardeners?" she asked. "Well, I'm a flower, and I won't be made to feel bad about it."

"A flower?"

"Don't take this the wrong way, Doran, but as a gardener you leave much to be desired."

"Tell me the right way to take that," said Hatch.

"Or maybe you're a flower, too." Samantha returned to her rack of clothes. "With two flowers, it's almost impossible to make a relationship work."

Hatch moved to the edge of the chair. He felt he was missing something important.

"I am determined to be full and complete," said Samantha. "I don't care if the world's breaking apart, I will be all I can be. I will have the magic and I will have someone who can make that happen."

"The magic."

Samantha sighed. "You wouldn't understand."

"You want me to shovel shit on you, help you grow?"

"Now that is unsupportive, and just what I'm talking about." She shook her head sadly, reached into the closet, and withdrew a pair of faded jeans. "At any rate, you were going to say something?"

"Some other time," said Hatch.

She gave him a disapproving look. "See? I show some interest and you close me down. Very poor gardening on your part." She pulled a duffel bag from under the bed, unzipped it, and began to stuff her clothes inside.

The area of Hatch's face around his eyes had begun to throb. "Taking a trip?" he asked.

Samantha didn't look at him. "I've decided to move out—or to stay moved out, I should say." She licked her lips. "I don't think you are quite what I need, Doran. If you were, I wouldn't feel this way, would I?"

Through the basement window above his shoulder Hatch heard the clap-clap of sneakers as someone ran along the sidewalk. How crazy to run after dark. In the distance, a truck beeped faintly as it backed up.

"At the very least," said Samantha, "I want to think things over. You should do the same." She sat on the bed and rubbed her hands on her thighs. "I am sorry to be so blunt, Doran. You do have some remarkable qualities, you know. You have potential. But we've never been terribly close, have we?" She paused, searching his face, but Hatch was unable to form any response at all. "I hope my decision won't interfere with our professional relationship," she said.

He stared at his hands. His fingers moved slowly and did not seem to be fully his own. "Odysseus always needs people who can contribute," he said.

"Well, Jocelyn can tell you I've been carrying the firm. Check the books."

Hatch looked up. "For the last twelve weeks, you have accounted for 62% of our revenue," he said. "For all of last year it was 29%. Impressive and appreciated."

Samantha's face fell. "You don't sound appreciative." She toyed with the damp strand of hair. "I have to keep this job, Doran. You know it is important to me to take care of myself. Besides, I'll never get a trading license on my own."

"I hope you find your gardener," said Hatch. He stood to leave. "I'll see you around the office."

"Oh, I am so glad!" Samantha beamed, but then her face grew somber again. "I mean, I'm relieved, you know. You must be, too."

Hatch trudged upstairs, utterly drained. In the kitchen, he found Marty shaking a few drops of bottled lime flavoring into a glass of water.

Mrooww.

The cat pushed between his feet. Hatch automatically poured a small dish of milk.

"Women," said Marty. "A lad never knows, does he?"

"What?" asked Hatch. "Were you listening to us?"

Marty's eyebrows jumped to his hairline. "No, and I never would, would I? But the expression on your face tells me all I need to know, Hatch."

The cat crouched over the bowl. Samantha came up the stairs, her duffel bumping on the railing and walls. Its wheels rumbled over the plank floor and then she was in the main room, chewing on her lip. Marty nodded. Hatch stared at the floor and frowned. She made a half-hearted wave and rolled the duffel through the front door.

"She'll be back," said Marty after the door had closed.

Hatch put the milk back into the refrigerator.

"You must consider what you'll say when she asks back in, Hatch. Meantime, give your head time to clear. As for myself, though it's early, I'm going to settle in with a book and get some shut-eye." He squeezed Hatch's arm and set off downstairs to the small sitting room which doubled as a guest bedroom.

Hatch listened to Marty rustle around downstairs while the cat finished the milk. He stared at the tall front windows and decided they could use new curtains. The current ones were worn. Dated, Sam would say. Perhaps he, too, had become dated in Sam's eyes.

The rest of the evening was a blur of ache and disconnected thoughts, and Hatch barely recalled sliding into bed. But in the early morning hours he started awake, confused and groggy, with poisonous longing flooding his heart. He sat up in the bed and squeezed the sheets in his fists.

Forget it. She's right, Sam's right.

A helicopter thumped overhead and faded. The cat, curled in a ball at the end of the bed, raised her head.

He adored Sam, but she was right, they had lacked a vital connection. It was a hard truth. She had faced it and he had not. But she had always surprised him, the way she could explode like a summer thunderstorm from a clear sky, or kiss him when he was angry, knowing he didn't want to be touched. She had surprised him even with their sporadic, spontaneous lovemaking...and his tears stung his eyes and he lay down and burrowed into his pillow and wondered how he had failed her. But had he? Of course he had. And she had wounded him to his core. In his turmoil he remembered the lilac paint and decided it would have to go.

Sunrise found him at his desk, searching the collector rags and tique listings for prospects. At one point, he leaned back in his chair and contemplated a photo of Mae, taken during the holidays after his first semester away at school. Mae was grinning while he held a glittery Christmas stocking on his lap. The photo struck a sad chord, and Hatch set it back on his desk just as Jocelyn appeared at his door.

"Marty stayed here last night?" she asked.

Hatch grunted but didn't look up.

"I met him on his way to Smyte's a few minutes ago."

"Probably."

"Okay, so I got some eggs and I'm making omelets. Do you want one?"

"No." He shuffled papers. "But thank you."

"I'll make you one anyway. Goat cheese, peppers, and prosciutto. It looked pretty fresh, the prosciutto. And I have bread for toast. Like real bread, not those soy boards."

Hatch frowned.

"We have to eat, Hatch." She took the chair in front of his desk. Her thick black hair bordered her heavy glasses, and his spirits fell another degree at the sight of her forlorn face. He wished for her to nag him about the bills, to wave the impossible numbers at him the way she always did. "Samantha is still staying with me," said Jocelyn.

Hatch nodded.

"She's been building up to this."

He shuffled more papers.

"I'm sure it's no surprise," said Jocelyn. "But I love her, you know. She's my friend, and it's like I have to be there for her. You understand."

"Sure."

Jocelyn twiddled her fingers. "I love you, too, Hatch. You know what I mean."

"Yeah. Thanks, Joss."

She straightened in the chair. "I'm cooking you an omelet, boss man, and you're going to eat it." She stood to leave, but paused at the door to his office. "Sam's my friend and all, but it was like crummy in the extreme what she did and the way she did it. It really was."

Hatch didn't wholly agree, and as Jocelyn's footsteps diminished in the hallway, he reflected that Sam had acted for Sam, the only way she had ever acted; he didn't consider it selfish so much as pure. Sam, in her way, was completely free and he respected it.

A short while later, he heard Big Ray in the main room talking to Jocelyn. Then the office door opened and Big Ray tossed his blazer on his desk and spun his chair around. "Okay," he said, "I'm on my way over and I get a call from my contact at the Met."

"The art thief?" asked Hatch.

"Charlene? No, this was Savoy, the guy who handles contemporary sculpture. Wants us to move a couple of pieces under the radar. I'm going to grab one of the Cochorans plus their truck. I'm meeting up with Savoy later this afternoon."

"Be careful. Knife or Crick, God forbid, may scare off your customer."

"Plus, I'm having a second meeting with my man with the egg collection," said Big Ray, locking his hands behind his head. "If I didn't know better, I'd feel the arrow of luck beginning to point our way."

Hatch paused. "Samantha may be able to help you. With the sculpture."

Big Ray coughed. "I meant luck for the business," he said with a stammer. "Look, brother, about you and Sam—"

"Jeez, was it on the news already?"

"She hasn't been herself." Big Ray made a dismissive gesture. "We've been expecting it, but hey, I'm glad she's staying on. She's really good, we all know it. I'll give her a call."

"She's been an asset for us."

Big Ray nodded and for a moment, they both looked away, staring into the corners of the office. Then Big Ray spoke. "Hatch, this business about K, working with your dad…"

"It's a lot to get your head around," said Hatch. His thoughts drifted to Kutznov and the artifact as Marty put his head in and announced the omelets were ready.

"It's just us four today," said Jocelyn when Hatch and Big Ray sat down at the workstation. "The others are off." She handed Hatch a mug of coffee. The aroma of eggs and potatoes and bread—real bread—brought a sharp pang of hunger, though he had vowed he didn't want breakfast.

"It'll take some doing to keep the tears off my plate," said Marty, perched over his omelet with a worshipful expression.

"Mine won't last that long," said Big Ray.

The cat glided over the workstation, moving from plate to plate and making soft *mroows*. "Eat, people, before it gets cold," said Jocelyn. She brought a plate from the kitchen and put it on her lap. "Can I cook, or what?" she asked.

"An angel'd pay double for it," said Marty. He halved a slice of toast.

Big Ray wiped his lips with a napkin. "Marry me," he said to Jocelyn.

"No," she said. "You aren't worth anything on a split." They others fell silent and Jocelyn cringed. "Sorry," she said.

Big Ray laughed.

"My fat mouth," said Jocelyn. "It's the shape of my foot sometimes."

"It's all cool," said Hatch.

They ate and told stories from the days when they'd all worked at China-Morgan and then the hedge fund. "Everybody had enough then," said Jocelyn. "Or most people. This is so hard now—but oh my God, listen to me complain, sitting here with a full stomach. I am a top-shelf idiot. I belong on my knees giving thanks."

It had been so long now, thought Hatch. He stared at his empty plate, wandering through his past. So many years with these same people. How he loved them. He wanted to tell all he had learned, and how his dad had died with courage and bravery. He could not. He was a plate spinning on a pole, wobbly and uncertain, and he didn't trust his emotions. He declared Odysseus closed for the day. There were smiles and gentle needling. Big Ray left to attend to his decorative eggs, and Marty returned to the guest room. Hatch and Jocelyn cleared the dishes and Hatch began washing them.

"Leave those," said Jocelyn.

"I don't mind," said Hatch.

"Dude."

"Go, enjoy the day, Joss. We'll settle up later."

"We are settled," said Jocelyn in a croaky voice. "You do a lot for us, Hatch. More than we deserve."

Her words touched him in a strange way and he had to stop for a moment. "I may have done more harm than good," he said.

She wrapped her arms around him and told him not to say such ridiculous things. Hatch patted her shoulder, his thoughts a galaxy away. After a moment, she drew away, wiping her eyes. "You asshole," she said. "You made me cry."

"I didn't mean to," said Hatch. "And I'm fine, I promise."

***

LATER THAT AFTERNOON, HATCH PUSHED HIS BED AND HIS furniture to the middle of the room and laid plastic sheeting on the floor. He was moving on. He had no fresh paint and no money to buy any, but he was moving on and this was the first step. He yanked the plastic, and as he worked his anger rose to a boil and he stopped and willed himself to laugh. The laughter felt like rusty machinery shifting in his chest.

So he wasn't perfect. He spread the plastic with his foot. So he was no goddamned gardener. He did have a business that needed saving. His mind bubbled like foam on a choppy sea, and he thought of food points and hoped Jocelyn and Marty had not blown too many on the omelets. He noticed the small clock on the bed table. He had given it to Samantha as a joke: the clock ran backward and had always made her smile. Slowly, he put his hands on his knees and doubled over, the pain palpable, a solid thing, inside and outside of him all at once.

Marty had left to grab a change of clothes and a few toiletries from his apartment across town in Murray Hill. Hatch was alone, and he gradually recovered himself and fixed tape to the plastic and replayed Kutznov's words in his mind.

He had no reason at all to doubt Kutznov, but the idea of Azazel and the Group chilled him to his core. When he thought of Samantha in his arms, however, and the taste of the omelet, and even the plastic stretched across the floor, all Kutznov had said became outlandish and surreal, an outrageous violation of his life. Yet the Group existed. The Group had unearthed an ancient, apocalyptic weapon. His dad had discovered and preserved its nemesis.

The familiar sense of dislocation swept over him, and again he discerned, at the edge of his hearing, the faint, melodic echo of chimes. How often had he remembered his dad over the past couple of weeks? Vivid, haunting memories. And what of his vision and his disorienting spells and his mad obsession with the artifact?

Adrestia, the goddess, touching him, summoning his attention, as she had from the night he had first met Ferret. It had always been about more than the million dollars, and now it came together in Hatch's mind with the force of a thunderclap. He gazed around for a moment, trying to assemble his thoughts. Then bolted for the stairs, taking two at a bound.

Find Ghost.

Upstairs, the front room was bathed in silvery light from the overcast sky outside. Hatch imagined Big Ray telling him he had lost his mind. Had he? Maybe. Probably. But it was already too late to stop, though he had only the whisper of a hunch.

But what about Marty?

He had promised Marty he wouldn't set foot outside the apartment. Too bad. This had to be done. He'd give Marty a call and explain.

Find Ghost.

Hatch bolted from the apartment and half ran to the corner. Subway? No. He was going through a rough time, but he wasn't suicidal. He hailed a hoo. The door whished open, and he climbed in, his mind as clear as fine glass.

"Central Park West and Ninety-seventh," he said.

CHAPTER 20

SAMANTHA TRIED TO RELAX NEXT TO KEE'S ROOFTOP POOL. She tilted her face toward the sun, which had just emerged from behind a bank of gray clouds. "I should be working," she said.

Kee, stretched beside her in a matching deck chair, had dozed off. It was just as well. He didn't sleep enough, and she didn't really feel like talking after her awful confrontation with Doran.

A small van blew its horn on the West Side Highway. She closed her eyes. "Move in with me, Sam, and let's be together," Kee had said. "You'll be safe. You'll have all you ever wanted. No p'outs or food points or travel restrictions."

It was true. Kee's world brimmed with obsequious servants and expensive cars and layers upon layers of security. It had brokers and personal trainers and private shoppers and chefs and extravagant charity galas. Kee's world had blossomed amid the collapse, but did he care? No. He was interested in games. And shaping the inner gamer. Through experience. Profound experience.

Did Kee even care about her?

Of course he did. Absolutely.

The warm rays touched her cheeks and forehead. Then the clouds drifted over the sun, bringing a chill. Doran didn't live in such luxury, but his apartment was quaint and charming. It was real. The old, heavy doors and shuttered windows and squeaking, plank floor and plaster walls had always made her feel warm and happy. Now, of course, the place was growing shabby with everyone traipsing in and out all day, Nathan's wires running hither and yon, the floor needing repair, and plumbing getting to be a problem.

God, she already missed it all.

But it wasn't the apartment, was it? No.

Overhead, a flock of birds scattered in flight. Next to her, Kee snored softly. He was quirky, but he felt like some kind of destiny, the way he had burst into her life. He was easy and open. On the other hand, one could only go so deep with Doran before reaching bedrock. When she told him she was leaving, for instance, he had not shed a single tear, had not yelled or thrown anything. Instead, he had quoted her sales statistics. He had said he hoped she found what she wanted. Goodbye and good luck, with never a batted eye.

But hadn't she been relieved?

Yes, oh, yes. She had barely been able to tell Doran she was leaving. She disliked scenes of that kind and appreciated his restraint. Criticizing him for it now didn't seem fair, but still she damned him for making her ache so. She suddenly missed having his arm around her at night, and the way he teased her, and always hopped out of bed to make her breakfast.

"A few million redbacks for your thoughts," said Kee.

"I am pondering the way life works," said Samantha.

"It works like it works."

"It works like I want it to. It had better." She managed a smile.

Kee stretched. "Life is about the future, and future looks like rain," he said. "How about lunch?" In his palatial kitchen —the main kitchen for the mansion, not the marble kitchenette with the wonderful brushed steel appliances in his suite—Kee produced containers of lettuce, tomatoes, cucumbers, carrots, slices of peppered filet mignon, gorgonzola cheese, and bottles of various dressings.

"Salad?" asked Samantha.

"Sure." Kee washed the lettuce and pulled it apart. "I prefer it for lunch or after I've worked out. Don't you find you aren't as hungry after a workout?"

"I used to eat salads almost every night," said Samantha in a reverent whisper.

"Then here you go. I have a nice burgundy somewhere." He opened a wine cabinet, withdrew a bottle, and decanted it.

"The lettuce is so crisp and fresh," said Samantha.

"I didn't tell you about my next game series. I think I was dreaming about it on the roof."

"No, you didn't."

"We're very close to having a demo out. It's about outer space. I think we can get the implants to simulate a bodily feeling of zero gravity." Kee began to hold forth on the coding challenges and the tangle of copyright laws and a legal action he was fighting in India.

"You know, Kee, I love art," said Samantha, "but I can't think of it all the time. You must give your mind a rest."

"I have to keep moving, but I'm tired, Samantha. I'm so tired."

"Tired? But you had a nap on the roof."

Kee poured two glasses of wine. "And between us, fear sinks me like a stone sometimes."

"Fear?"

"What if I can't come up with more great games or develop a better implant?"

"But you mustn't allow fear into things. It's a negative force."

"This is a pretty serious business we have going here. I didn't tell you, we are sifting through the feedback on the last several implant updates. Clearly, we are getting a thumbs-up from the gamers, as we expected, but the updates seem to provoke irritation and rambunctiousness."

"Really?" asked Samantha, cutting a spinach leaf. "How will the planet cope?"

"You tease me, but we're seeing a tendency toward real aggression. It isn't good for business."

"I've heard talk of more riots," said Samantha with a coy look. "Do you think they'll blame you?"

Kee frowned. "Our work at the Institute depends on continued gaming success, Samantha. The Institute is why I do all this, as I've told you a million times. It scares the hell out of me, the idea of failure." He began to stalk around the kitchen. "It is all about who and what we are, about improving the mind and the essence of a person through gaming."

Samantha stifled a yawn.

"You don't consider this a good thing?" Kee's eyes seemed to bore through her face.

"I adore healthy minds," said Samantha, a little flustered.

"All consciousness is connected, Sam, but I believe you and I have a special bond. Maybe an eternal bond."

Eternal? Samantha wasn't sure what to say. Eternity struck her as an awfully long time.

Kee set down his glass and put his hand on her arm. "Can't you see, this is my blueprint, my mission. I wish I could describe the rush I feel when I—I mean, this is critical for the future of humanity, Sam. I'm convinced of it. I fell in love with you because I knew you felt what I felt."

Samantha, awed by his intensity, struggled to gather herself. She took hold of his hand and pulled him close and kissed him. "I believe what I see in art is what you feel when you make your games," she said.

Kee kissed her back. "Yes. Art is transcendental. It speaks to our permanent parts."

"Precisely." Samantha touched the side of his face and kissed him again. He tasted like wine and salad and she was sure she tasted the same, which wasn't bad. This wasn't the time to dwell on it.

"You have something on your mind." Kee ran his finger along her thigh.

"No."

"It's me, Sam. I'm here for you."

Another kiss. "You'd take it the wrong way," she said.

"Impossible."

"It's why I brought you the Urbans, Kee. To you, in particular." She spoke in a soothing voice, pushing aside a rush of panic and desperation. "This thing about the inner essence of a person—you see, dear, I know little about it, really, but I know you have it. Very strong essence, I mean."

Kee ran his fingers through her hair.

"And I just know you can see what I can see in those Urbans," she said, quelling a mad impulse to flee from the kitchen and return home—wherever home was. "I know you value Urban's superlative technique, the way he hints of something bigger than life."

Kee kissed her neck. Her shoulder. "Tell me what you want me to do, Sam," he said, "and I'll do it."

CHAPTER 21

"LOOK, I KNOW YOU DON'T LIKE IT," HATCH TOLD MARTY as the hoo began to move north, "but I have unanswered questions." He held his phone away from his ear and heard, therefore, only a few of Marty's most emphatic phrases: "damned pig-headed"..."waving the cape at Blue"..."death wish."

"It has to do with the artifact," said Hatch, putting the phone back to his ear, "I know who I have to talk to."

The afternoon traffic gridlocked to a stop before Hatch had traveled more than a few blocks. Horns cried out. Marty, still at his apartment across town, refused to countenance the idea of Hatch going alone to Central Park. "I'll meet you there," he said. "The Ninety-fifth Street gate, was it? Now listen, Hatch, you'll leave your hoo this minute and slip into a shop or a bar with a rear entrance."

Hatch rolled his eyes.

"Pass a bill or two," Marty continued, "get out the back into the alley or courtyard, then find another hoo and meet me at Ninety-fifth. Let's not tempt fate more than we have to."

Hatch ended the call with no intention of taking Marty's advice, but then reversed himself and decided it might save time to walk around the gridlock. He paid off the hoo and jogged down 12th Street. The snarled traffic had resulted from the collision of another hoo with a death cart. The death cart lay askew on the street, split almost in half and missing two wheels, while the wrecked hoo rested partially on the sidewalk. A boy, probably the death cart's driver, pounded on the hoo and shouted indignantly at the stopper trying to pull him off.

Hatch crossed West 4th Street and scanned the storefronts, finally ducking into a Municorp-sponsored sensitivity training center. The sign over the door read:

FREEDOM FOR DIVERSITY
Subject to Approval of the Designated Diversity Classification

Hatch walked through a darkened lounge area with carpet and suede furniture. Several people, their heads shaved and wearing one-piece suits or loose smocks, occupied a couch and chairs. E-sexuals, Hatch guessed. As they gestured and laughed, he vaguely recalled that e-sexuals, rejecting the tried and true physical methods, preferred to use pituitary drugs and electronic body implants to stimulate and share sexual sensation. Toward the back, he encountered a young person who might have been a woman—or mostly woman—with a pretty face, straight black hair, and a distinct blue tint to her complexion.

"Oh! You're *white*," she said—or tre said (Hatch was unsure of the correct pronoun)—in a distinctly male voice. "How retro! Or are you just siwhite?"

"I'm sorry, si—"

"Simply white. Out of the womb that way. We can help you with that!" The mostly-woman flashed a smile full of silvery teeth. "Take a seat wherever you like, but you really aren't supposed to be back here."

"I need to leave by the rear door," said Hatch. He had hoped to charm her—or trer—but was as unsure of the dynamic as he was of the gender term; he resorted, therefore, to the tried and true, the ultimate unisexual concept: cash. He flashed redbacks, the last of his thin hoard.

"Keep your money," said the mostly-woman. She flushed a deeper shade of blue. "You're too cute to be a totally bad guy."

"I'm not a bad guy at all," said Hatch. He followed her along a narrow hallway cluttered with cabinets and sporting a bulletin board full of notices printed in bright colors.

"Sure you can't hang around a while?" she whispered.

"Another time," said Hatch.

Mostly-woman smiled again and let him through the rear door. He crossed the courtyard to Jane Street and made his way to the avenue, where he grabbed another hoo and ordered it to Central Park. "And be quick about it," said Hatch.

"New York Transcorp requires strict observation of all statutory speed limits," replied the hoo.

***

DARTHAM RECEIVED SETH'S CALL JUST AS THE GCI receptionist was scanning his in-chip. "I don't have no time to talk," said Seth. "I'm supposed to keep an eye on his apartment, which is one effin hard chore. He went somewhere up the West Side the day before yesterday and I lost him. Blue's going to flay me if it happens again."

"Who are we talking about, Seth?" asked Dartham. "Do you mean Doran?"

"Who else? It's what I do now. I watch Doran for Blue and I talk about Doran to you. Doran, Doran, Doran."

"That is what I am paying you to do," said Dartham. For the past few days, Dartham had been squeezing Seth—and Helena, for that matter—for any information on Robert Hatcher Doran (not Hayes, as it turned out). He did not intend to let up.

"These houses on Doran's street are flat against each other," said Seth. "There's nowhere to hide. I walk up and down the street all day, and I'm tryin' to follow him now but the traffic's all jammed up. Blue'll kill me if he don't get the artifact."

"Is that so?"

"Uh…"

"Where are you now, Seth?" asked Dartham.

"Uh, Eighth Avenue and Jane, I think—rats, he just got out of his cab. I got to go, man. I can't lose this guy." Seth clicked off. Dartham arrived a minute later at his desk and put Helena on it.

"The Municipal Service Corporation cameras are partially operable at Eighth Avenue from Jane Street to Bleecker Street," said Helena.

"Calculate a ten minute walking radius from Jane and Eighth, and keep expanding it in real time, please," said Dartham. A tinted circle appeared on his computer monitor and gradually expanded. "And use whatever muni cams you have to face-match the Hatch Doran we profiled earlier."

"In process," replied Helena. "I have no current matches."

Dartham played with the possibilities. If Doran had hopped in another hoo, he was already long gone from Helena's circle. Another minute passed.

"In process," said Helena. "I have no current matches. I am examining archived municipal camera records for the past twelve minutes."

Dartham twirled a pen in his fingers. How did a small-time tique broker like Doran become involved with people not even Blue wanted to cross? Was Doran a patsy? A low-level errand boy? A deep player of some sort? Judson Blue had murdered a man to identify Doran, and Dartham began to wonder if Doran was somehow the linchpin of this whole mess.

Moreover, Seth had confirmed Blue's desire for the artifact —which Dartham already knew, having heard Blue himself say it a dozen times through the bug. Dartham idly twirled the pen. Blue, trying to punch above his weight and play both sides, pretending to be working for Dartham while chasing the artifact for himself.

"I have no current matches," said Helena. "I am examining archived municipal camera records for the past fifteen minutes."

Intimations of approaching pandemonium touched Dartham's mind: he had Doran and Blue, combined with what he had learned from Hansen and Shel Kirk. He had Terry Bronsun on the warpath, as Marcus Hansen had put it—Terry having called twice in the past twenty-four hours wanting updates, getting increasingly impatient for Dartham to show progress. But what information did Terry really have? Dartham didn't know and he disliked operating in the dark. "There is no solid evidence of anything yet, but we are getting close and I've got the Blue on a leash," he had said to Terry, wanting to keep his cards close until he was ready to lay them on the table.

Or so he told himself.

Dartham indulged in a moment of self-pity. Just what in the hell was he involved in? This business about the Azazel technology and the true nature of the Group had come as a harsh blow. But he remembered what Shel Kirk had said about order. Kirk, fingering the holster.

Forget it, Dartham told himself. Grow some backbone. Blue was jerking him around, trying to gain leverage by grabbing the artifact. He knew Blue would not lightly tangle with the Group in this fashion, and he knew that he, Dartham, in Blue's place, would do exactly the same. But he was not in Blue's place, and such misbehavior had consequences. When all this was finished, he planned to teach Judson Blue a painful lesson about insubordination. In the meantime, however, someone was going to end up with the precious artifact, and Dartham intended to be that someone. He therefore had to remain close to the action, and Seth and the Blue looked like his best bet.

Through his windows, the office towers seemed decrepit under the gray-black sky. Yes, he wanted to do his job and live in comfort. He wanted an easy ride. Who didn't? On the other hand, it had been a long time since he had kicked some serious ass. Too long. A tingle of excitement rose, like sap running up a tree.

Helena informed him that she had no current matches. "Keep digging," he said.

***

WHEN HATCH ARRIVED AT 95TH STREET, MARTY WAS WAITING with an overnight bag slung over his shoulder. He surveyed the p'outs lounging against the park wall. "I feel like I'm being watched by a pride of hungry lions," he said.

"Faith, faith," said Hatch as they headed north toward 97th Street.

"We've little else, it seems," said Marty. "This whole business has my tuning fork ringing."

Hatch had planned to approach the park entrance and ask for Street Hammer, but they found their man at the Tudor building where Hatch had met him before, wearing a flat cap and blue shades and sitting in a nylon folding chair.

"Look what washed up on my beach," said Street Hammer. He slipped a phone from his pocket and tapped something on the screen.

"I want to see him," said Hatch. "The man I talked to before."

"Let me tell you about all the things I want, bruh." Street Hammer laughed. "The man figured you'd be back. Put me right here on this sidewalk to look for you."

"Then let's go."

"You don't know what you fooling with," said Street Hammer. "I'm supposed to tell you to run along, give you one more chance to save your ass. I know you not going to take it."

"We don't need much time, Street," said Hatch. "How'd the man know I'd come?"

"The man has mysterious ways." The phone in Street Hammer's pocket chimed. "Last chance," he said. He stood and folded the chair. "I take you to the man, the game's got to play."

"Let's go," said Hatch again.

Street Hammer raised an eyebrow over his shades. "The bag?" he asked Marty. Marty handed it over and Street Hammer rifled through it. "I know you packing something," he said. "You give it or I take it. If I take it, I keep it."

Marty reluctantly handed over a small truncheon he had strapped to one ankle and a switchblade he had fastened to the other. Street Hammer took the weapons, hefted the truncheon in his hands, and grunted. He returned the overnight bag, frisked Hatch and Marty, took their phones, and directed them toward the park.

Across the street, they waited for several minutes until a white van with the Electricorp logo arrived at the park entrance. Street Hammer watched it turn in a circle and stop. "You want to see the man, this is how you do it," he said. He tapped on the passenger window of the van. The window lowered and he handed the truncheon, knife, and phones to whomever was inside. Then the rear doors popped open and Marty and Hatch, after a quick glance at each other, climbed in. The van was crammed with electronic equipment, a couple of small drones, and several rifles locked in a steel cage. Three seats were bolted to the vehicle's floor, and a metal panel separated them from the driver's compartment. After Hatch and Marty had each taken a seat, the panel opened.

"Why'd you bring the sidekick, Doran?" asked the driver.

"He's one of my partners," said Hatch. "You're the same guy I talked to in the barn?"

"What a genius you are."

Hatch knew him only by his voice. The frizzy beard and shades were gone, and he now wore thick-framed glasses and an Electricorp hat. Hatch cocked his head toward the front of the van. "This is Ghost," he told Marty.

"The same as Blue mentioned?" asked Marty.

Ghost turned. "I know all about you, Shannon, just like I know everything about your whole bang-up crew—Odysseus, or whatever you call it. I figured you'd come alone, Doran, but hell, it probably doesn't matter."

"Tell me why Ferret wants the artifact," said Hatch.

"Ask him yourself when you give it to him."

Hatch pulled himself forward toward the front of the van. "Kutznov said he and I were out."

"Kutznov was trying to scare you off. He also didn't like the way Ferret brought you into this without consulting us. It's not how we work." Ghost tapped his fingers on the wheel. "We had to vet you ourselves before we let you near our business. Now you can finish the job, like you've told half the goddamned world you want to do, or you can leave right now. It's up to you."

Marty sighed. Hatch shot him a warning glare. "How'd you know I'd come?" he asked.

"Jesus, Mary, and Joseph," Marty whispered.

"I bet Kutznov you'd be back crying at our doorstep like a hungry stray," said Ghost. "He wouldn't take my wager." Ghost checked the outside mirror. "You sure you didn't get yourself followed?" He pressed the ignition button and cool air filled the van. "Leave if you want to, Doran, but it'll mean I went to a hell of a lot of trouble for no reason."

"We're in," said Hatch, sensing Marty's stare on the side of his face.

"We've wasted too much time," said Ghost. He closed the panel, sealing them in the rear of the van.

Marty gave Hatch a severe look. "Not to put your ice cream in the oven, lad, but you are an open book." The van made a turn, and Marty raised his hand before Hatch could respond. "Let me concentrate on where he's driving us."

They jounced along, making a series of turns and stops. Hatch heard the sounds of traffic and occasional shouting. Marty was certain they had crossed one of the East Side bridges. More turns followed, and several tight circles and a long stop. A horn. A Policecorp loudspeaker in the distance. More circles, this time in the opposite direction, and then they drove straightaway for several minutes.

Marty shook his head. "He scrambled me with all the circling around. I'd say we're somewhere in Queens."

Ghost opened the rear doors and Marty and Hatch stepped out into an empty receiving area. They followed Ghost through a door into the disused lobby of a vacant office building. Through the windows, Hatch glimpsed a weedy parking lot surrounded by high, razor-wire fence. An old interstate highway was visible in the distance. Ghost hustled them along to a pair of white double doors which appeared new and freshly painted, in marked contrast with the rest of the building. There he submitted to a retina scan, and a steel door opened to reveal an inner, windowless area completely enclosed within the larger facility. At one end was a second van, this one gray and unmarked, pointing toward a closed exit door. The center of the room contained a cage bristling with electronic equipment. Ghost tapped a code on a small keypad, unlocked the cage, and rolled a chair to the console.

"You may have been followed by Judson Blue's people," said Ghost after checking a small computer display. "The Group is probably not far behind."

"How do you know that?" asked Hatch.

"Ferret and I know what we need to know. We've been working under Judson Blue's nose, so I had someone inside the Blue well before you came along. The same Blue who knew zilch about our business before you went running your mouth."

Marty studied the corners of the caging and ran his fingers along the steel mesh. He caught Hatch's attention and indicated several bundles connecting by colored wiring. "This whole place is rigged to blow," he said.

"Blue has gotten soft and therefore he's vulnerable," said Ghost. "But he's also unpredictable. The Group's breathing down his neck, and he means to have the artifact." Ghost gave Marty and Hatch a grave look. "Blue murdered one of the gatekeepers over in Chelsea last week. In cold blood, and just to get your name, Doran. Blue is crazy, and he has no honor.

We're going to deal with him, but that's not today's business. The Group also has a guy involved in this, a former Colonel named Dartham. He's a different breed altogether, but he also wants the artifact." Ghost stuck his thumb at his chest. "I don't intend to let either of them get it."

Marty stared off into the gloom.

"Blue can bring a lot of people," said Hatch.

"If he does, we'll fold our tent and pick another time."

Marty looked up. "The point is, Hatch, this man Ghost wants everybody at his party," he said. "He's hunting scalps, or so I'd guess." Marty gave Ghost a hard look. "Tell me I'm wrong."

"He does have it in for the Group," said Hatch. "Told me so himself."

"It's a pickup and delivery," said Ghost. "And it's a stage play for the stage players. I have some books to balance with the Group."

"Does Ferret know?" asked Hatch.

Ghost scowled. "Ferret's a control freak. He doesn't like to improvise."

Hatch took a chair a few feet away from Ghost. "Why does Ferret want the artifact?" he asked.

"You never quit, do you?" Ghost fiddled with a mouse, and one screen went dark. "After all these years, Ferret believes he can activate it, use it somehow."

Beyond the brightly lighted cage, the sealed, interior room lay in shadows. No sound penetrated from outside. Ghost flicked on a radio receiver or computer of some sort covered with thick metal plating. A screen flashed green, blocky letters on a black background. "We go in two and a half hours," he said, slipping on a pair of headphones. "You may want to take a nap or say your prayers. I've got someone I have to talk to."

CHAPTER 22

BACK IN THE WEST VILLAGE, CAMO AND SETH HAD HOLED up in a run-down food dispensary, eating rubbery sandwiches and syrupy sweet artificial apples. Camo finished his call with Ghost and took a minute or two to review what Ghost had instructed him to tell Blue.

"Who was that you were talking to?" asked Seth. "You said something about an incinerator?"

Camo made a throat-cutting gesture for Seth to shut up. He called Blue on his other phone. "Yeah, we're back near Doran's place, but we lost him," said Camo. "Again."

"You mean Seth lost him," said Blue. "That's twice in a week. What a dickhead."

Blue sounded irritable and out of sorts, but Camo needed him to focus. "Listen, JB, I have word that the transaction Doran came to us about, the delivery of that artifact, is going down tonight."

"I ought to plant my steel-toed boot right up Seth's sorry, stupid ass," said Blue. Camo sighed and let Blue run on. A vision of Lindi on a sunny beach formed in his mind, but he didn't allow it to linger. There'd be no beach and no Lindi unless he did Ghost's bidding, which meant luring Dartham into the trap so Ghost could kill him. Blue was still ranting about Seth when Camo's words finally struck home.

"Wait," said Blue. "Did you say tonight?"

"It's a rumor," said Camo. "But I think it's a good one."

"What do you mean, a rumor?"

"I got a mole inside Pachetti's organization. I slip him a few bills, he keeps me posted." It was a total fabrication, but Camo was reading from Ghost's script now and he needed Blue to swallow it.

"Pachetti's guy knows about this transaction how?" asked Blue.

"It's one of Pachetti's bodyguards," said Camo. "He says Ghost is tight with Pachetti. There's been some loose talk over there."

"Ghost and Pachetti, eh? Damn."

"So I'm told just today."

"We'll twist Tony Pachetti's left nut all the way to Sunday when this is over. Wise guy, messing around in our space."

"The source may be wrong, JB. We don't know what time, exactly, but we're pretty sure where: the downtown incinerator."

"With Doran on the move, we have to assume your source is good," said Blue.

Camo agreed. He omitted to mention, however, that he not only knew the transaction was on for tonight, but he knew which entrance to the incinerator to use and knew where to be so Dartham would see them. Ghost had been specific and detailed in his instructions.

"This could be a setup," said Blue. "I want more people involved."

Camo could hear Blue's gears grinding and he wanted to put a quick stop to it. "Too many people, too many ways for it to go FUBAR," said Camo. "I got Seth, and we're headed over to the incinerator now."

"You know I don't like to handle ops like this on the fly," said Blue. "I'd feel better with a few more people on the perimeter." The gears continued to grind. "But what the hell, you're the best man I've got, Camo. You want to swap out Seth?"

"No. He'll do what I tell him."

Camo listened while Blue jabbered on, telling him what he already knew about lines of fire and elevation and working from shadows. Then Blue mentioned Dartham. Camo, stunned, had to ask him to repeat it.

"What I said, Camo, is I wouldn't be upset if Dartham caught one. You know, by accident. Some crossfire shit. Fog of war and all that."

Now Blue wanted to kill Dartham? Christ. "Dartham is Bronsun's boy, JB."

"Accidents happen is all I'm saying."

Camo rubbed a spot on his forehead between his eyes. The good Colonel had a rough ride in store. Ghost wanted to off the man, but Ghost was Ghost. Camo, on the other hand, had no intention—none whatsoever—of taking out one of Bronsun's people. That shit was miles above his pay grade. "I'll see what I can do," he said.

Blue was happy. Camo ended the call and gave Seth a suitably limited view of the landscape. "Now, you're going to call Dartham and tell him about the incinerator," said Camo.

"I don't know nothing about Pachetti," said Seth.

"Forget Pachetti. Just call and tell Dartham what I told you to say."

Seth fumbled with his phone, dropped it, and had to punch in the number again. Camo listened while Seth filled Dartham in about the incinerator, mumbling and uh-huhing and cringing like a whipped dog.

"What's the man say?" asked Camo when Seth finished.

"Dartham says for us to get out of the way. Says leave it to him."

Camo chuckled. "This ought to be fun."

"Dartham's a tough old bastard," said Seth. "I'm no good at this complicated stuff. Maybe I shouldn't go."

"Don't be a wuss," said Camo. "You're perfect for the job."

CHAPTER 23

Marty and Hatch huddled outside of the cage in Ghost's hideaway. "We've no cards to play here, the way I see it," said Marty.

"Ghost is putting the artifact in my hands," said Hatch. "That's the bottom line for me."

"You're going to be the piñata at Ghost's party, sure. But Ferret'll run us all to ground if we fail him now, and who'd blame him?"

"It's not Ferret. Ghost is right, Blue is the complicating factor. And this guy Dartham. Sounds like the Group is closing in now."

"You two stop gabbing," said Ghost from inside the cage. He had headphones over one ear and was fiddling with what appeared to be a short-wave receiver.

Hatch walked over to the cage entrance. "I want to see it. The artifact."

Ghost whirled in his chair. "Why?"

Hatch paused. "My dad died for it."

"Learning about your daddy patched you back up, did it?"

"What can it hurt?"

"It's not just some museum piece, Doran. Kutznov probably left you with the impression it's some kind of ancient technology—and who knows, maybe it is. But I have a different idea, and so did Ellis Beckham. We think this Azazel weapon is actually a portal of some kind, and the ugly, beastly shit coming through it has given us the world we're dealing with now. So your daddy's artifact—Adrestia, the goddess, as he called it—is probably a portal, too. You want to use it, you have to *hope* it's the good guys talking back to you. You have to *hope*, but you don't *know*, and your dear old dad didn't either. All I'm saying is, you let your mind get touched by it, it may not get right again."

"I'd already figured that out," said Hatch. "But who is Ellis Beckham?"

"He was Caterpillar's head physicist for the last eight or ten years of the project. Every university in the country blackballed him for thinking outside the box—academia frowns on that, as your pappy could've told you—but those are just the kind of people Caterpillar wanted. He and your dad were close. They passed a lot of evenings talking about the multiverse, time travel, all kinds of weird shit."

"So they murdered Beckham, too?"

"No. You know him as Ferret. You want to piss him off, tell him I told you his name." Ghost laughed, a hoarse, scraping sound, and checked his watch. "Get in the cage," he said. "Shannon, too."

Hatch and Marty took the two chairs. Ghost cuffed and blindfolded them. "What's all this for?" asked Hatch.

"My peace of mind," said Ghost.

Hatch heard soft, beeping sounds and the hum of an electric door. Ghost returned, removed the blindfolds, and unlocked Hatch's cuffs while leaving Marty's hands fastened. He had placed on the console a rectangular box with rounded corners, constructed from a midnight blue metallic substance. Intricate symbols etched in fine lines of silvery-gold covered its surface. Ghost touched a diamond-shaped figure near the upper corner and the top panel of the box irised open and disappeared within the box's sides. Inside, a set of prongs extending from the box's inner walls held in place an oblong, football-shaped object.

Hatch forgot where he was. He saw only the artifact.

"We never figured out what the box was made of, but your father noted that these symbols"—Ghost indicated the exterior etchings on the box—"these symbols tended to shift and change under various light frequencies." He pressed a rune-like spiral in the uppermost corner of one of the box's sides. The prongs extended and lifted the artifact out of the box. "Go ahead, Doran, take it. Your daddy's dear goddess. She won't bite, though who knows what else she might do."

The artifact was lighter in weight than Hatch expected. Its obsidian surface scarcely reflected light and, like its container, was covered with precisely engraved figures. Hatch held the artifact in his hands, and the etchings glowed and pulsated as if a living light had awakened inside; and with the shifting light came a vibratory hum, more sensed than felt. A profound sluggishness descended over Hatch, and he lost all but rudimentary command of his hands and arms. He hardly noticed: the artifact had entranced him entirely. It had grown warm to the touch and it shimmered at the boundaries of his perception, the curve of its edges diminishing in clarity when he tried to focus on them.

Ghost was saying something—"I told you, Doorrraaann…"—his eyebrows creeping above the top of his glasses while the world around Hatch slowed to a crawl. Ghost's lips continued to move, but slower now. The corner of his mouth inched upward into the beginning of a smile before stopping altogether, as unmoving as a photograph. And Hatch saw Marty, frozen, statuesque, and bound to his chair.

Visions surrounded Hatch, moving and lifelike images, seen as if presented on scrim; he perceived a mélange of colors, scenes of earth in a far earlier time, gorgeous, mountainous landscapes, and an elegant city perched beside the sea. And then the artifact spoke in his mind, and he sensed an ancient intelligence of staggering power.

We are observers and friends,
Not of your realm.
See those of your earth
Who lived long before you.

And Hatch observed multitudes of people dressed in bright rainbows of color going to and fro, and he heard shouts and laughter and the familiar melody of chimes. Below, and in the distance, great ships gathered in the harbor while others sailed on the far horizon. Then, in an instant, an ominous precognition laid hold of him, and he knew that everything before him was marked for destruction.

Montgomery Doran had ears to hear.
So do you.

As one jerking out of a nightmare, Hatch fought his way to the surface of his awareness.

"I tooold yoooou," Ghost was saying in a deep, slurry voice, "this thing will screw around with your head." His mouth finished curving into a smile, and his movements returned to normal. "It had no effect on me, of course, but Kutznov held it once and swore never to touch it again."

Hatch cradled the artifact. All he had seen had passed in a sliver of an instant. The artifact's fuzzy outline held his gaze, and he had to remind himself to breathe.

"Shaken, were you?" asked Ghost.

Marty gave Hatch a concerned look.

"You know why your father gave his dear Adrestia to Kutznov?" asked Ghost.

"To keep it safe," said Hatch. He had intended to speak clearly, but his words emerged in a mumble.

"No," said Ghost. "He gave it to Kutznov because it told him to. The artifact, the one you're holding in your hands, it told him to."

***

DARTHAM ARRIVED AT THE INCINERATOR WITHIN AN HOUR of receiving Seth's call, but he was not about to rush into a robotic waste furnace without a plan. He parked at the end of Warren facing the Hudson, his vehicle hidden by a pockmarked wall surrounding the rubble of a demolished building. The park trees had long since been cleared, and beyond the south wall of the incinerator lay the inky surface of the Hudson River. Every minute or so, the massive incinerator heaved, making a muffled *shoomp-clack-paahhh*. Dartham's nostrils rebelled at the pungent odor, which penetrated his SUV even with the windows raised.

He surveyed the incinerator facility. A high wall with three vehicle gates surrounded the structure, and no exterior vantage point permitted observation of more than a single entrance. Though he had ordered Seth to keep the Blue away, Dartham knew they would come. He also knew that the parties delivering and picking up the artifact might enter and exit by vehicle or on foot or even by boat, from the docks on the river side where they brought in the refuse. It was altogether too many points to cover. He needed to be close to the action. He had to get inside.

Fine. The vehicle gates were open, and entering the facility itself posed no serious problem: Dartham's pulser would cut practically any lock or door in existence. Moreover, he doubted the place was even locked, since the parties involved were probably sophisticated enough to disable the security systems without a fingerprint, digital or otherwise. Moreover, Seth was not responding to calls, and this weak clue suggested he might already be inside, his cell reception blocked.

So Dartham would cast his lots and wait inside.

He sent a remote message to Helena and a moment later his cell vibrated. "Central Helena, Core AI. Your call is secure, Tom."

"Helena, can you interface with the Policecorp drones? I need you to capture their surveillance of lower Manhattan around the downtown incinerator."

"Checking." A moment passed. "Covert penetration of drone data is not possible," said Helena. "A cyber intrusion has temporarily disabled the drone fleet. However, I can deploy my own drones, if you wish."

"No," said Dartham. "I cannot have the operations people involved. Except for you, this is off the books."

"Understood."

"I need an interior diagram of the downtown incinerator facility."

The requested diagram appeared on Dartham's screen, and he ended the call. He did not know what time the transaction would occur, but he figured on a window of time ending before the section gates closed at midnight. It was almost nine p.m. and dark now, with the clouds thick and heavy overhead.

Dartham zipped his pulser into his jacket pocket. He checked his .45 automatic, much his preferred weapon, and tucked it in a back holster. His mind was sharp and clear, and he was ready for action. Only the lack of full situational awareness nagged at him, but tonight his training and experience would have to do.

The incinerator rose before Dartham, a vast, shadowed bulk against the black sky. Sometime during the next few hours, the artifact would be somewhere inside its walls. It was Dartham's duty to get it and to bleed anyone who stood in his way. And when he was done, he would walk out of the incinerator with the artifact under his arm and present it to Terry Bronsun.

It's what an old soldier would do.

***

THE ENCOUNTER WITH THE ARTIFACT LEFT HATCH FEELING lightsome, and with a sense of drifting on clouds. In a daze, he watched Ghost place the artifact into its box, free Marty from the cuffs, and unlock the cage.

"It's almost time," said Ghost.

Marty rubbed his wrists and gave Hatch an inquiring look.

"I'm fine," said Hatch.

Ghost called up a diagram on his computer. "This is the downtown incinerator." He ran his stubby finger along the central portion of the diagram. "The handover happens here."

"You want Hatch to go *inside* the incinerator?" asked Marty.

"Clever, isn't it?" Ghost's face gleamed with satisfaction. "The incinerators are automated. There are no workers. The place is secure enough not to need guards, but not close to secure enough to keep us out."

"Isn't it like a thousand degrees in there?" asked Hatch.

"It's a mechanized plasma furnace," said Marty. "It isn't fit for humans."

"You creampuffs," said Ghost. He tapped the screen. "There are two furnaces. One is sealed off underground, and that mother runs at 2,700 some odd degrees. Complete molecular deconstruction. So, yeah, you don't want to mess with that baby. The other, upper furnace handles the preliminary burning. That's the only one you'll have to deal with. It's no worse than a backyard grill, for Christ's sake. You could sit in it if you had to."

Hatch studied the diagram.

"I know every square inch of the place," Ghost continued. "There is no staff, but they designed the interior for maintenance and engineering people to get in when necessary. You may drop a few pounds of sweat, but you probably won't burn very much."

"It's not a problem," said Hatch.

"Once you're inside—see this marker here—you'll find a secured door," said Ghost. "It leads to the incinerator control area, and it will be unlocked. Once you're in, proceed along this walkway, clearly marked as Passage 5." Ghost indicated a complex network of crisscrossed hallways. "You follow it to here, this junction with Walkway F1."

"Passage 5, Walkway F1," said Hatch.

"F1 is really an enclosed catwalk. When you get to it you turn left and go to the end, to what is labeled here as the F-Ledge." He gave Hatch a serious look.

"The F-Ledge," said Hatch.

Marty shook his head. "F-Ledge, and right beside the furnace?" He trailed off in a string of profane muttering.

"The ledge does run along the edge of the outer furnace, Doran. It's about eight feet high and it looks down over this open area here."

The F-Ledge reminded Hatch of a theatre stage. The open area Ghost referred to was where the audience would sit, had there been seats. Unfortunately, he suspected his audience was apt to be well-hidden. Ghost confirmed it. "The F-Ledge is the only way to get across to the exit Ferret's people are using," he said. "Now, Blue's people—there will be two of them—will be here in the open area. You may not see them." Ghost tapped the screen with a serious look. "I assume Dartham'll be nearby. That's one bet I'm making. The other bet is that neither Dartham nor the Blue will expect you on the F-Ledge so close to the furnace."

"And if your bets are wrong, God forbid?" asked Marty.

"The point is, they can't climb up to the F-Ledge. Therefore, they can't follow Doran after he crosses it. You,"—Ghost addressed Marty—"need to stay outside. Ferret's people will have a small truck here, on the river side of the facility. When it leaves, you go home and celebrate your payday. We've disabled all the area street cams. They'll be spooling archived footage."

"I'll be inside with Hatch," said Marty.

Ghost shrugged and turned to Hatch. "Now you're going to proceed along the F-Ledge, like I said before. Halfway across, you'll be able to see Ferret's contact man at the far end, some guy named Hop. The F-Ledge dumps you into a receiving area and that's where he'll be waiting. This Hop guy is not coming out on the F-Ledge, is that clear? You have to make it all the way to him."

"I've met Hop," said Hatch. "He's a sweetheart."

"If Hop isn't there, Hatch is getting the hell out," said Marty.

"Hop'll be there," said Ghost.

Marty took a step toward Ghost. "You'll make sure of it, and with the truck idling outside."

"It's cool, Marty," said Hatch.

"You're putting Hatch up there to tip-toe along the edge of hell itself," said Marty. "We know Blue wants the artifact and we know this fellow Dartham wants it. You're dangling Hatch and the artifact as bait."

"He's getting paid," said Ghost.

"Not to give you a table dance next to a mechanical lake of fire with God knows who shooting away at him," cried Marty. "Give it a think, Hatch, It's wacked, if you ask me."

"It's a million bucks," said Ghost. "He can damn well work for it. I have a jacket for you to wear, Doran, which will protect your tender skin from the heat. As for the other stuff, let me take care of it." Ghost squinted through his thick glasses. "Anything happens to you, people will answer to me and to Ferret. It's a good insurance policy, but it's the only one you've got. I told you where I stood with the Group. Dartham is part of the Group and he's going to walk right into my arms."

Marty said something about the rabbit at the hound race and told Ghost it wasn't worth the risk.

"I'll be hunting the Group as long as I live," said Ghost. "Tonight Doran will walk his ass across that F-Ledge and help me do it." He pointed at the diagram. "Blue's people and Dartham will use the primary doorway here or"—Ghost traced his finger to a service door at the far end of the diagram —"if not, they will enter here. None of this affects what you do, Doran, but like I said before, this is where you might see them." Ghost pointed again to the open area in front of and just below the F-Ledge and the furnace.

"So I'll only be able to see them—and be visible to them—when I'm on the F-Ledge," said Hatch.

"That's right."

Marty cursed under his breath. Hatch made out the words *eejit* and *arseways*.

The computer chimed and Ghost swiveled to examine the screen. Hatch glimpsed an invoice or statement of some kind written in Japanese. Ghost grunted and returned to the diagram. "Now, finally, there's a catwalk running over and above all this," he said. "See, it parallels the ledge where you will be, but from above and behind the open area."

"Here's what he says next," Marty told Hatch. "Anyone making a go at you will have to cross beneath the catwalk."

Ghost gave Marty a cross look. "I will be there to cover you," he said to Hatch, "with clean lines to anyone who tries to stop you. You focus on getting to Hop and delivering the artifact to Ferret. I'll keep you safe and sound."

Hatch studied the monitor.

"Have we lost our brains here?" Marty asked.

Ghost appeared to run out of patience. "Listen here, Shannon, Doran said he wanted in. Now he's in. I know who you are and I know some of the gory things you did for dear old Ireland. I'm still not sure why you're here, but this is how it happens tonight."

"Marty, I'm good," said Hatch.

Ghost shut down his computer. "Let's go," he said.

Marty was still grumbling to himself when he and Hatch seated themselves in the rear of the second van. Like the Electricorp vehicle, it had no windows and the front seat was sealed off from the cargo area. Ghost tossed Hatch a heavy, fireproof jacket. He then gently wrapped the box containing the artifact in black quilting, fastened it with a rubber strap, handed it to Hatch, and closed the van door. A few moments later, they heard the mechanical door rumble open. The van lurched forward and made a sharp turn before picking up speed.

Marty studied Hatch with narrowed eyes. The van bounced over the broken pavement and slowed, probably for a bridge toll. "You're plotting something," said Marty.

Hatch didn't want to discuss it, not in the van. He held the box close. After a few minutes of tranquil driving, Ghost suddenly accelerated, putting the van through a variety of quick turns and then coming to a dead stop for several minutes. When they resumed movement, Ghost drove at a normal pace. A short while later, he stopped the van and slid open the metal panel separating Hatch and Marty from the front seats. Sporadic rain drops plopped on the windshield.

"Either I'm getting more paranoid in my old age or we got followed again," said Ghost. "Probably the Blue, just like before, but I shook them." He gestured. "This is North End. Down there, at the end of Murray, is a building with red-brick facing. You enter through the maintenance doors and go down the stairway to your left. At the bottom of the stairway, veer left again, which is west. This will take you underground into the incinerator. When you reach the staircase marked as an emergency exit, you will go up until you reach the secured door we reviewed earlier."

"I remember," said Hatch.

"You will enter the incinerator at 10:25 p.m. You got a watch?"

"How are you getting in?" asked Hatch, wriggling into the fireproof jacket.

"Don't worry about it," said Ghost.

"You're going to let us walk out of here, into the street, carrying the artifact?" asked Hatch. "We could run. We could disappear."

Ghost's eyes met Hatch's through the rearview mirror. "It's a block away, the building entrance, and I'll be watching you. Could you pull a fast one? Sure. But what are you going to do with the artifact, Doran? Sell it? To who, Ferret? Please.

To the Group? You wouldn't live a day. On the other hand, you could pocket a million just for taking a quick walk on a ledge. But go ahead and run if you want. I leave you to Ferret's tender mercies. As for me, I got paid already. The wire cleared before we left my place."

Marty grumbled some more. Hatch tightened his grip on the box.

"Now go," said Ghost. "Right down the block there. I'll have your truncheon and your Cub Scout knife shipped back to you, Shannon. Your phones have already been destroyed, which is how it goes."

They climbed out and Marty slung his overnight bag over his shoulder. Hatch thrust his head back through the van door. "What you're saying is, I'm going to stand on a ledge in plain view with two different sets of people gunning for me. And I'm going to be covered by a man who's already been *paid*?"

"Unless I change my mind," said Ghost.

The van door hummed closed.

CHAPTER 24

DOWN MURRAY STREET IN THE SOFT FALL OF RAIN, TO THE building Ghost had indicated: Marty and Hatch passed through the rusted double doors and into a maintenance area containing a few cans and moldy boxes and the remnants of a broken forklift. Though the light was dim, they spotted a doorway opening to a stairway and felt their way through it to the landing. Their arrival triggered a series of weak, motion-sensitive lights, and at the bottom of the stairs another doorway opened into a narrow passage extending toward the incinerator.

The air was close and moldy. Hatch motioned for Marty to stop. "Listen, we can't both go into the incinerator," he said.

"You aren't fool enough to think you're doing this alone," said Marty.

Hatch tucked the box under his arm. The fire-jacket was heavy and uncomfortably warm. "I've botched a few things recently, Marty. I don't want you to be the next victim."

"I'll not be anyone's victim, lad, but I'd feel better if I was the one on the catwalk, keeping an eye on Ghost—and on you."

"I was thinking we need a decoy," said Hatch, unstrapping the black quilting from the artifact's container. "See if this will cover your overnight bag. I say we part ways inside the incinerator. Once I'm on the F-Ledge, you draw their attention. Get rid of the strap and make sure they see you carrying this."

"And someone will have to follow me," said Marty. "They won't risk letting me go."

"But they also have to watch for me."

"Bit of a shell game." Marty's brow wrinkled.

Hatch checked the time and set the box on the floor. The air was moist, and scratching sounds came from inside the walls. Water gurgled through a nearby pipe. "My dad understood, Marty," he said. "He understood what happened in the past."

"I'm sort of left to play all that by ear," said Marty. "There is much I don't grasp about this artifact and what it does, but the cast of characters going after it tells me a lot."

Hatch struggled to clear his mind. "It's everything, Marty, and everything depends on it. But we have to shave the odds or I may not come through this."

The corners of Marty's mouth turned down. "I'll not hear it."

"I'm cool with it, all right? It sounds deranged, but when I was holding the artifact…" Hatch stopped, trying to find his words. Sweat beaded on his forehead and ran down his nose. "Ferret and Ghost, they're on the right side, but I cannot let the Group have the artifact. Dad pretty much gave his life for it, and I may know why."

Marty's face was chiseled and craggy in the weak light. He made no argument, but silently took the quilt from Hatch. "It's a bad idea," he said at last. "I feel it in my bones. I should stay and help in there."

Hatch leaned over and put his hands on his knees, his arms trembling with nervous fatigue, his earlier confidence blown away like dust. He had never quit on anything. Never quitting was all he had ever had to cling to, but fighting until the end had never seemed such a sad, uncertain prospect.

"Listen, Marty," he said, lifting the box. "I know what I have to do, but I'm going to be exposed. You have to draw at least one of these guys off my back or I'll never get out of there."

**

DARTHAM HAD STUDIED HELENA'S DIAGRAM, AND ONCE inside the incinerator he took his bearings. As expected, the main entrance had been unlocked. He was, indeed, pitted against sophisticated players, able to covertly invade Municorp's security systems at will. He touched his .45 again and crept along a lighted hallway until he reached a door painted in deep violet. The incinerator bristled with hazard warnings and flashing lights. The periodic *shoomp-clack-paahhh* of the incinerator sent vibrations through his feet.

Beyond the painted door was a long, rectangular machinery room with low lights spaced at long intervals. Here the incinerator's grinding and puffing was loud and immediate, giving Dartham the sensation of being caged with a deadly beast. He made his way toward the center of the facility, holding close to a row of tall, metal cabinets. Their darkened gauges stared outward like a host of dead eyes. High above, a network of catwalks crisscrossed in the darkness.

Shoomp-clack-paahhh…

The odor was foul and almost overwhelming, and a burst of heated air flooded the machinery room after every exhalation of the incinerator. Dartham began to sweat. He heard a clatter of metal, and from a few yards ahead the sound of voices: Seth, crouched and talking to another man who was dressed in camouflage. Beyond them lay an open space with an access ledge running about eight or nine feet off the floor. Beyond the ledge beat the fiery heart of the incinerator.

Shoomp-clack-paahhh…

A burst of heat, and Dartham stepped back, concealing himself about thirty feet behind Seth and the other man.

Good. He had the favorable position. Maybe luck would smile on him in this mindless, automated hell.

Dartham was beginning to like his odds.

***

MARTY AND HATCH JOGGED ALONG THE TUNNEL UNTIL IT intersected with a finished underground hallway, part of the incineration facility's emergency exit system. At 10:25 on the nose, they reached the stairs leading to the incinerator, opened the secured entrance door at the top, and stepped into machinery room at the opposite end from where Dartham had entered.

Shoomp-clack-paahhh…

They moved stealthily down a corridor with metal walls and spaced lighting: Passage 5, according to the sign. Hatch indicated the sign and pointed for Marty to proceed in the opposite direction. Marty shifted his quilt-wrapped bag, gave Hatch a clap on the shoulder, and disappeared behind the tall rows of metal cabinetry.

Hatch, holding the box with both hands, continued along Passage 5 at a trot. The cycles of the incinerator and the intervals of relative silence between them had begun to register in a corner of his mind. He passed an entrance with steps rising to Walkway D1 and then, further along, to Walkway E1. Another hundred feet and he arrived at Walkway F1, the one leading to the F-Ledge. Hazard signs in several languages and with garish flame shapes decorated the entrance.

Hatch squeezed the box tighter in his arms and climbed the steps to a landing enclosed by orange caging. About thirty feet ahead, Walkway F1 and the caging ended. Hatch emerged on the ledge, still out of the sight of anyone below. The furnace opened.

Shoomp-clack-paahhh…

A wave of heat swept over the ledge, searing Hatch and causing him to fear for his lungs. He almost dropped the box as he went down in a crouch.

Oh Jesus the heat.

The furnace closed. The ledge vibrated with the grinding of hidden machinery. Then came a faint pop, a gunshot, followed by the quick burst of a pulser. High above and to his left, someone clattered along the catwalk. Hatch moved forward, risking visibility and catching a glimpse of Marty, hooting madly and racing along the catwalk with his quilt-covered bag held high in his arms. Shouts and curses erupted from below. A figure rose from the floor and took off across the open area in pursuit of Marty—it was one of Blue's men, the kid who had mentioned Piano Man—two more shots cracked and the kid fell gasping on the floor. Had Marty had also been hit? Hatch closed his eyes and shrank back out of sight.

The kid cried out for help. More shouting, this time from just below him. Hatch crouched.

Shoomp-clack-paahhh...

The cycle started again and drowned out what may have been another gunshot. Hatch crept forward and peered over the open area. In the shadows, thirty or forty feet away, he spotted another of Blue's men, the one who had met them at the door the day they visited. Camo. Camo was right below him, waving a gun, his back to Hatch.

Hatch drew a deep breath.

The F-Ledge was at least twelve feet across, much wider than Hatch had expected. With every cycle, the furnace beside the ledge opened to reveal a sea of flame worthy of Dante. Hatch rose in his crouch, anticipating the cycle and wondering whether he could survive standing next to the furnace when it opened.

Shoomp-clack-paahhh...

The heat burst forth and spread and dissipated. Hatch crept along the ledge, exposed now. At the far end of the ledge, some forty yards beyond the furnace, he spotted Hop waiting with a couple of Ferret's goons and gesturing for him to come on. On the floor of the open area below, the kid lay unmoving in a pool of blood. The air was almost too hot to breathe. Hatch poured sweat. His heart made drum rolls.

Another shout sounded from below and Camo, still turned away from Hatch, raised a gun. Hatch broke into a run, unable to hear his own footsteps. More shouts—he was too damned slow in the heavy jacket—gunshots—Hatch ducked—*move move move you silly ass*—he risked a quick glance down from the ledge and saw Camo, face down and unmoving on the floor. The furnace began to grind. A third man in a leather jacket leapt into the open area and two-fisted a gun directly at Hatch.

"My name is Thomas Dartham," he yelled. He had Hatch dead in his sights. "Put down that box, son, or I will shoot you. Please do not test me. I will do it."

The furnace roared. The ledge shook like it was fighting to hold back the monsters of the abyss. Choices and choices. None remained. No time to keep turning it over in his mind. A verdict was called for and Hatch would now provide it and probably die in the process. He needed another ten or fifteen seconds.

"Put it down, Doran."

The box seemed to have come alive in his hands, and its etched symbols slithered and gleamed with light.

"Who are you?" Hatch shouted.

"Put. It. Down."

Hatch moved to the edge of the furnace, extended his arms, and held the box over the closed pit. He thought of his dad. He may have prayed.

Dartham ran forward, his pistol still raised. "Listen to me, Doran. You are way too smart to drop that box. Do not even think about it."

Shoomp-clack-paahhh...

The furnace opened. Dartham moved toward the ledge. Hatch was slammed by a wave of heat so intense he thought his eyeballs were melting. Flames roared like the sick hiss of a pit of rattlers and drowned out Dartham's shouts. Gunshots cracked and something brushed Hatch's back.

Hatch heaved the box into the furnace, watching it arc through the air and glimmer as it dove into the flames and vanished.

Another gunshot and Hatch flattened himself on the ledge. Dartham shouted, and Hatch expected a hail of bullets to crease him or put his lights out in an instant; he expected to die, having forgotten that Dartham had no angle on him now. He inched away from the incinerator's heat and peered over the edge. More gunshots, just audible, and the front of Dartham's jacket exploded open. Dartham went down and didn't move for a second. Then he rolled over and squeezed off two quick return shots into the darkness above and behind him.

Hatch scuttled across the ledge, got to his feet, and took off running. He covered the remaining thirty or forty yards to the receiving area where Hop had been waiting. It was empty now, save for a few maintenance vehicles; Hop and his people were nowhere to be seen. Through an open door, Hatch heard a truck rumble away. He zig-zagged around the vehicles and raced into the outside lot. The wind off the Hudson struck him like an arctic blast. He turned and ran through the incinerator's gated entrance, praying Marty was safe, and then raced further still, north along the old River Terrace to an open area near the incinerator. There he stopped, his chest heaving, and ditched the jacket. When he took it off, he discovered two long rips along the upper back.

Bullets.

The son of a bitch Dartham had shot him.

Hatch's drenched shirt clung to him—he was covered with blood!—no, no, it was only sweat. He ran his hands all over himself to make sure. He was not hit, but the world had tilted in shifting shadows and darkness, and Hatch staggered, hopped up with adrenaline and braced by the cold air. He began to run again, scarcely aware of his footsteps clapping on the concrete. To the south, from in front of the incinerator, an engine started to life. Headlights stabbed the darkness, and a car spun its wheels in a screech and shot toward him.

Hatch cursed.

Was it Blue? Somebody from the Group?

He ran on and passed a truck parked next to a pile of crates. He leapt over a bundle of trash and stomped through several bulging garbage bags. The car swerved around the corner behind him. He darted into the street, headlights sweeping his back and casting his own shadow far ahead of him; he ran further still, hoping to reach the corner with enough time to hide or find some way to shake them. The car squealed to a halt. Shouts. Cries to stop. Footsteps. Two figures silhouetted in the headlight beams were gaining on him, and then one of his pursuers grabbed his arm while the other spun him around and forced him against the rough facing of the corner building.

"Wait a second, Haze," said one of the men. "This ain't Dartham." He had a pointed nose and dead little lizard eyes that scanned Hatch from head to toe.

"He's that punk came in and met with Blue," said Haze. "You remember, Lewie, about two weeks ago." Haze was tall and powerfully built, with a long, horse-like face. He shoved Hatch. "Where is it? Who'd you give it to?"

Hatch didn't answer, and his silence earned him a punch in the midsection. He doubled over, unable to breathe. Good God. His switchblade. He remembered he didn't have it. Haze punched him again and threw him to the ground.

"Ease up for a second," said Lewie. "Let's make sure he don't have it himself before you finish him off. Blue'll have our hides if we shoot his artifact."

"Dartham's the one we're after," said Haze.

Lewie searched Hatch. "He don't have it," he said.

"We got to go find Dartham," said Haze.

Hatch pushed himself onto his hands and knees, now aware of what was coming. He was dizzy and his heart swelled with unexpected fury.

"Stand back," said Haze, producing a pulser from his belt. Its metallic barrel glinted in the headlights and its end glowed burnt orange. He leveled it at Hatch who, in his rage, did not see Crick Cochoran materialize from the darkness. But he saw the blur of a metal bar as Crick swung it downward on Haze's wrist, and he heard the soft, snicking sound of pulped bone. The pulser went flying. Haze screamed. Hatch scrambled into a sitting position and tried to breathe. Crick put his six-and-a-half feet and three hundred pounds into a mighty roundhouse swing of his bar that caved in Haze's skull and sent him flying.

Lewie, his mouth agape, turned and ran—right into Big Ray, who wrapped him in his arms and body-slammed him to the pavement. Lewie groaned and tried to pick himself up, but Big Ray kicked him over told him to stay put.

Hatch got to his feet but couldn't stand straight.

"You all right?" asked Big Ray.

Hatch nodded. Still damp with sweat, he began to shiver. Crick, a toothpick dangling from his lips, stood over what remained of Haze. He idly nudged Haze's flattened head back and forth with the toe of his boot, keeping his foot out of the black blood spreading on the pavement.

"Where's Marty?" asked Big Ray.

"He left," said Hatch, still recovering his breath. "Tried to draw them off me."

Big Ray looked around, his hands on his hips.

"I assumed they were from the Group," said Hatch, still trying to breathe. "They're just a couple of Judson Blue's flunkies."

"Which means we don't need to hang around," said Big Ray.

"Listen, Ray," said Hatch. "Thank you, man. I mean it."

"Thank you doesn't begin to do it," said Big Ray.

At that moment, the man called Lewie tried to run, but Big Ray seized him by the arm and reeled him in. Then he administered a hard, leather-gloved right hook that left the man sitting dazed on the ground. "I told you to stay there," he said.

Crick Cochoran was losing interest in playing with Haze. He spun the bar in his hands and spat the toothpick onto the street. Then he approached Lewie, stepped into another swing of his bar, and almost knocked the man's head from his shoulders. Blood sprayed the adjacent building wall.

Big Ray and Hatch grimaced and looked away.

Crick delivered a few additional blows for fun. When he had finished, he gave both of the mangled, misshapen heads several pokes with the bar.

"Crick's truck is around the corner," said Big Ray. "You ran right past us."

Crick Cochoran walked over, put his hand on Hatch's shoulder, and peered into his face with a look of tender concern. "You all right, little bruh?"

Hatch nodded. "Yeah. Thanks, Crick." He hoped his voice didn't sound shaky.

Crick flashed a broad smile full of gold teeth. "Let's scare up some chow," he said, swatting Big Ray on the back. "I'm fucking starved."

CHAPTER 25

A FEW DAYS LATER, BIG RAY LEANED BACK IN HIS CHAIR AND rested his feet on Hatch's desk. "Like I said before, Marty called us from Central Park—this was before you got there. I was with Crick, and we were on the way to the Met to pick up that sculpture I told you about."

Hatch folded a note he had written and began searching for an envelope, shuffling through the papers, books, clocks, pens, ancient thumb drives, and sundry other items cluttering his desk.

"Marty ordered us over to the park," said Big Ray. "Told us to lay back and keep a sharp eye out. After you two left in the Electricorp van, we followed, keeping as far back as I dared."

"So you said."

"You think it was easy?"

"I know, I know, you lost us twice in the traffic," said Hatch. He sealed the envelope and stuck it in his desk. "Upper left hand drawer, Ray. When the time comes."

Big Ray lowered his feet and rested his elbows on the desk. "The time isn't coming, Hatch." They stared at each other for a moment. Big Ray looked away.

"It's just a note, telling you how to handle a few things when I'm gone," said Hatch.

"Which, God willing, will be in about forty or fifty years."

Hatch's chair squeaked. Big Ray winced. "I left you the apartment," said Hatch. "And everything in it."

"Nothing for Crick?"

Hatch cracked a smile.

"So, anyway, we followed you to Ghost's place—did I tell you this part?" asked Big Ray.

"Several times."

Big Ray put his feet back on the desk. "We sat there for what, two hours? Crick isn't exactly your passive sort of guy. It was a pretty manly accomplishment to keep him from storming the place. Then, lo and behold, the van exiting the building was different from the one that carried you in. A quandary: follow or don't follow? Then I almost lost you again downtown."

A patch of clear sky showed through the window above Big Ray's desk. "Ghost knew somebody was following us," said Hatch. "He thought it was the Blue."

"Look," said Big Ray, "this last will and testament stuff gets to me. Contrary to the many thousands of things I may have said in the past, I don't like seeing you give in this way. It shakes my assumptions about the world."

"I'm a realist."

"Since when? Three days now, and we've seen no sign of Ferret."

"We will," said Hatch. "Or I will. Trust me."

"Then go to ground. Get your butt up to Havensville, hide out on your grandmom's farm. You still have it."

"I screwed the man over, Ray. It may not look too smooth in retrospect, but I couldn't let the Group have the artifact. I told Marty as much before we went into the incinerator. But one more second and that guy Dartham would have finished me off and climbed the ledge. Maybe Ghost would've stopped him, maybe not."

"Too many maybes," said Big Ray. He drummed his hand on his thigh and then stood and began straightening a few items on his own desk. He cast a sideways glance at Hatch. "Did you talk to Samantha?"

"No."

"Five Urbans."

"I heard."

"How did she net a mandate for five Urbans? And coaxing that Bickerman guy to pay six million. It comes to a million bucks in commission for dear Odysseus."

Hatch was quiet for a moment. "She is a devotee of the Lama," he said. "Lama Ravi Pearl. He's all about how belief shapes reality, or something like that."

"Then I'm interested in reading him," said Big Ray, and catching Hatch's glance, he added, "out of curiosity." He paused. "By the way, Jocelyn's putting together a celebration tomorrow night at Vinnie's."

"You think I'm unhappy about the Urbans because of what happened with Sam?"

"Did I say that?"

"I'm not," said Hatch. "It's a terrific score. It's true, we were cooked, but once we were finally broke, I quit worrying about it so much."

"And you don't have to now, either. Not for a while, anyway."

"If we're having a celebration, there's someone I'd like to invite. You remember meeting Caroline Atherton last year?"

"Let Jocelyn know."

Hatch nodded. Big Ray folded his arms and leaned against his desk. They remained in silence for some time, gazing into their separate corners. "You heard anything from Marty?" Hatch finally asked.

"You know how he gets." Big Ray picked up a small beanbag ball and began tossing it up and down. "Said he needed a few days."

"He's pissed off at me. Again."

"All that time he spent hiding behind the incinerator—an odorous task, as he mentioned several times—and he never saw you come out."

"That's not it," said Hatch. "He disagreed with my decision."

"He'll come around."

"That may take months," Hatch looked at Big Ray.

Bog Ray caught the beanbag. "Stop pretending you're going somewhere."

Hatch took the drawer key and tossed it to Big Ray. "Left hand drawer, Ray. On top."

***

BIG RAY LEFT FOR THE EVENING, AND HATCH HEADED TO Smyte's for an early dinner. A sweet breeze rustled the tree limbs as he strolled along, and he took in the play of soft light and the low, indistinct conversation of those he passed. He perceived everything afresh, as if he had never walked this street before, and he savored the expansion and contraction of his own clear breathing and the rush of blood through his veins. How fragile, how ephemeral it all seemed, life appearing and vanishing like a spark leaping from a bonfire into the night.

Hatch meant to live as long as possible, but he knew what he had unloosed. Ferret, in particular, had a true grievance, one which would require settlement. And yet, as he continued past Ms. Rochambeau's house, he felt strangely recollected inside. A few doors further, he passed a mother sitting on her stoop and joggling a toddler on her knee. Two other children chased each other, squealing happily in the cool of late afternoon. Hatch nodded at those he met and continued on until he reached Smyte's. And there he almost walked into Hop, who was leaning against the fender of one of Ferret's black SUVs.

Hop opened the rear door. Hatch did not resist. He climbed in and sat alone in the back. As before, on the night when he had first met Ferret, Hop took the front passenger seat. The driver locked the doors, circled the block, and the familiar neighborhood slid by and was gone. They crept through the traffic and over the rotted pavement, finally reaching the West Side Highway; driving faster now, they headed south toward the tip of Manhattan, the skyscrapers standing at shabby attention as they passed. They entered the tunnel beneath Battery Park and emerged into the traffic inching north on the FDR Drive. The upper half of the sun lay huge and fading on the horizon, and the traffic had begun to glimmer on the distant bridges.

They left the highway and entered the downtown canyons, and Hatch watched the people walking along the sidewalks or pedaling bicycles on the street or darting past in death carts. He saw faces of delight and despair and even puzzlement, alight with the last gleam of the day. How bedraggled and grubby it was, but he loved all of it, even in its dirtiness and even in its pain; he loved all of it for the indomitable life shining from it.

They meandered through the narrow streets and Hatch made peace with himself. He had acted as he thought he should act, and he knew the world owed him no reprieve, owed him nothing at all. The world spun in silence, and it rarely listened or took questions. The world had given him a body and a brain and a place to be, a place at once so frightful and so beautiful that heartbreak was its only possible end, for what heart could hold the love or the grace or the horror? Whatever he had made of his journey in the world was on him, for the world had incurred no obligation; but what might he owe the world? Mae used to tell him to find the song he had brought and sing it, and maybe finding his song and belting it out with all the joy and anger and indignation and gratitude inside him was the only way to repay the world in full. It was something to consider, if he ever had another chance to do so.

They reached the center of downtown, not far from Wall Street. The driver slowed as they approached a boarded-up restaurant.

"That door right there, under the green sign," said Hop.

They stopped. For Hatch, everything had begun to move in slow motion, and on the sidewalk Hop took him by his arm and steered him toward the restaurant. The driver came around and raised the metal roll door covering the entrance, making a loud, metallic clatter. Hatch and Hop stepped inside. The roll door slammed shut behind them as Hop escorted him down a dark hallway and into a closed-up dining room which had seen neither food nor drink in ages. Hop's grip tightened. A row of tall booths stood against one wall and Ferret sat alone in one of them.

"Here he is, boss," said Hop, and Hatch noticed the fatigue in Hop's voice and how worn his face appeared.

Ferret glanced at Hop and nodded, once. An ancient ceiling fan squeaked overhead. Hop shoved Hatch in Ferret's direction and left the room. Ferret dumped a contraband cigarette out of a box and cracked his lighter. Hatch eased into the opposite seat. Ferret squinted at him through a cloud of smoke, and then exhaled a plume which drifted upward and disappeared at the touch of the fan.

"I hired you to deliver to me the artifact," said Ferret. "Ghost brought you to fulfill your assignment. Are we agreed on those facts?"

Hatch nodded.

"And you stood in view of my man and you threw it into the flames."

"Yes."

Ferret looked at the cigarette he was holding between his fingers. The thin, blue-gray ribbon of smoke wove its way upward. The dining room, done in old plank and hardwood, was stained in black and dusty with neglect. A thick spiderweb stretched over the corner above the booth.

"I couldn't allow the Group to have it," said Hatch.

"And you make these decisions now?"

"I knew that much."

"We plunder the treasures of the world and we sell them to the Group, Hatch Doran, for they are convinced that in every ancient scroll or plate they might add to their occult knowledge. What we do is execrable and indefensible, except that we seek to make the Group fund their own destruction, just as they have engorged themselves on the blood of the people." Ferret stopped. He seemed unwilling to follow tangents. "Do you know what the Group is doing now, while we sit here?" he asked.

Hatch didn't answer.

"No, of course you do not know. The downtown incinerator is closed. The Group, using their substantial control of the Municipal Service Corporation and the Police Corporation, will assure it remains closed while they sift through the many tons of ash and charcoal."

"So? What can survive that heat?"

"Nothing—certainly not the corpses that the Homeland Labor Corporation feeds into the furnaces day and night—nothing except, of course, the goddess artifact." The fan squeaked. Ferret smoked. "You see, Hatch Doran, the artifact cannot be destroyed—at least, so your father and I came to believe."

Hatch closed his eyes.

"The box you tossed away contains what your father somewhat facetiously named Adrestia. Within the artifact itself resides a spherical crystal of unknowable provenance—or so said the ancient writings, for no one in our time has ever opened it and perhaps no one can." Ferret flicked ash. "I was once a physicist," he continued, "and I was, to my eternal discredit, instrumental in unraveling the mystery behind the horrid Azazel. When I had done so, I urged Azazel be returned to its vault and locked away for all time."

"You didn't think Group could handle Azazel."

"No one *handles* Azazel. The device is a portal to another realm, one occupied by a profound and yet subtle evil of extraordinary intelligence. Azazel exerts an instant influence over those it chooses to touch. You or I might experience nothing in its presence, but others with different ambitions and inclinations might be swept away by the dark possibilities it offers. Azazel has infected the Group with dreams of inconceivable power, dangling before their eyes visions of a world they might control to the last degree, a world harvested for their benefit and ultimately scrapped of all but themselves and those they need to support them. Of course, they cannot see that Azazel, left to its own, will eventually lay waste to the planet, as our freezing, trembling earth testifies."

Hatch swallowed. His throat felt crusty and dry.

"So we shall not excuse the Group as good people under malign influence," said Ferret. "Azazel takes nothing that is not given it, and the Group, lost in delusion and fearful that it might fail in its predations, eagerly partners with its otherworldly master. I tell you these things so that you might grasp the enormity of what you have done. For I believe our Adrestia also represents a link with another realm, and poses an existential threat to the Group's plans. Do I know this for sure? No. I cannot. But I have pondered the ancient writings, and the artifact has called to me, has touched me, and these things have left me with my convictions. Perhaps we cannot defeat Azazel on our own, but its mere existence has drawn to us the possibility of assistance."

"Adrestia." Hatch swallowed again, trying not to gag.

"The goddess of balance," said Ferret. "The artifact summoned your father as it summoned those in antiquity, and it calls us now. All this I feel in my heart." Ferret touched his chest and rested for a moment against the back of the booth. "But after half a lifetime pondering the enigmatic materials we recovered in Antarctica, I believe Adrestia will work through us only if we first *choose* to save ourselves."

Hatch tried to calm his roiling stomach. "Why didn't you tell me about my dad?" he asked.

"I did not think it was the proper time. Andrei Kutznov disagreed."

"I deserved to know."

"Your behavior suggests otherwise. You acted foolishly and accomplished the very thing we sought to prevent." Ferret took a deep draw on his cigarette and its end glowed brightly. "Each of us, in our own way, is dedicated to bringing the Group to its knees. We do not fear for ourselves, neither do we aspire to the Group's power. But we have seen the evil of a world held hostage, and we know something of what is intended."

"Tell me," said Hatch. "Please."

Ferret dismissed the request with a flick of his hand. A miniature smoke ring hovered in the air and gradually disintegrated. "I chose you because I believed you had it in your heart to resist, and because—as I told Ghost—I hoped you might, over time, help further this cause your father died for. He is in many ways the founder of our effort."

"You're saying Ghost is—"

"He is part of our organization, yes."

"But you *paid* him for the artifact."

Ferret's face was as hard as the wind side of a granite mountain. "Twenty million international dollars, to be exact."

Hatch was stunned. "International dollars?"

Ferret flicked ash on the floor.

"That translates into…160 million redbacks," said Hatch.

Ferret sighed and looked away into a dusty corner of the restaurant. "It is a complicated affair," he said. "Ghost provided cybersecurity for Project Caterpillar, and his skills have served us well in the years since. The Group murdered his friends—including a woman he loved—and now, though he dismisses vengeance as a motive, he cares only about destroying the Group in turn. That and making money. Little else exists for him in life." Ferret paused, his face tight, his eyes pale and hard. "So I bought the artifact from Ghost, and he now is happy with his bulging pockets."

Hatch heard footsteps and a door close in the hallway outside the dining room. "You're going to kill me," he said.

Ferret squinted at him through the smoke. Hatch held his gaze.

"If the Group recovers the artifact—and I assure you, Hatch Doran, I will know if they do so—then I will have to take it back from them," said Ferret, speaking quietly. "Such an undertaking would be dangerous and very costly for those involved, perhaps in an ultimate sense." He looked intently at Hatch, his eyes bordered by deep creases. "Do you understand the gravity of what I am saying?"

"Yes."

"If the time comes, I will require you to assist in this endeavor."

Hatch closed his eyes and nodded.

"You have committed a grievous wrong," said Ferret. "Such things must carry their price. Yet you are Montgomery Doran's son, and he was my friend. His life was noble and so may yours be. I cannot know." Ferret stubbed out his cigarette on the table and flicked it away into the gloom. "I am growing old, you see, and I trust very little now that is not of the heart. All I truly know anymore is I know almost nothing at all."

CHAPTER 26

JAMAEL HIGHTOWER, ALSO KNOWN AS THE TOWER, SAT alone at a linen-covered table in Azure's dining room. Five or six of the Blue stood talking in low tones at the kitchen entrance nearby, but not one dared to sit because the Tower was cracking down, restoring discipline to the Blue. Camo had been a good man, rest his soul, but he had taken a casual approach to order within the gang. "Look at the meetings," Tower had complained to Camo a couple of weeks earlier. "The guys spread all over, interrupting, thinking they got something to say instead of keeping their holes shut and doing what they supposed to do." Tower had been an army sergeant and he valued discipline. "Nothing good happens if we get all loose in here," he had said.

Camo had blown him off, had said this was the Blue, not the American Homeland Army. Tower hadn't liked it, but it was Camo's call. Now, after Camo had eaten a couple of hot ones at the incinerator, it was Tower's call.

One of the boys walked over. "JB's on his way up," he said. The Tower nodded and straightened a few papers on the table. The boy returned to the wall and stood, just like Tower wanted.

The real problem, Tower thought, was that Judson Blue was showing a few cracks in his own foundation. JB needed to pull out of the dive. Camo's death had body-checked the man, no question, and losing the kid, Seth, had put a shade over everybody. Then they had Lewie the Nail and Haze, mauled to death a few blocks from the incinerator, their faces flat turned into pizza by nobody knew who. Lindi, Blue's woman, had taken the whole thing poorly, moping around, snapping at everybody. But the sad fact was, people took the hit now and then. Sometimes some brothers and sisters went down.

But it was Dartham, Terrence Bronsun's old hump, who worried Tower. Rumor was, the man had survived whatever went down in the incinerator, and Tower didn't see anything good in the news. Dartham had come into this room a week or so earlier and had told Blue who he was and what he wanted, and Blue had tried to play him. Dartham didn't strike Tower as one of those country club colonels who'd let it ride, and every time the front door creaked open he expected to see Dartham walking in and looking to settle up. Which led to another issue: JB had gotten loose, too, running around without bodyguards, not staying inside. It was another problem the Tower intended to fix. Add it to the list. The nub of it was, Tower considered himself better able to manage the Blue than Judson Blue himself, and several times every day he found himself mulling it over.

"It's Blue," called out one of the boys. The Tower stood.

"Tower, where are we on the Moroccan shipment?" asked Judson Blue, striding into the room.

"Due in late in the day tomorrow. We'll have people to meet the boat, and it'll go straight to Upper East soon as we have it."

Blue nodded. "Let's hope Bronsun appreciates it."

The Tower said he was sure the man would enjoy his goods.

"I have another matter," said Judson Blue. "Let's go outside, get some air."

The Tower stepped closer to Blue. "I'd feel better we talk here, JB, maybe go downstairs."

"Don't be such an old woman," said Blue.

An old woman? All right, then, it was JB's call. The Tower followed him through the front entrance and onto the sidewalk under the canopy. It was about ten o'clock at night, and Tower glanced toward the corner and noticed the man he had put there was gone. Tower couldn't imagine what would make somebody who'd been ordered to stay in a place just up and leave. It pissed him off, but this was still the Blue's neighborhood and the street was quiet.

"Listen, I've been thinking, Tower," said Judson Blue, "This asshat Doran, I want him gone."

"Word is, he's protected, JB. Ghost or somebody got his back."

"He's not protected if I decide he isn't."

"I don't figure him for the one who took out Camo and Seth or even—"

"We lost four men in that shit parade," said Judson Blue. "Maybe Doran did it and maybe not, but we will not stand down. We take him out, spread the word, and people'll think twice about dealing in our house without permission."

Tower shrugged. He appreciated Blue's point, but if was him, he'd let the whole mess go. It was stupid to pick a fight with the global boys. Better to move on to the next job.

Judson Blue walked to the end of the canopy and balanced on the curb. He seemed to be thinking about something. The Tower checked the opposite corner and found nobody there, either. Both his men probably off in some pussy den, leaving the street open. He shook his head. He would have a word with those men, for real, and after that they'd beg to stand on their corners the rest of their lives. The Tower took another look around and then moved over next to Judson Blue.

"Something Camo told me," said Blue. "We have some open business with Tony Pachetti. I say we get rid of Doran and trade a few blows with Pachetti. It'll give everybody a lift."

"We deliver Bronsun's goods tomorrow, those scrolls from Africa or wherever, then spread some coin to everybody, that'll give the lift."

Judson Blue opened his mouth to reply, but as he leaned forward and began to turn toward Tower, his head exploded and everything above his eyebrows vanished in a spray of pink and gray mist. Glass shattered. Something sandblasted the side of Tower's face. A long section of Blue's skull shot straight up, hit the canopy, and fell back into his open brainpan. Blue collapsed like a marionette whose strings had been cut.

Shit—Tower tried to move—*ohshit*—he dove behind the concrete planter next to the door—he hadn't even heard the shot, but whoever did it was about to take him out too, finish him off, this is it now—*shitohshit*—he fumbled for his gun and then he heard someone yell from across the street, a man hanging out of a second floor window of the old hotel across from Azure.

"Let's see the gun, lad," cried the man in the window. "Pull the clip and scatter the bullets. Do it now and maybe you'll live to tell what you've seen tonight."

Tower hesitated, but only for a second. Even at night, the lights from the street and windows showed Tower that the shooter had a wild thatch of gray hair, a face as mean as hell's doormat, and a rifle dead-aimed at him. The man looked vaguely familiar. Then Tower remembered: it was the old bird who'd come in with Doran to see Blue.

Glass littered the area under the canopy. Azure's front door began to open, but Tower waved the gang back inside, away from this goddamned kill box. He raised his hand toward the shooter. He knew the planter wasn't big enough and if the guy could shoot, he was toast. Tower didn't like bad bets, and Blue was gone, anyway. Tower pulled the clip from his gun, fed out the bullets, and flung them down the sidewalk along with the empty clip. He realized the side of his face and his shoulder were spattered with Judson Blue's blood and brain matter and bone shards. In a daze, he tossed his gun aside.

"Now be a good man and go inside and tell everyone this was for Peter Adagio," shouted the man in the window. He looked hateful and he gestured with his rifle. "D'you understand, now? Peter Adagio!"

CHAPTER 27

WHEN HATCH OPENED THE DOOR TO VINNIE'S PUB, THE music and general hubbub hit him like a breaking wave. Jocelyn waved and danced over to greet him. "Come on, have a drink, boss man. Relax for a change."

"I am relaxed," said Hatch.

"So, we're not going under," said Jocelyn, "thanks to—anyway, who cares about the reason, right?"

Nathan shoved his way between them, angry and looking daggers at everyone. "I'm out of this place," he said.

"Party hasn't even started," said Jocelyn. She narrowed her eyes. "Wait a minute, you're *not* going to the demonstration."

"It's the only way anything's going to change," said Nathan. "People are asleep. We're going to wake them up." His expression hardened. "One way or another."

Jocelyn turned to Hatch. "More riots," she said.

"The March of the Eyes," said Nathan, working his jaw. "If we don't expose the secret government"—he stopped and blinked at Jocelyn—"you could stand to be more supportive, you know."

"Stow the craziness, metal head. Without me to keep you straight, you'd be bus fodder already, a smear on the pavement, the way you walk around in those goggles."

Nathan blinked again and then stormed away.

"He like unironically believes that garbage," Jocelyn said, watching him leave. "He's gotten belligerent lately, Hatch, which is not like him. Makes me wonder about those games... anyway, in case you didn't know, Samantha's got the tab tonight."

"She really came through for us," said Hatch.

"But did you hear? She was like attacked this morning— p'outs or something, who knows—not two blocks from the apartment."

"No, I didn't know. Is she—"

"*She's* not hurt," said Jocelyn. "She like dislocated the guy's knee. Did you know she has had martial arts training? A stopper saw the whole thing. And oh my God, the victim—can you believe I'm calling a robber a victim?—he like couldn't move after she kicked his leg or his hip or whatever." Jocelyn paused and switched tracks again. "I'm sorry about your project, Hatch, whatever it was. I wish it had worked out."

"It worked out, Joss. I'm here."

She tugged his arm and smiled. "Shall we dance? You won't be so edgy after I give you a spin."

"Maybe later. I'll be back around."

"No, you won't. I know you, Hatch." She blew him a kiss and returned to the other dancers.

A hand fell on Hatch's shoulder. It was Vinnie. "I want to tell you about that girl with all the dark hair, the one who was just here," he said. "Jocelyn, she calls herself."

"You better bring your A-game with her," said Hatch.

"I know the other one, the tall one, looks like some kind of model."

"Samantha."

"She kind of reminds me of cat woman," said Vinnie over the music. Samantha, wearing a tight, black leather outfit, was holding a colorful cocktail and talking with Jocelyn. "She comes in here about five o'clock, this Samantha, and tells me what it's going to be," he continued. "Plates of food, drinks for all you people, yah-de-yah. Then a few minutes later, that one"—he jabbed a beefy finger toward Jocelyn—"shows up and starts in with me on the tab. I haven't put out one glass, but there she is in my face, asking me the cost per drink and can't she get a discount for the group and doesn't it mean anything to be regulars. This girl I haven't seen one time in my life. But you're good people, so I think about it and give her a number. She says it's too high."

Hatch watched Samantha throw back her head and laugh. "Jocelyn keeps the trains running, Vin."

"Stretches every redback until it screeches," said Vinnie. "I get it. I tip my hat."

"Have one on us," said Hatch. "The cat woman is paying tonight."

"You think it's a little stuffy in here, Hatch? I got to turn on more air."

Vinnie disappeared. Delia brought Hatch a seltzer and he thanked her. Madam Fray's soft voice pulsed through the crowd.

> *The famished gleam in the tiger's eye*
> *Purple roaring ancient skies*
> *Through eyes as old as time I see …*

Hatch elbowed through the crowd, many of whom seemed to have no connection to Odysseus. He bumped into Marty, and a stilted moment followed. Hatch set his drink on a table and Marty's mouth twitched into a smile. They embraced, slapping each other on the back, and when they moved apart, Hatch noticed the tear in Marty's eye.

"Look at me," said Marty. "Weepy as a lost pup."

"Not at all."

"Raymond posted me on your chat with Ferret. We knew it had to be faced, but I had a feeling you'd pull through it."

"There's more to come."

Marty nodded and grew serious. "I've had some time to reflect on the matter, Hatch. I can't say I fully understand what you did at the incinerator, but you were decisive and you listened to your heart. It couldn't've been easy."

"I didn't see any choice, Marty. I still don't. I've gone over it a thousand times."

The music pulsed and Madam Fray sang:

> *The sweet lamb sleeps*
> *Beneath the stars*
> *I hear the wisdom of the world*
> *Sung in Creation's harmony*

"Don't wallow in it, lad," said Marty. "Put it in your rearview."

Hatch ushered Marty into a corner away from the noise. "Listen Marty, I don't remember if I properly offered my condolences regarding Peter Adagio. I feel partly responsible, and I'm sorry. He was a friend of yours."

"It was none of your doing. And it's true, he was a friend. The words are much appreciated, Hatch."

"And his wife?"

"I visited her just this morning. She's bearing up. And Peter himself, I'm sure, is resting easy now."

"I heard Judson Blue was killed last night," said Hatch. "Ray said the cops wouldn't even go to the scene, that Blue's people had to bring in his body."

Marty rattled his drink. "Well, it is the Blue's neighborhood, as we know."

"Karma, I suppose."

Marty's eyebrows rose. "Actually, it was a rifle bullet, a hollow point boat tail"—he smothered a cough—"that is, so I hear. At any rate, Blue's demise is the city's gain."

Caroline Atherton appeared and took Marty by the arm. "Oh, Hatch, how wonderful to see you." She kissed his cheek. "Thank you for asking me to your party."

Compliments and laughter all around, and Hatch said, "I'm glad you came, Caroline. You know Marty?"

"We met a short while ago," said Caroline, beaming. "He claims to be quite the dancer."

Marty bowed. "I was once known to shuffle around a bit, though it was long ago."

"You still owe me a drink," said Caroline. She gave Hatch a playful poke, then tugged at Marty's sleeve and pulled him into the crowd. Hatch retrieved his seltzer and drifted over to the bar. The pub had filled, and the inevitable marijuana cloud had formed along the ceiling. Above the bar hung a lifeboat floater ring made from cast iron—a running joke of Vinnie's—and as Hatch contemplated it, Vinnie slipped past like a dancing rhino. "Coming through," he cried, carrying a pitcher of beer toward a table occupied by Knife Cochoran, Big Ray, and two women Hatch did not recognize. Across the pub, Samantha was in deep conversation with Crick Cochoran and another woman. Crick held a smoking joint, his eyes half closed, a smile of happiness spread on his lips.

Hatch looked away, glancing at the pub's rough brick walls and honey-varnished wood. The sight of Samantha, her face aglow, her movements so unconsciously graceful, tugged at something inside him. He looked again, and she was watching him, flashing him a sweet smile. A moment later she joined him at the bar.

"Can't we have a breath of air?" she asked. "It grows so warm once they all light up."

"I heard you took out a mugger," said Hatch. "Glad you weren't hurt."

Samantha looked perplexed. "A troubling intrusion, but I am at a loss to say what it means." They stepped outside and stood a few steps from the door. A couple walked by holding hands, and Samantha chewed on her lip and watched them pass. "Look, Doran, I've been thinking quite a lot, so I'll just blurt it out. I don't think we should be in such a hurry to be apart."

"Really."

She took him by the arm and turned to face him. "You know, you aren't so bad," she said. "I never thought so."

"I could've been better for you, Sam."

"To be candid, I am a bit confused right now, and confusion can attract all sorts of chaos into one's life, don't you agree?" Her brown eyes had grown large and expectant. "You and I had some times, didn't we? I could do with what we had, Doran. What do you say? Let's give it another go."

"No."

"What?"

"No, Sam."

"But I expected you'd be happy!"

Hatch shook his head. "What you want doesn't exist."

Samantha crossed her arms and sighed. "I *am* sort of between worlds at the moment."

"I don't think I am."

"No, you're not, Doran. There is something awfully peaceful about you now. It's just what I need." She searched his face. "It's pure magnetism between us. Hasn't it always been?"

"Yes," said Hatch. "It has."

"You can't deny it. And you can't disapprove of me for wanting a better world."

"But aren't you wiser for being in this one?"

Samantha huffed. "You aren't trying to rub my face in it, are you?"

"Never."

"You can be rather grim, love," she said. "But you need me, you know. I keep you from drowning in it all."

"Come back to earth, Sam, if you want to. See things as they are."

"Don't be ridiculous." She blew a strand of hair off of her forehead. "I refuse to let all this mess touch me. I never consented to any of it. Anyway, as for the Urbans, you are welcome. I've kept us afloat. Again."

"Thank you," said Hatch. "And Ms. Franklin is happy?"

"The client is pleased." Samantha smiled.

"And Kee Bickerman, of all people."

Samantha's expression lightened further. "He wants me to attend his gala, the Third Bickerman."

"You'll be hobnobbing with the movers and shakers. The *owners*. That's terrific, Sam."

"It is?" Her face fell for a moment and then brightened again, and she gave him a sly look. "Yes, I suppose it is. As for you, gorgeous, you'll change your mind about us. I've only to wait awhile. Until then, I'll see you 'round the office." She gave him a knowing smile and went back into the pub.

When she opened the door, the uneven clamor of laughter and conversation and the thrum of music swept over him. Then the door closed and tranquility returned. A bracing wind circled through the street and cooled his face and hands. He remained outside, leaning in the doorway while people passed on the sidewalk. In the thin frame of sky visible from the narrow street, a few dim stars winked in the night. Hatch closed his eyes and breathed the precious air.

***

CAROLINE SMILED AND LAID HER HAND OVER HATCH'S. "Nevermind my chatter. You are distracted. I'm boring you to death, I'm afraid."

"Not possible in this life, Caroline," said Hatch, meaning it. They had been conversing at the bar, and Caroline's upbeat spirits had given Hatch a lift. "I'm happy to see you."

She withdrew her hand and gave him a pleased look. "Marty has danced me off my feet," she said, "and I haven't even asked about your little soiree with...our friend."

Hatch said something about all being well that ended well. The smoke was getting to him, however, and when Caroline, after another pleasant half hour, left to rejoin Marty, Hatch signaled to Big Ray. Outside, they waited for a hoo.

"Clouds coming in," said Big Ray.

Hatch looked up. "I see a few flakes."

"And the middle of June, too." Big Ray shook his head. The hoo arrived and they directed it to the apartment. The hoo informed them that Policecorp had issued a civil disturbance warning.

"Another Eye Brigade riot," said Big Ray, as they began to roll.

"I worry about Nathan," said Hatch.

"People going to do what they're going to do, partner." They wound through the maze of downtown streets. "So we're all getting our pockets filled. Any plans?"

"Couple of cans of paint. I'm thinking antique white. You?"

"A case of cabernet, maybe. Speaking of, when we were reorganizing the storeroom last week, I found an old bottle of port you probably didn't know you had. Graham's, I believe."

"I wonder if they're still around."

"This bottle's still around, though it'd be a waste to drink it with a lightweight like you."

The hoo veered north, past a graffiti-covered expanse of gutted shops, sex parlors, low-end gambling dens, and an odd restaurant or two. A motley crowd shivered on the sidewalks and spilled into the street. A pair of armored Policecorp cruisers idled at one corner.

"I keep thinking of everyone back at Vinnie's, laughing and partying," said Hatch.

"You don't approve?"

Hatch shrugged. "Maybe they're right to be happy. Maybe being oblivious is the last justifiable philosophy of life, but I can't accept that." He considered again the monstrous Azazel, able to make anything, anywhere, disappear. "The old world really is gone, isn't it?" asked Hatch, taking in the ruined streetscape.

Big Ray didn't answer, and they continued on until the hoo stopped in the middle of the street. Hatch felt a soft jolt. "A tremor," said Big Ray. "They had a big one in China yesterday. And did you read about the temple in Shanghai, disappearing in a flash of light? *Boom*"—Big Ray pantomimed an explosion—"and it was gone. No debris, not a scrap of anything. Nathan said they've scrubbed the internet, but you can still find the odd video of it."

Hatch paid off the cab.

"This freaky stuff gets to me," Big Ray continued. "Buildings disappearing in a flash of light. That convoy of trucks in Germany last year, same thing—a bright light and then gone. Whenever it happens, you get earthquakes and weather, and then a week goes by and you never hear another word. Down the memory hole like it never happened." Big Ray opened the hoo door. "If they weren't so crazy I'd join the Eye Brigade myself."

They left the cab and as they approached the apartment, a man wearing a Stetson hat stepped from the shadow to meet them. A wrap of white bandages showed beneath his flannel shirt, and his arm rested in a sling. "We were never properly introduced," he said to Hatch. "My name is Thomas Dartham. I believe we attended the same party the other evening."

"You killed Blue's people," said Hatch. "And you tried to kill me."

Dartham's face was pale and drawn. "I did not kill anybody, son, though I did attempt to wing you. I do not usually miss."

"I thought they finished you off, too."

Dartham spread one hand. "Yet I still roam the earth, seeking whom I may devour." He smiled, and deep crows-feet appeared beside his eyes. He turned to Big Ray. "You might want to keep a space between you and your partner," he said. "He is a little hot to the touch these days, if you will pardon a weak joke." Big Ray gave Hatch a questioning look. Hatch eyebrow-shrugged while Dartham gazed into the distance. "Those incinerators run so hot and are so toxic that it will be awhile before we can start sifting for your box," he continued. "You have created a headache for me, Hatch Doran, but I will find my artifact if it is there to be found. Still, I am amazed to see a small-time tiques shuffler like you playing the lead in such a momentous production."

Hatch wasn't in the mood for it. He shouldered past Dartham and went up the steps.

"I don't like unanswered questions, Doran, and I make it a point not to leave them that way." Dartham lifted his hand and a lone snowflake fell into his palm. "Another storm is coming," he said. "Now, if you'll excuse me, I have an appointment to go stare at a bottle. But I cannot escape the notion that we will be seeing each other again." Dartham touched his hat and limped stiffly away.

Once inside the apartment, Hatch retrieved his dad's chalice from his desk and Big Ray fetched a small wine glass from the kitchen cabinet. The cat, mewing at Big Ray's feet, followed them downstairs to the storeroom.

"Dartham. That was the guy from the incinerator you told me about," said Big Ray, arranging two folding chairs on either side of a plastic file container.

"He's Group," said Hatch.

"That's just wonderful." Big Ray removed the dusty bottle of port from its shelf. Hatch grabbed a crowbar, pried open a corner section of the stone floor, and withdrew an old rucksack from the compartment beneath. He loosened the leather cord and carefully removed the artifact.

Adrestia. The goddess.

Big Ray shook his head. "What you and Marty pulled off," he said. "Marty prancing right out of the incinerator with that artifact in his bag. I'm lost in admiration, when I'm not worrying myself sick about it."

Hatch was still mulling over the significance of Dartham's appearance when the artifact came to life. A greenish-gold light shimmered and shifted over its surface, and a slit appeared, stretching from end to end and then widening to reveal a round crystal nestled inside. The crystal became pure light, soft and translucent, suffusing the storeroom and causing the shelves and boxes around Hatch to fade and almost vanish. Big Ray had ceased any movement at all. The light pulsed thoughts—or words—which resonated throughout Hatch's mind:

We are observers and friends.

Hatch's surroundings had shifted and grown dreamlike. He squeezed his eyes shut, frustrated by his sudden inability to formulate his questions. "But who are you and what are you?" he managed to ask. "What is your purpose?"

Time for you grows short.

What did that mean? "Can you do something about this Azazel machine?" asked Hatch. "I need to know how all of that works and what I'm supposed to do."

That which you call Azazel is one and many;
Azazel is old as you measure time,
And roams the invisible realms seeking conquest,
Bringing destruction and death.
For Azazel fears there is not enough,
As do all who do not understand the universe.

"Not enough?" asked Hatch. "Enough what?"

Enough to eat!
Every tear
Or burst of anger
Or rush of terror
Or impulse to murder or harm
Feeds Azazel,
Who shapes worlds to nourish itself in its blindness.
Azazel is the eater and the master of your realm,
And cares not what ruin it brings.

Then, as had occurred in Ghost's hideaway, a scene of extraordinary vividness unfolded all around, and the core of

Hatch's being rang with the laments of a billion souls trapped in a feast of fear and horror. In a single instant, he glimpsed fierce battles and a thousand ships scattered on the boiling seas and mountains shaken against a black sky. He was overcome by a shared sadness, profound and almost overwhelming, and he trembled as he watched the people flee to their underground sanctuaries. He felt on his own skin the searing heat and the touch of the poisonous winds. The beating of hearts surrounded him and merged with his own, hearts hidden and mourning their lost world, hearts hidden beneath the shattered earth.

> *More than twelve thousand solar orbits ago,*
> *Azazel came to your planetary realm.*
> *We assisted humans of that time,*
> *And a remnant survived.*

The immediacy and clarity of Hatch's vision left him shaken. He felt a deep kinship with those he had seen, running for shelter as the earth around them cracked open and the air grew black and sulfurous. He marveled at their intelligence and refinement, and he wondered, too, how he could know such things. "It's what Kutznov was talking about," he said. "You cannot allow that to happen again."

> *Humanity plays Azazel's game of its own will.*
> *We will not interfere with what you have chosen,*
> *Lest you trade one master for another.*

"Then what's the point?" asked Hatch. He saw Big Ray as if through a golden fog, a statue grasping the bottle of port. "Are we just the ham in some cosmic sandwich? Is earth a giant chicken coop? An ant farm? You've been tapping on my shoulder and beating on my brain since the night I first met Ferret. I know that now, but I don't know why. And I don't know how to stop the Group. Do you want me to throw bombs? Assassinate somebody? Join the Eye Brigade?"

Sure,
If you are ready to exit the body.

"You mean die? Well, that's just hunky-damned-dory. So we're all just supposed to knuckle under?"

You knuckled under long ago.
You cannot overthrow your masters,
For you have nothing with which to replace them;
You would bring greater chaos and suffering
And harsher masters in their stead.
We suggest you focus on Azazel.
We will assist
If you are up for the ride.

Hatch put his face in his hands. Conquest. Death. Food. Poor Azazel was hungry. Good God. "So am I supposed to activate you somehow?" he asked, hearing the note of desperation in his voice. "Am I supposed to press a button and make you shine a light on Azazel and cause it to vanish? Just tell me, what's the game here?"

The game is slavery and slaughter;
Azazel prepares to act,
And senses us but cannot see.
Are you in or out?
Will you risk the sacrifice?
Every action draws its own reaction;
Choose and let your choice reveal your path.

Choose? Hatch began to say that he did not understand how one person was to stand against a force as powerful as the Group or evil such as Azazel. But Big Ray was nudging him, and Hatch found himself trying to awaken, as if he had been in a deep sleep.

"Hey, did you see it?" asked Big Ray.

"Are we in our out?" asked Hatch. "We can't..."

"What do you mean? We can't what?"

Hatch stared at him. His trance had not fully dissipated. "Slaughter..."

Big Ray shook Hatch's shoulder. "You're slurring. Pull out of it, Hatch."

Hatch started, as one fully awakened. "Did I—was I talking?"

"The thingy there in your hands, it flashed like a camera. I mean, it blinded me for a second. Did you see it?"

The storeroom was as quiet as falling snow. The artifact was closed and dark. Hatch eased it into the rucksack. "Ray, when you examined the artifact, did you experience anything out of the ordinary?"

Big Ray took a seat in the other chair. "Yeah, fear. Cold, hard, pants-wetting fear. I can't imagine why."

"Marty said he didn't experience anything, either."

"You've put yourself through too much. Your circuits are a tad fried, methinks." Big Ray poured a little of the port into his glass and, at Hatch's nod, into the chalice.

Hatch tied the rucksack, rolled the flap, and set it gently into the corner storage nook. "In Ghost's hideaway, he let me hold the artifact—this was before we went to the incinerator."

Big Ray swirled the port in his glass.

"I don't know how to describe it, Ray. I sensed an intelligence, old and deep but vibrant, energetic. It was—it is —joyful and caring, if that makes sense. It just happened to me again. This sounds nuts, I know, but I conversed with it."

Big Ray studied his glass. "Look, take a few days off. Get some sleep."

"It makes me wonder if Dad had the same experience." Hatch was tempted to tell Ray all Kutznov had said about the Antarctica and Azazel and the artifact, but he didn't. The cat jumped onto the file container between them and delicately sniffed the bottle. "In the end, that's why I couldn't give it to Ferret," said Hatch.

Big Ray leaned forward. "Look, Hatch, I never asked, but you went back to the park hoping to retrieve the artifact, didn't you? And when you got it, you knew Ferret wasn't going to take you out."

Hatch looked down. "I went back to the park to find out why Ferret wanted the goddess. I hoped Ghost would tell me. I didn't know he had rescheduled the pickup. A lot of cards fell just the right way."

"Come on."

"Come on yourself. And no one can know what Ferret will or won't do."

"But you had the bargaining chip." Big Ray waited a little longer, and when Hatch didn't answer, he shrugged. "Anyway, it'll be an interesting conversation when you tell Ferret you have it."

"If I tell him."

"What do you mean, if you tell him?" Big Ray leaned forward. "Here's how it's going to play, Einstein. This Dartham guy is going to poke around in the ashes, and when he doesn't find what he's looking for, he's going to get downright proctological with us. We'll have to work with Ferret to save our skins."

Something rustled behind one of the boxes. The cat jumped down to investigate.

"We have a few days, maybe a couple of weeks," said Hatch. He contemplated the file boxes and the crates of old books set against the wall, the fossils of his life thus far.

"So, a toast," said Big Ray. "One which is overdue." Hatch reached for his chalice, and Big Ray said, "To your dad."

Hatch hadn't expected it, and Ray's gesture brought a sharp ache to his throat. "I was angry at him for so long," said Hatch. "But the truth is, I loved him so much." He raised the chalice. "To Dad."

"To Montgomery Doran," said Big Ray.

"And to a job unfinished," said Hatch.

Big Ray hesitated. He set his glass on the file box. "What job, exactly?"

"Dad was the first to understand the artifact. Now I have it and it has a purpose. Forget Ferret. Forget Dartham."

"A purpose."

"Damn straight." Hatch drank the port.

"And what, you think you're going to fulfill its purpose?" asked Big Ray.

"I'm just saying it's a chance to play a different game." Hatch reached for the bottle. "We've all got to sing our song, brother."

"Sing our song?" Big Ray looked incredulous. "Whatever that means, it cannot be good. In fact, coming from you it scares the bejeezus out of me. I don't get it, haven't you learned anything at all?"

"Yes."

"Doesn't sound like it from where I sit."

They argued while the cat scuffled behind the boxes, chasing its prey. In a hidden corner of the storeroom, a mouse hesitated and the cat pounced with claws flexed. Big Ray jabbed his finger at Hatch, who shook his head. A drop of blood welled up on the cat's claw. High above Manhattan, the cold night spread over the joyful celebration at Vinnie's Pub and the sirens and bullhorns punctuating the Eye Brigade demonstration. Deep underground, the Azazel device shuddered, registering a slight tremor on the seismological graphs. But in the space beneath the concrete in Hatch's storeroom, the artifact of Adrestia, the goddess of equilibrium, brightened. Its light danced before slowly subsiding.

Big Ray drained his glass. "You are hopeless, you know that?" he asked. "Beyond hopeless."

"No," said Hatch. "I don't think anything is."

THANK YOU FOR READING
THE AZAZEL SYNDROME

If you would like to receive an email when the next installment of the Azazel series is released (and it is coming soon), please visit www.jekennedywriter.com and join the mailing list. I will never share your address, and you may unsubscribe at any time.

If you enjoyed *The Azazel Syndrome*, please consider leaving a review at Amazon or Goodreads. Even a brief review would be greatly appreciated. Thanks very much.

ACKNOWLEDGEMENTS

My deepest thanks to Robin Samuels at Shadowcat Editing for her suggestions and corrections (any remaining errors are wholly my responsibility); to Lieu Pham at Covertopia.com for the cover design and to Guido Henkel for the formatting; to those who read and critiqued the manuscript for their astute and pointed observations; and most of all to my family, for their incredible assistance and support.

J.E.K.
Peachtree City, Georgia
August 2018

www.ingramcontent.com/pod-product-compliance
Lightning Source LLC
Chambersburg PA
CBHW031704170626
46808CB00005B/1604